"The plain truth is I'm disappointed in myself—I'm angry."

The anguish Pete saw on her face tore at him. "I hate to disillusion you, Mary Elizabeth, but you're only human, and humans sometimes feel the way you do. If you got a kick out of being pregnant in your situation, then I'd really think you were nuts. But being disappointed and angry?" He shook his head. "Welcome to the human race, princess."

He watched relief enter her eyes, felt it wash through her body.

"It took courage to do what you did. Going to Florida isn't running away. You deliberately chose to give up your home, your job and your family for this baby, and in my book, kid, a person can't get any more heroic."

"How'd you get to be so nice?" Her smile trembled.

"Mary Elizabeth—" he released her and pushed away "—I'm a lot of things, but nice isn't one of them."

"Stupendous, then."

Pete got to his feet. "That's more like it."

Dear Reader,

I have to admit, I had an ideal research arrangement during the writing of this "Nine Months Later" story. My daughter was expecting her first baby, which allowed me to become intimately reacquainted with pregnancy and its many joys and woes.

One of those joys was a baby shower that I hosted, an affair my daughter really, really wanted. Not for the presents, she said. She merely wanted a get-together with friends and family to celebrate her pregnancy. She was especially looking forward to the stories women typically swap at showers, about morning sickness and bloated ankles, stretch marks and fifty-hour labors.

I didn't fully understand until the day of the shower, when thirty women were gathered in my living room. And there in the middle of them was my daughter, enthusiastically swapping stories with the best of them. Entering the sisterhood of motherhood.

It's difficult to explain my feelings at the time. I just know I was suddenly very glad I'd had the shower and given my daughter her moment.

For as joyous as pregnancy is, it can also be a frightening time. Ready or not, one's life is about to change, drastically and forever. I can't imagine going through it without a wide net of support—a loving husband, friends, family. Not only do they minimize the terror of impending motherhood, through their joy they expand one's own joy, as well.

Writing *Three for the Road* gave me a new appreciation for the importance of support systems. My pregnant heroine has no one. Not only is Mary Elizabeth unmarried, she's also leaving home, job and everyone she's ever known. I found this a most distressing situation! The mother in me wanted to throw a shower for her, surround her with friends and family who'd assure her she was not alone. The writer in me gave her Pete. I hope you approve.

All the best,

Shannon Waverly

Shannon Waverly

THREE FOR THE ROAD

Harlequin Books

**TORONTO • NEW YORK • LONDON
AMSTERDAM • PARIS • SYDNEY • HAMBURG
STOCKHOLM • ATHENS • TOKYO • MILAN
MADRID • WARSAW • BUDAPEST • AUCKLAND**

ISBN 0-373-70660-X

THREE FOR THE ROAD

Copyright © 1995 by Kathleen Shannon.

THREE FOR
THE ROAD

PROLOGUE

CHARLES DRUMMOND STARED at his daughter over his reading glasses. "How far along are you?"

Mary Elizabeth swallowed. "Nearly three months."

"Nearly three months," he echoed, his long patrician face set in distaste.

"I'm sorry," she said on a broken whisper.

Removing his glasses and tossing them onto the desk, he got to his feet and began to pace. "How could you do this, Mary Elizabeth?" He didn't raise his voice. A Drummond never did. "How could you bring such disgrace to this house?"

Above his meticulously groomed gray head hung a family portrait painted seventeen years earlier, one year after he'd been named president of the Deerfield Institution for Savings and two years before his wife's death. The five Drummonds presented as perfect a family image as ever there was, even to the extent that the artist had inadvertently painted Mary Elizabeth's eyes blue instead of brown, to match everyone else's.

"But no one cares about such things anymore." Mary Elizabeth spread her hands. "Times have changed."

Charles stopped pacing. A muscle jumped in his cheek. "If you believe that, you're more a fool than I thought."

She flinched.

"People talk, Mary Elizabeth, especially about families like ours. And they never forget. Ten years from now, twenty, they'll still remember you as the Drummond girl who got pregnant before she was married.''

This wasn't the way she'd envisioned their conversation. She'd entered this library hoping they'd discuss her situation like two rational, enlightened adults. She hadn't come looking for easy answers; all she'd wanted was his love and support during a difficult time. When would she ever learn?

Charles reseated himself in his leather chair with a long disgruntled sigh. ''Have you set a date?''

''For what?''

''A wedding, of course. Have you and Roger set a date?''

Her breath stalled. ''No. Roger doesn't even know.''

''Well, what are you waiting for? Are you afraid he'll refuse to marry you? He won't. He's an extraordinarily decent young man.''

''Father, we broke up seven weeks ago. It's over between us.''

Charles breathed out a bitter laugh. ''Apparently not.''

''But I don't want to marry Roger. We don't love each other.''

''You made your bed, Mary Elizabeth...or do you think you're so extraordinary you should be excused from doing what's morally right?''

''No, of course not, but I don't see the point of raising a child in a loveless home.''

''You should be grateful to be so lucky. Roger has a good job and a secure future at the bank. He doesn't have any vices that I can see...well, any *other* vices.'' His hard blue eyes flicked briefly to her waist. ''He comes from a pleasant family....''

But Mary Elizabeth was still shaking her head. ''Marrying under these circumstances, he'd feel trapped. He'd resent me and the baby. I don't want that.''

"What do you intend to do, then, have it out of wedlock?"

"I . . . yes, that's an option."

Charles shot her a crippling look. "Over my dead body."

"But—"

"I don't care if certain segments of society have relaxed their standards, or that unmarried mothers are as common these days as the married variety. Drummonds do not belong to that vulgar trash."

Mary Elizabeth glanced at the painting, blinking away tears. It seemed she'd been receiving lectures all her life on how Drummonds did or did not behave. Once again, she didn't measure up.

"Tell me, what sort of social life do you expect to have, burdened with a child?"

She misunderstood his remark as rising from concern and was about to reassure him when he added, "Who do you think is going to be interested in you now?"

A piercing pain sliced right through her.

"It isn't merely that you're pregnant, although Lord knows that's a formidable enough reason for any man to avoid getting involved with you. After all, who wants to take on another man's child?"

Mary Elizabeth's breathing had become so labored it felt as if someone had stuffed a rag down her throat.

"It's also the fact that you've obviously had intimate relations, and by remaining unmarried, you're all but announcing to the world that those relations were meaningless. From there, I'm afraid, it's an easy leap for people to see you as indiscriminate and promiscuous. In plain English, Mary Elizabeth, they'll see you as cheap."

With each word he leveled at her, Mary Elizabeth felt smaller and dirtier. She sensed she ought to say something in her defense, but her will to act seemed to have deserted her. On a level she hadn't wanted to acknowledge, she knew her father made sense.

"I hope you realize I'm saying these things only because I'm concerned about your future happiness. I want to see you settled, with a family, in your own home. But if you continue to follow this path, I don't see how that's possible." Charles smoothed a palm over the desk blotter, wiping away imaginary dust. "Now, you might argue there are lots of broad-minded men out there who'd be interested in you, but don't kid yourself, Mary Elizabeth. Most decent men still want to marry a 'nice' girl, no matter how liberal they claim to be, and I hate to say this, but the label that's usually attached to the sort of woman you aspire to being is—" he cleared his throat "—'used goods.'"

In a mature, detached part of her brain, Mary Elizabeth marveled at her father's ability to manipulate her emotions. Equally astonishing was her inability to stand up to him. But it wasn't really such a mystery; they'd had a lifetime of this sort of confrontation to perfect the pattern.

Unfortunately, knowing what was happening still didn't prevent her from being reduced to a helpless bundle of shame and guilt. She could only lower her eyes and hope she didn't break down before she reached her room.

Charles folded his hands on the desk blotter. "Have you considered terminating the situation?"

Mary Elizabeth blinked, rising out of her pain. "No."

"And why not?"

She reared back in sheer incredulity. Her father had been a pro-lifer as long as she could remember. But apparently the "morally right thing to do" existed on a sliding scale, depending on how close to home an unpleasant situation struck.

"I just can't."

He shook his head. "Ah, Mary Elizabeth. You've always been a burden."

She looked down at the Persian carpet, remembering other times, other lectures, when she'd stood just so. Yes, she'd been a burden to him, not as studious as his two other children, not as well-groomed, never as well-behaved. She'd tried. Lord, how she'd tried. But evidently there was simply something inherently wrong with her.

Charles pinned her with a look of renewed determination. "Tell Roger."

She shook her head.

"If you don't, I will."

Panic engulfed her. "You can't."

"I most certainly can. If you insist on having this baby, then, by God, you'll have it married. You'll give no one reason to gossip." Not for a second did he doubt his ability to persuade Roger to marry her. Neither did Mary Elizabeth. Apart from the fact that Roger idolized Charles, he enjoyed his job far too much to cross his employer.

For one brief moment, Mary Elizabeth regained her normal adult perspective and saw her father's attitude as absurd and archaic. She was twenty-seven years old, for heaven's sake. She was an educated, accomplished woman in a professional career. He had no business dictating her decisions, especially one that was so important. And that was why, when he offered her one last alternative—the choice to go away, have the child and give it up for adoption, a choice she was already leaning heavily toward herself—she said no.

"No?" Charles jerked his head, as if her impudence had struck him a physical blow.

"No."

In a most uncharacteristic loss of control, he flung a priceless paperweight across the room. It hit a plaster bust of Winston Churchill, leaving the statesman without a chin. "Damn you, Mary Elizabeth! You're just like your mother."

Mary Elizabeth frowned. She didn't understand his comment and would have let it go—if he just hadn't turned so red.

"What do you mean, I'm just like my mother?"

He continued to stare at her, saying nothing, but a look came into his eyes, an angry determination she thought she'd seen over the years now and again, a look almost too fleeting for her to be sure it had been there before it moved on, always leaving her trembling and relieved when it did.

"Tell me." She shot forward, gripping the edge of his desk, challenging him, finally.

This time the look in his eyes didn't pass. It settled in and focused, like the cross hairs on a rifle.

"Why am I like my mother?" she persisted. "Tell me."

And he did.

CHAPTER ONE

KEEP MOVING, DRUMMOND. Don't think. Just pick up the carton and go!

Mary Elizabeth obeyed her own command, ignoring her fatigue and mounting anxiety, and carried the last of her bedroom things down the wide, elegantly turned stairs.

But at the open front door, a surge of sadness blindsided her and caused her to hesitate. Outside, at the top of the circular brick driveway, basking in the golden September sun, was what might appear to be an ordinary eighteen-foot motor home. To Mary Elizabeth, however, it was her future.

Behind her rose the dignified, twelve-room Georgian where she'd lived all her life—her past. Her very definite, no-coming-back past. Her throat tightened and her eyes threatened to well up again.

Fortunately, Mrs. Pidgin chose that moment to come lumbering down the hall from the kitchen. The poor woman was already upset enough and didn't need to see Mary Elizabeth breaking down, too. She pulled in a fortifying breath and smiled before turning.

The short, sixty-year-old housekeeper was carrying two plastic grocery bags by their straining handles, their weight seeming to tip her blocky form side to side as she walked. Like a windup toy, Mary Elizabeth thought with painfully deep affection. She only hoped the woman didn't end up like most of those toys, overbalanced and on her side.

"What's all this?" she asked. They'd already packed the RV with more than enough food to get her through her trip from Maine to Florida.

"Just a little extra. You never know."

Mary Elizabeth suppressed a smile. Mrs. Pidgin was fussing over her as if she were setting off on a months-long journey in a covered wagon instead of a three-day zip down the interstate.

"Thanks, Mrs. P. But I wish you'd stop worrying. I'm going to be fine."

"Of course you will. Of course."

They both looked at the foyer floor, unable to hold each other's gaze, then hastily headed out to the motor home.

Inside the vehicle, Mary Elizabeth threaded her way through the kitchen, down the short passageway with the bathroom on one side and storage cupboards on the other, to the bedroom at the rear. With a grunt of relief, she dropped the box she was carrying onto one of the two twin beds—already overburdened with her belongings.

The motor home was a marvel of storage compartments, but in her haste she hadn't packed as efficiently as she could have. She'd do that later, when she had more time. Right now she felt compelled to hurry. Charles had gone to the bank this morning, giving no indication he'd be returning to see her off, but Mary Elizabeth didn't trust him anymore. She especially didn't trust him to keep from speaking to Roger.

Although Charles abhorred the idea of her staying in town, pregnant and unmarried, he didn't like her going away so abruptly, either. People were bound to wonder what had happened here to cause such unseemly behavior, he said. He also worried about her accidentally running into people they knew during her pregnancy. And what if she decided to return with the baby some day? His lack of control over the situation bothered him, and she knew he'd started thinking of telling Roger again. To Charles, marriage was still the best solution to the problem.

Mrs. Pidgin was fitting a package of six single-serving quiches in the freezer compartment of the refrigerator when Mary Elizabeth emerged from the bedroom.

"Here, let me help." She dipped into the bag, pulled out a deli container of lobster salad and tossed it into the refrigerator.

Mrs. Pidgin closed the freezer. "I don't suppose there's anything I can say that'll make you change your mind." It was a question, a last-ditch hope. She was the only person other than Charles who knew why Mary Elizabeth was leaving. She was the only person, period, who knew where she was going. Mary Elizabeth had told Charles Chicago, in case he decided to come looking for her, but she didn't want to drop off the map entirely. She wanted someone here to know where she was if a family emergency arose.

"Change my mind? Afraid not, Mrs. P."

The housekeeper's face looked pained. "Well, I can't really say as I blame you. Your father's behavior this past week has been unforgivable."

Mary Elizabeth worked at keeping her expression set. The past week had been difficult, that was for sure. Charles had found a reason to make each day hurtful and exhausting. He'd continued to harp on her pregnancy and denounce her choices, and always he wondered what people would say if they knew. The barbs that especially dug in, though, probably because she was already frightened and insecure, were the ones regarding her ability to survive on her own.

Charles accused her of having no real job skills or practical experience, and said the only reason she'd landed the curatorship at the local museum five years ago was that he had used his influence with the board. She'd never find another position like it, he said, just as she'd never find another man like Roger whom, coincidentally, Charles had also "provided" since he'd arranged their first date.

Mary Elizabeth didn't know what she would have done without Mrs. Pidgin. The woman had always been an ally and a comfort, but never more so than this past week.

Mrs. Pidgin had accidentally overheard the tail end of the conversation between Mary Elizabeth and Charles in the library, the part about Eliza Drummond's affair and Mary Elizabeth's true parentage, and had followed Mary Elizabeth up to her room afterward. There a shattered Mary Elizabeth had broken down, letting the shock of Charles's revelation give way to grief.

When she'd eventually brought her tears under control, she'd filled Mrs. Pidgin in on the rest of the conversation and the full scope of her dilemma. Mrs. Pidgin had been shaken when she learned of Mary Elizabeth's pregnancy, but she'd controlled her reaction well, better than Mary Elizabeth had when she learned the housekeeper had known all along about Eliza's illicit romance. Despite Charles's order not to tell anyone, Eliza had confided in Mrs. Pidgin. Mary Elizabeth could understand why. In time of trouble, a more loyal and nonjudgmental friend couldn't be found.

At present, that friend was folding the empty grocery bag with exaggerated care, distracted by her continuing worries.

"I just wish you weren't taking the camper," she said, frowning. "Such a big, difficult thing to drive." She tucked the folded bag into a drawer crammed full of embroidered tea towels and cutwork napkins. "It would be a lot easier if you left it here and let my Alfred sell it for you. You could take a plane then, have a moving truck transport your things. That way you could relax, take more things with you, too."

With a sigh, Mary Elizabeth reached into the second grocery bag. "I thought you understood, moving vans are expensive. So are plane tickets. Besides, I don't need any more things." She wasn't sure of much these days, but she was certain that taking the RV was the right choice. Not only would it get her and her possessions to Sarasota economically, but it would also become her home once she got there.

Chloe, her old college roommate, lived in Sarasota, and when Mary Elizabeth made the decision to move away from the northeast, she'd immediately called Chloe. Her friend had said she knew of a trailer park a few miles from her house that might take her in. Mary Elizabeth hoped so. She didn't want to impose on Chloe, who was a newlywed. Neither did she want to encumber herself with the expenses of an apartment until she was secure in a well-paying job, and that might be a while. In addition, things might not work out for her in the Sarasota area, and what better way to move on than to simply turn an ignition key?

With the groceries finally put away, she started for the door, eager to get the last of her belongings and be on her way.

"Stop a minute, will you please?" Mrs. Pidgin grasped Mary Elizabeth's wrist. "I won't keep you long, I promise." The housekeeper tugged her gently toward the front of the RV. Mary Elizabeth took the driver's seat, swiveling it to face the other.

"All right, so you're going, then."

Such a note of finality, Mary Elizabeth thought. She looked down at her clenched hands. A faint band of white skin, left by Roger's engagement ring, was still discernible against her light tan. "Yes," she said softly.

Mrs. Pidgin sighed. "You have to promise me you'll be careful on the road. Florida is so far away, and you haven't had that much experience driving or being on your own."

It was useless to remind Mrs. Pidgin that she'd had her license for eleven years and never been in an accident. The woman worried as only a person could who'd never driven or traveled—irrationally.

Besides, there was a grain of truth to what Mrs. Pidgin said. Mary Elizabeth hadn't traveled much. She'd bought the motor home a full year ago, but since then had taken only four weekend trips, all within New England.

"Please don't worry. The trip takes only three days, four if I drive very slow, and it's major highway all the way. What could possibly go wrong?"

The older woman stared deep into her eyes. "A lot," she said, her voice grave.

"Don't talk like that," Mary Elizabeth chided mildly. "You're scaring me."

"Good. That's good. The crime rate being what it is, you should be scared." The housekeeper tipped to one side so she could slip her hand into the right pocket of her blue cotton housedress. "I have something I want to give you." She pulled out a small plastic figure and set it on the dash.

"A St. Christopher?" Mary Elizabeth bit off a laugh.

"Ayeh."

"But he was kicked off the saint roster almost thirty years ago."

The woman's look said she didn't want to hear it. Mary Elizabeth closed her mouth and gave the icon, protector of travelers, a welcoming nod.

Mrs. Pidgin pulled a second item from her pocket, a square blue envelope. "I have something else."

Mary Elizabeth gazed at the envelope. "What is it?"

"Something from your mother. She gave it to me before she died. She told me I was to give it to you only if Charles did something like he did this week and you found out he wasn't your real father."

Mary Elizabeth's fine-boned jaw hardened. "What makes you think I want anything from her?"

"She was your mother, Mary Elizabeth, and no matter how upset you are with her now, you still love her. I know you do." Mrs. Pidgin placed the envelope on Mary Elizabeth's knee. "Here. It isn't much, but it belongs with you now."

Giving in to curiosity, Mary Elizabeth opened the envelope and pulled out a yellowed photograph. "Oh." The sound she made was barely audible.

"Ayeh, that's him, your real father. A handsome fella, wasn't he. You have his eyes."

Mary Elizabeth gazed at the man in the photo with a mixture of fascination and denial. He was slim, good-looking, young. A carpenter's belt, heavy with tools, hung around his hips. Behind him rose the Drummond house with its sun room under construction.

Swallowing, she slipped the photograph into her open purse on the floor. "Thank you," she said quietly.

"Wait. I have something else." Mrs. Pidgin grunted as she tipped to the right, pushing her hand into her left pocket this time.

Mary Elizabeth's eyes popped when she saw what the woman pulled out. "Where did you get such a thing?"

"Oh, it isn't a real gun."

Mary Elizabeth looked at her skeptically.

"Believe it or not, this is only a toy, a water pistol. My Alfred bought it for our grandson, but Judy wouldn't allow him to keep it."

"I can see why. It looks so real." Mary Elizabeth gazed at the lethal-looking toy. She'd heard such things existed. She'd even read about them being used in robberies, but she'd never actually seen one before. "And you want me to..."

"Yes, take it. Here." The housekeeper placed the water pistol in Mary Elizabeth's lap. "I wish I had a real weapon to give you, but—" she shrugged "—this might work if you're ever in a bind."

Mary Elizabeth stifled the urge to laugh. She thought Mrs. Pidgin's fear of traveling had put her over the edge, but she said a polite thank-you, anyway, and slipped the gun into her purse.

Mrs. Pidgin breathed a sigh of relief. "Good. Now, another thing..." She dug into the pocket again. Mary Elizabeth was beginning to feel decidedly like a knight in a medieval tale, being given magical gifts before setting off on a quest.

"Here's my cousin's phone number in Orlando and my sister's in Gainesville. If you ever need help, anything whatsoever..."

Mary Elizabeth nodded. "I'll call. I promise I will." She took the slip of paper and filed that in her bag, as well.

"You have enough money?"

"Yes, and my credit cards, too. Don't worry."

Mrs. Pidgin took Mary Elizabeth's smooth, slender hands in her plump, work-reddened ones. "I have only one more thing to ask." Her voice lowered. "If things don't work out for you, you've got to promise me you won't let pride prevent you from coming back."

Mary Elizabeth turned her head and gazed out the windshield toward the perfectly sheared shrubs gracing the perfectly manicured lawn that surrounded Charles Drummond's perfectly perfect house.

"I can't promise that," she replied hollowly.

"I know it hurts now but—"

"Hurts? Learning you aren't who you always thought you were doesn't 'hurt.' It's more like having your entire world turned inside out." Or maybe, she thought, like discovering that gravity doesn't work anymore. Your footing is gone and you're spinning away from everything that's familiar, out of control, with nothing to hold you safe.

Turning, she saw that the housekeeper's red-rimmed eyes had filled again.

"But such a big step."

Mary Elizabeth pulled her hands away and placed them tentatively on the steering wheel. There was nothing tentative about her voice, however, when she said, "I have no choice. I have to go. There's nothing left for me here. Charlie's in London doing graduate work, and Susan has her own family to keep her busy. We were never close, anyway. All I have, really, is you."

Mrs. Pidgin wiped her eyes and rasped a string of curses, all directed at Charles Drummond.

"Don't be angry with him, Mrs. P. It couldn't have been easy for him all these years, either. Every time he looked at me, he must've been reminded of my mother's infidelity. Actually, he did more for me than anyone in his position was obligated to do."

"Ayeh," Mrs. Pidgin affirmed bitterly. "All those insulting lectures, all that criticism ... and the restrictions he imposed! It's a wonder you didn't choke on all he did for you."

Mary Elizabeth shook her head. "He was instilling values, Mrs. P. Punctuality, neatness, frugality. I have no complaints. Just the opposite. I led a privileged life here. Just look at the house where I was raised. I had the best clothes, went to the best schools...."

"Only because he was afraid. If he didn't give you those things, same as he gave your sister and brother, people might wonder why he'd singled you out. And if there's one thing your...Charles can't abide, it's having folks think anything's wrong here. He's the proudest fool I ever met."

"You're right. And that's the reason—one of the reasons—I'm leaving. I don't want him feeling shamed or unable to hold up his head in town just because I refuse to get married."

"Just? There's no 'just' about it."

"Right again. Getting married is hardly a trivial step." Mary Elizabeth smiled, trying to shift the conversation onto a more cheerful path. "Besides, it's past time for me to leave the nest. I'm practically ancient, Mrs. P." But the brightness slid from her voice when she said, "I need my independence. I want to finally be free."

The two women fell quiet. Outside the motor home, birds chirped noisily in the maples that bordered the property. The foliage looked played out, even a little tired. The calendar might say it was still summer, but the sky was too blue, too dry and clear. Change was in the air.

Finally, the older woman said softly, "You'll call me when you reach your friend's, won't you?"

"Of course. And you won't tell Charles where I've really gone until I tell you it's safe?"

"Ayeh." Mrs. Pidgin gazed at her a long, worried moment. "Well, I can't think of anything else, so maybe we should get on with your packing. Is there much more?"

"Only the rocker from my room and the cat." Mary Elizabeth rose and the woman followed. But at the door of the RV, Mary Elizabeth turned. "Before I go, I'd like you to know..." She fidgeted self-consciously with the buttons on her jacket. "I mean, what I want to say is..." She swallowed, and then simply wrapped Mrs. Pidgin in a fierce hug. The woman patted her consolingly while tears streamed down her wrinkled cheeks.

"I know. I love you, too, Mary Elizabeth."

EVEN THE PHONE BOOTH brought a smile to Pete Mitchell's eyes. You just didn't see those things anymore, only the open half-shells that looked like something out of *Star Trek* and didn't exactly encourage a guy to linger or say anything personal.

The glass bi-fold door closed with a familiar squeak-thump, recalling hot summer nights, cheap after-shave, and dialing Sue Ellen Carlisle's number while friends serenaded him with cat calls and whistles from the drugstore corner.

Pete lifted the receiver, noted the rotary dial and got the urge to call everybody he knew. He called his office.

Outside the booth, morning sunshine glittered over the dewy, deep green lawn in front of the Rest E-Z Motel. Old Adirondack chairs, ignorant of the fact that they had become a hot new item in backyard furniture, dozed under a stand of maples and birches.

Pete lowered himself to the booth's small metal bench as the call went through. He tried to cross his legs, rest his right ankle over his left knee, but his long limbs kept knocking into things.

He heard a click, and then, "Mitchell Construction."

"Brad?" he said, surprised to hear his brother's voice.

"Pete?"

"Yeah."

"Hey. How ya doin', man?"

"Great. What are you doing answering the phone?"

"Oh, I thought I'd goof off, sit around and drink coffee. My boss is gone for ten days."

Pete knew Brad was kidding, at least he hoped he did, but that didn't stop his stomach from tightening. They were already two weeks behind on the McKenna house.

"Did the shipment of drywall come in?"

"Hey, you're on vacation. You're not supposed to be thinking about work. Remember?"

Pete sent a daddy longlegs flying off his boot with a flick of a finger. "So, did the drywall come in?"

His brother chuckled. "No. I just called, though—that's what I'm doing here at the office—and it's on its way. Should be here tomorrow."

"Good. Get the men on it right away, as many as you can spare."

"I will." After a short pause Brad said, "So, did you get it?" His voice contained a smile.

As did Pete's when he replied, "Get what?"

"The measles. Jeez Louise! You know what."

Pete laughed. "Yeah, I got it."

Brad whooped. "Oh, man! That's great. So, tell me about it. Is she as sweet as the ad promised?"

"Sweeter. What a beauty, Brad. I even brought her into my motel room with me last night. Couldn't get enough of looking at her."

"Good price?"

"For a mint-condition '53 Triumph, the exact same model Brando rode in *The Wild One*? Yeah, it was a good price. Well, a little steep. The old man knew what he had. But she's worth it."

"I can't wait to see it. Where are you now?"

"Still in New Hampshire, west side of Lake Winnipesukee, about forty miles south of where I bought the bike, although I must've put a hundred and forty on it yesterday up in the mountains." He paused, his sharp builder's eye sweeping the grounds.

"I wish you could see the motel I stayed in last night, Brad. Separate cabins, each about the size of a garden shed, painted this bright fifties aqua. It's the genuine article, too, not some fake retro setup with an eye on the nostalgia buck. I'm calling from a phone booth outside the motel office 'cause there aren't any phones in the rooms."

"And you're having a good time?"

"The best." He hadn't taken a vacation like this in so long he'd forgotten how much he enjoyed being on the road, totally alone and freewheeling—how much he needed it. His construction business had thrived this past year, and he'd been working full-tilt all that time, unaware of the wear and tear on his body as well as his spirit. But already he felt better, and he'd been gone from home a mere two days.

"Only you, Pete. Only you." Brad laughed. "So, are you still going to ride her home?"

"That's the plan." That had always been the plan. Pete had flown up from Tampa on a one-way ticket, with only a duffel bag and a certainty of his luck.

"What I'd like to know is," Brad said, "what are you gonna do with one more antique motorcycle?"

"Love her, cherish her, till the road runs out for either one of us, what else?"

Brad chuckled. "That reminds me, somebody stopped by the apartment yesterday who maybe wishes you'd think about *her* in those terms."

Pete was glad his brother couldn't see his face. He suspected it had fallen to somewhere around his knees. "Sue Ellen?" he asked, trying not to hesitate. Hesitation might give his brother the impression he cared more than he did.

"Uh-huh."

"What did she want?"

"Came by to hand-deliver her reply to our wedding invitation."

"Cutting it close, wasn't she?"

"Sure was. Jill had to call the country club last night with a final count."

Pete swallowed. "So, is she coming?"

"Of course. She is Jill's cousin, after all."

Pete got to his feet and moved around the phone booth like an agitated tiger in a too-small cage. Two teenage girls, walking slowly in his direction and trying to pretend they weren't checking him out, giggled.

Brad said, "I'm reluctant to give people advice, especially my older and so-much-wiser brother, but now that her divorce is finalized, this might be a good opportunity for you to explore the possibility of getting back with her. She's a gorgeous lady, Pete, and if you ask me she's still real interested in you."

"No, she isn't."

"No? Then how come she's been calling you three times a week? How come she's been coming by the office?"

"She's thinking of renovating her house, dummy."

"A house that was built only six years ago? Come on, Pete, open your eyes."

Brad was getting a real kick out of this. So were their sisters, Pam and Lindy. They saw it as the ultimate romance, Pete and Sue Ellen, high school sweethearts, getting back together after fifteen years of unfortunate separation.

Pete saw it as a good time to hit the road.

"Listen, kid, I'm not interested in getting back with Sue Ellen, and I don't want any matchmaking going on at your wedding, hear?"

"Yeah, I hear."

No, he didn't. Pete could tell his brother was smirking.

"Look, just because you're getting married doesn't mean everybody around you should do the same. Hell, you're getting as bad as your sisters."

"It might not be a bad idea to start thinking about settling down, too, Pete. I think I saw a few gray hairs on your head the other day."

"Yeah, well, they're my gray hairs and I'll thank you not to worry about them. Hell, I'm never going that route again. Once was enough for a lifetime. For several lifetimes."

A few seconds of uneasy silence followed, then Brad said, "Not to change the subject, but when can I expect my best man to get home?" The reminder of Pete's disastrous marriage had effectively killed the discussion. Pete felt his equanimity return.

"Do you need me sooner than Friday? Not this Friday. The one before the wedding, I mean."

"Of course I need you. I'm getting as nervous as a turkey in November."

Grinning, Pete picked at a small tear on the right knee of his jeans. "Well, hell, I'm hardly the guy to have around if what you're looking for's support. My advice would be to give up this deranged idea of marriage and come on the road with me."

"You just haven't met the right girl yet," Brad replied righteously. "Wait till you do. You'll be eating your words."

"Don't hold your breath."

"And don't you go sounding so sure of yourself. But to answer your question—no, I don't need you. Just be here the day before the wedding. We have to pick up our tuxes and go to the rehearsal."

"Sure enough. How's the rest of the family holding up?"

"Good. Pam has decided to have the rehearsal dinner at her house."

"That isn't necessary. You know I offered to take everybody to The Sand Dollar."

"You've done enough, Pete. Besides, she really wants to do this."

"Well, in that case... Has Lindy's husband made it into work this week?"

"So far."

Pete sniffed. He didn't like his brother-in-law a helluva lot. The guy had a serious drinking problem. But he was family, and so, when he said he needed a job, Pete gave him a job.

"How are Abby's tonsils?"

"Pete, will you stop worrying about the family, already!"

Pete almost said he didn't know how. He'd been at it too long. But that might come out sounding like a complaint, which it wasn't, so he just shut up.

The two teenage girls were nearly abreast of the phone booth now, walking stiffly, eyes straight ahead. Pete slouched a little—enough to look disreputable, yet not so much that he'd slide off the bench—and sent them his sexiest half smile and a slow nod hello. Their eyes rounded and their faces turned red as thermometers about to pop. As soon as they'd passed, he sat up, laughing to himself.

"So," Brad said, "what are you going to do with the rest of your vacation?"

Pete felt a warmth like new love melt over him. "I plan to hit the back roads, do my Jack Kerouac thing, look for America in the slow lane."

"Man, do I envy you."

"You should. I don't have to shave or change my socks for the next nine days if I don't feel like it."

"Have fun, but do me a favor? Take a shower before crossing the town line, okay? I'm not sure even I could stand you that ripe."

"I'll think about it. Take care, Brad."

"Hey, you will be here by Friday, right?"

"Yes, I'll be there. Have I ever let you down?"

When Brad answered, his voice held more emotion than Pete had intended to elicit. "Never, big brother. Never."

"So, okay." Pete uncoiled from the seat. "Till then, hang tough. Jill is worth it."

"I know."

"I hope so." Pete ran callused fingers over the heart-enclosed initials someone had scratched into the black paint of the phone. "Don't let this get around, it'll kill my image, but I'm the one with every reason to be envious."

Brad was quiet awhile before mumbling, "Thanks, Pete."

"For what? See you Friday."

He hung up quickly, but continued to stand there staring at the phone. He'd added that remark about envying Brad merely to bolster his brother's confidence and get him through the prewedding jitters. But just for a second . . .

In general, he was happy with his life. He liked his work, enjoyed his freedom, wasn't looking for any more responsibility than he already had, certainly not the kind you got saddled with in marriage.

But just for a second he thought he'd felt something, like a faint pang of hunger, an intimation there could be more.

He gave his head a little shake. Well, of course he knew there could be more. He always had. That was why he'd asked Sue Ellen to marry him when they were just eighteen. As things turned out, she broke up with him before they quite made it down the aisle, but that didn't alter his view of marriage or keep him from marrying Cindy Barstow half a year later.

Pete curled his hand into a fist and pressed it against the phone-booth wall. Cindy. The biggest mistake of his life, a classic case of marriage on the rebound. At twenty-one, though, he'd believed he was in love again.

Cindy was cute, sweet and affectionate, and she fell for Pete very hard, very fast. By their second date they were making love and she was saying, "I love you," which was exactly what his shattered ego had needed then. Three months after that they were married.

Cindy had another endearing trait that had bolstered his self-image, a soft feminine helplessness that made him feel strong, protective and needed. Like a rescuing knight.

But it didn't take long for her dependence on him to wear thin and for him to see how draining it was. He began to resent her. He wanted a partner, a helpmate, someone who could occasionally nurture him when he was down—not a little girl.

He soon discovered other things about her that were equally annoying. There were her constant small "tests" to prove he loved her—calls in the middle of the day, for instance, to ask him to leave work to pick up something at the market for her, usually when he was most involved in an important project. She also made unreasonable demands, like having him account for all his time. And then there was the way she said "I love you," with that plaintive little question mark at the end, her way of asking him to reassure her he loved her, too. Constantly. On the phone, during dinner, in the middle of the night.

Only months into their marriage, he knew he'd made a mistake. Cindy was desperate for love, starving for it, and that scared the hell out of him. Although she claimed to love him, all he saw was her fierce need to *be* loved, a need that soon became a bottomless pit. No matter what he did to reassure her, her emotional needs remained unsated and insatiable.

How they'd lasted two years he'd never know, but finally there came a day he couldn't take it anymore. The ante in Cindy's games had risen to the point where, if he didn't walk out, he felt sure that dark bottomless pit of her insecurity would swallow him up. In the end it almost did, but that was a time in his life he didn't like to dwell on.

The only solace he derived from looking back on his marriage with Cindy lay in the fact that they'd never had a child. He'd wanted one, but not with her. Lord, not her. He couldn't imagine a child growing up with that woman.

After that, Pete was pretty well soured on the idea of marriage. Oh, he'd had relationships with other women, some serious, most too casual even to remember. But marriage? No, never again.

Aside from being incurably gun-shy, he simply liked his freedom too much. Single, he could come and go as he pleased, see whom he wanted—or not. He could smoke smelly cigars, eat chili for breakfast, or drop a bundle on a bike that was forty years old. No one would be at home waiting to chew off his head.

So, why was he suddenly feeling twinges of envy for his brother? And why hadn't he felt those twinges while Sue Ellen was still married? He didn't want to marry anyone, even her. She might have been his first love, maybe even his best love, but, no, not even her. She'd hurt him too much when she broke up with him to marry that guy she'd met in college, and he still blamed her for the consequences, his marriage to Cindy.

Cindy. Sue Ellen. They were a mess from his past he'd just as soon forget. And that was exactly what he was going to do. Pete pushed away from the phone, opened the bi-fold door and stepped outside. He had nine days until the wedding, nine glorious, freewheeling days before he had to deal with Sue Ellen again and his interfering relatives. In the meantime—he smiled—it was time to get back on the road.

ALL THE WAY OUT OF TOWN Mary Elizabeth cried. Tears obscured her vision so badly that, turning a corner, she drove over the curb, nearly hitting a mailbox, and a block after that she ran a red light. By the time she reached the highway, the floor around her was littered with tissues, and the fluffy orange cat lying on the seat beside her was eyeing her with aloof disdain. But she couldn't stop.

She was leaving behind everything she knew—her family, her friends, her job and hometown—and was going to a place that was totally unfamiliar. The climate, the architecture, the landscape, everything in Florida would be different.

But then, everything in Maine felt different now, too. Learning she wasn't who she'd always thought she was had changed things. Charles wasn't her father anymore. Susan and Charlie were only half sister, half brother. Aunt Julia wasn't even her aunt. And her mother? Mary Elizabeth reached for another tissue from the box on the dash.

As had happened innumerable times that week, the moment when Charles had informed her of her true parentage replayed itself in her mind. Again she felt her initial shock, the confusion and numbing incredulity that had prevented his words from really registering for several minutes. It was sort of like watching the demolition of a high-rise building, she thought. Hearing the boom of the explosives, seeing the jolt through the structure—and then that strange moment when the building simply hangs in place, mortally wounded but still appearing sound, right before dropping story by story into a thundering cloud of devastation. That was how she felt every time she recalled the destruction of her world.

She wiped her eyes, but they filled again almost immediately. Oh, this had to stop. She couldn't afford to dwell on her illegitimacy anymore or wallow in self-pity. Facing a solitary drive down the entire Eastern seaboard, she needed to be alert, defensive and tough, even though in all her life she'd never been any of those things. Growing up affluent in a quiet New England town, she'd never had to be.

But after several minutes of focusing on her trip, her sadness had been replaced by fear, fear of the journey, fear of the unknown. No, that wouldn't do, either.

"How hard can it be, huh, Monet?" she asked the fat feline riding beside her. "People make this trip all the time—college kids on spring break, retired folks." She blotted her eyes one last time and pocketed the tissue. "I have Triple A insurance, my route clearly mapped out, even the best campgrounds to stay in each night. I've got food, shelter, credit cards, everything I need. And," she said with added emphasis, "it's only three days."

Morning sunshine warmed her left shoulder as she drove down the highway heading south. She relaxed into the warmth, flexing her stiff neck to one side and then the other. "Actually," she said, addressing the cat again, "the drive isn't hard at all. I-95 all the way until we reach Daytona. Just one long road. Amazing, isn't it? Then at Daytona we'll cut across Florida to a highway that runs down the gulf side of the state straight to Sarasota. The gentleman I talked to at Triple A told me that only New York and Washington might give us trouble, but if we avoid those cities during commuter hours, we'll be okay. And once we reach Florida everything's going to be more than okay. It'll be great. I've got a job interview lined up already. My best friend'll be there. The weather'll be forever warm...."

The cat gave her a look that said he'd had enough bothersome conversation. He settled his chin on his paws, closed his yellow eyes and went to sleep.

Mary Elizabeth shrugged and turned on the radio, trying to find a classical station. When she had, she settled back.

But a few minutes later her mind had wandered again, away from the music to the countless school concerts Charles had sat through when she was a girl. He'd attended her plays and art exhibits, as well. But he'd usually grumbled beforehand, looked impatient during and been irritable after. At times she'd thought she was merely being overly sensitive, but now she knew better. Now a lot of Charles's behavior made sense. So did his words. *You've always been a burden, Mary Elizabeth*. A burden. More than she'd ever suspected, apparently.

It must have been terribly difficult raising a child who was the taunting proof of his wife's infidelity, a child he clearly didn't want and had hoped Eliza would give up for adoption. And how maddening it must have been when that child, given every advantage, had continually failed to live up to the Drummond name.

Or maybe she had, she thought, but in his pain and resentment Charles had simply refused to acknowledge it.

Mary Elizabeth's fingers tightened around the wheel. She wished she'd seen things in that light when she was younger. Instead, she'd spent her youth trying to win his approval and love, trying, always trying, but growing increasingly certain that in some mysterious way she was inferior and deserved to be treated differently from her brother and sister.

Damn! It shouldn't have been that way. Her mother should have told her about her illegitimacy instead of keeping it a secret. It would have explained so much. Besides, it was her very identity her mother had withheld. And what if there was some unpleasant surprise lurking in her gene pool such as heart disease or diabetes? It was only right a person be told such a thing, or at least be given the opportunity to find out. The likelihood of that happening now was slim. Mrs. Pidgin had told her that after her biological father left the area, her mother had never heard from him again. No one knew where he was or if he was even still alive.

Mary Elizabeth came to with a start, realizing she'd done it again. She'd fallen into thinking about Charles and her illegitimacy when her mind ought to be on the road. With a determined effort she put them from her thoughts, reached for the radio and turned up the volume.

She stopped at a roadside rest area south of Boston shortly after noon to feed Monet, who thought he was human and insisted on three meals a day. Although anxiety had destroyed Mary Elizabeth's appetite, she knew that for the baby's sake she ought to eat, as well.

While she was putting together a lobster salad sandwich, she realized her stomach was knotted with a curious new tension. Her hands trembled with a nervousness she couldn't quite define.

She was opening a cupboard to look for her copper tea kettle when the thought abruptly hit her: survival. That's what this nervousness was about—preparing her first solitary meal, in the first home that could truly be called her own. It didn't matter that she'd prepared innumerable meals before. This one cut through time and all common sense to feelings that were obscure and primitive. The need to survive. The fear that she wouldn't, just as Charles had predicted.

Conscious of her every move, she found the kettle, set it on the propane stove and turned the knob. Ridiculously, her heart leapt when a flame appeared.

She considered going out to a picnic table with her food, but an eighteen-wheeler was parked nearby, and while the driver was probably just having his lunch, too, she felt it was wiser to stay inside.

She sat instead at the small kitchen table and cranked open the window to catch the fresh September breeze. Gazing outside at her unfamiliar surroundings, her stomach suddenly clenched again. She was alone now, truly disconnected from everything she knew, and she *felt* alone, *felt* disconnected.

But there was simply no way she could have stayed in Deerfield. Feeling alone and disconnected wasn't nearly as bad as having to deal with Charles. Or with Roger, she thought. In a town as small as Deerfield, Roger would have found out about her pregnancy sooner or later.

Mary Elizabeth picked up her sandwich and took a small, tasteless bite. Charles was right; Roger *was* a decent person, and although he and Mary Elizabeth didn't love each other, he'd want to marry her. He'd think it was the right thing to do.

It wasn't. She'd never been more certain about anything in her life. It wasn't her own happiness she was considering, although she'd always assumed she'd marry a man she was in love with. It was the child's welfare that concerned her. Roger would feel trapped in a situation he hadn't planned and didn't need or want.

Of course she wouldn't have to marry him, despite her father's considerable influence on both her and Roger. But even single, Roger was sure to resent the child. Maybe not at first. At first he might ask for visitation rights, maybe even insist on paying child support, but eventually he would feel he'd been dealt an unfair hand, especially when he met a woman he wanted to marry. He'd resent having to explain this embarrassment from the past, this bastard. He'd resent having to justify the drain on his time and his wallet. The child would become an issue between them. His wife might even be jealous and ask him to stop seeing the child altogether.

No, Mary Elizabeth didn't want any baby she brought into the world to grow up like that, resented and unwanted by its father—the way she'd been raised.

She regretted not being able to tell Roger she was pregnant. Fathers had their rights, and what she was doing to him was morally wrong and probably legally wrong, as well.

But whatever guilt she felt was dwarfed by her conviction she was doing the right thing for the baby. And in the end, would it really matter whether Roger knew or not? She planned to give the baby up for adoption, anyway.

Taking a sip of tea, she let her gaze wander the motor home, crammed full of her possessions. She'd brought along most of the necessities to start a new life, but she'd also brought some frills. The Steuben goblets she'd inherited from her grandmother, her Crabtree & Evelyn clothing sachets, nearly twenty years of needlework, even her Salem rocker. She knew personal, homey touches had little to do with survival, but she needed them, anyway. Her soul needed them.

Mary Elizabeth smiled softly, her sense of well-being returning. She might be alone now, detached from home and everyone she knew, but ultimately she'd be okay. She had this RV to comfort her and shelter her from all the wide-open unknowns beyond.

And she had a tiny life growing inside her, she thought, placing her hand on her stomach. As always, that realization intensified her resolve. She *would* reach Florida, she *would* make a new life for herself. And she *would* provide a happy future for the baby. There would be no more talk of abortion, no more pressure to marry a man she didn't love, no more fear that that man would begrudge and mistreat his own child. The legacy of resentment stopped here.

She finished her lunch, washed her dishes and, with fresh determination and optimism, got back on the road.

Mary Elizabeth's spirits remained buoyed through most of the afternoon, down the Massachusetts interstate, into Rhode Island and on through Connecticut. She played the radio, listened to a book on tape, and when she got tired of that, simply drifted along with her thoughts.

She pulled into another rest area just before New Rochelle. Traffic was bumper-to-bumper on the opposite side of the highway, commuters leaving New York for their homes in the suburbs. And while this side of the highway was relatively free-flowing, she knew she'd hit similarly clogged arteries once she reached the city and the lanes outbound south.

Instead, she parked the RV and passed the hectic rush hour over a leisurely dinner of quiche, salad and crisp bottled water with a twist of lemon. For dessert she had tea and a slice of Mrs. Pidgin's spice cake.

Feeling replete, she took to the road again at dusk. With any luck she'd reach the recommended campground in New Jersey around seven-thirty. She smiled, struck by a childlike sense of anticipation.

Everything was going well. The tires were humming, *she* was humming, the cat had even awakened to keep her company again.

And then she reached the Bronx.

There, highway signs and exit ramps became so confusing that before she knew it she'd gotten off I-95 and entered a labyrinth of streets that seemed to have no way out. It was, by far, the most frightening terrain she'd ever seen, except on "NYPD Blue." She drove in circles, went down blind alleys and sped past loitering, leather-clad gangs. Occasionally she thought of her St. Christopher riding solemnly along on the dash, but mostly her prayers just went up to anybody who'd listen. She wanted to find her way out, but more than that, she was terrified of breaking down. All along the dark, potholed streets, cars lay stripped of everything but their shells. She didn't want to think about what had happened to their owners.

Eventually, and for no reason she could discern, she did find the highway again. But by then she was so weak from having adrenaline rushing through her system, she didn't even care that she was heading in the wrong direction, back toward Connecticut. And when, a few miles later, she realized she wasn't even on I-95, that didn't matter, either. She was on a major highway, she was going somewhere, and that somewhere wasn't New York City.

She took the first exit she came to that displayed the symbol for lodging. It was nearly nine o'clock.

She braked at the end of the exit ramp, peering first to her right, then to her left, wondering which direction to take on the dark two-lane road. Wondering, too, why there weren't any signs. The billboard on the highway had promised a luxury motel three miles east off the exit, but which way was east? She was so tired she didn't know up from down anymore.

She slumped over the wheel, dropping her forehead to her knuckles. She didn't need this. For the last half hour, the only thing keeping her going was the thought of bringing this cumbersome vehicle to a stop and crawling into bed.

Ah, well, she sighed, sitting up. It was only three miles. If she chose the wrong direction, how long could it take to turn around and backtrack? She flexed her shoulders, did a quick eenie-meenie, and went left.

The road was dark and narrow and arched with trees. She passed a cottage set back from the road, a small restaurant and several acres of corn field. After that there was nothing but woods.

She glanced at her odometer several times, and when she was satisfied she'd covered more than the requisite distance without finding the motel—or any other signs of civilization, for that matter—she decided to turn around.

Almost too tired to see anymore, she swung the camper across the road, her headlights cutting a white tunnel into the trees. She shifted and carefully backed up, red brake lights casting an eerie glow over the roadside brush at the rear.

Given the length of her vehicle and the narrowness of the road, however, Mary Elizabeth was forced to go through the maneuver again, cutting across and backing up. Still, the turn wasn't complete, and she wished she'd waited until she'd come upon a driveway or crossroad.

This time would do it, though, she was certain. Forward. Back. Back a bit more...

Without any warning, the rear end of the motor home dropped with a thud. Mary Elizabeth's teeth banged together, while somewhere in the nether regions boxes tumbled. "Oh, God!" she whispered as the engine stalled.

With fingers that quivered, she turned the ignition key and pressed her foot to the gas pedal. But even as she was doing so she knew she was wasting her time. The back tires spun futilely, kicking up dirt and pebbles that hit nearby tree trunks like buckshot. The RV didn't budge. Panic flooded her as she gripped the wheel. Her blood pounded. What was she to do now?

After turning off the engine, she found a flashlight and slipped outside to investigate. Just as she'd suspected, she'd backed the RV right into a roadside ditch. She clutched the top of her head as if it might blow off. How could she be so stupid?

Okay, don't panic. This isn't a problem, she assured herself. *You've got AAA, and they come to the rescue anywhere, any time. Right? Right. All you have to do is find a phone.*

She peered up the road one way and down the other. All black. Just cricket chirps and bullfrog noises mixed with the thick, woodsy smell of humus. This was definitely not her idea of New York. Or was she back in Connecticut? Well, it wasn't her idea of Connecticut, either.

She climbed into the motor home again, brushed her hair, put on lipstick, found her purse, stepped outside, locked the door and, with a shuddery sigh, pocketed the keys.

The solution was easy, she told herself. She'd simply walk back the way she'd come and phone for a tow truck from the restaurant she'd passed just off the exit.

But when she stared down the dark empty road and remembered she'd be on it for more than three miles, her heart grew faint. She reminded herself that every journey, no matter how daunting, begins with a single step. She pulled in a breath and set off.

When she finally reached the restaurant, her legs were ready to give out. But what was worse, now that she'd gotten a good look, she realized it wasn't the sort of establishment she'd ever walked into before. It wasn't the sort she ever wanted to walk into, either.

It was low and dark and seedy-looking. The gravel lot surrounding it teemed with pickup trucks and motorcycles glinting lurid neon color from the beer signs flashing in its windows. Over the door a string of multicolored Christmas lights outlined a peeling sign left over from happier or more hopeful days. Starlight Lounge it read. The *I* was dotted with a star.

Mary Elizabeth looked across the road to the lone cottage huddled beneath a dense grove of pines, pines that made an almost human sighing, and her mind filled with visions straight out of a Stephen King novel.

She glanced from the cottage to the restaurant and back to the cottage again, feeling truly caught between the proverbial rock and a hard place. She decided on the restaurant. At least it was a public building.

As soon as she opened the door she was hit with a wall of country music and cigarette smoke. The next moment she realized she'd made a serious mistake.

CHAPTER TWO

PETE GOT A BAD FEELING the moment she opened the door.

He was sitting along the far leg of the U-shaped bar, near the back exit where he could keep an eye on his bike and still watch the room. He was trying to mind his own business, catch a little of the American League play-off, finish his beer and ribs, and be on his way. He still needed to check into that motel he'd seen up the road. His body ached and his eyelids felt like sandpaper despite the protective glasses he'd worn while riding.

Still, it had been a good day. No, make that a great day. He'd traveled some of the prettiest country he'd ever seen, the weather warm and dry and sweet. But even better was the riding itself, the sense of freedom that came from the open road, a motorcycle, and no agenda to meet. Time seemed to peel away from his thirty-six years as he'd ranged the wooded hills out of New Hampshire and down the Berkshires of western Massachusetts. By early evening, when he'd reached Connecticut, he'd felt eighteen again. Had the urge to buy a pack of Lucky Strikes and try out a few lines from *Rebel Without a Cause*.

Stifling a grin, Pete picked up his thick glass beer mug and took a cool sip.

Over the rim of the mug, his glance returned to the young woman at the door, poised on the threshold, surveying the clientele. His good humor dissolved. Damn! What was she doing here? He lowered the mug and gave serious thought to slipping out the back door.

It wasn't such a bad place, really. A working-class bar, unapologetically masculine. The patrons seemed to be mostly regulars, guys from the nearby town, here to kick back with a cold brew, watch the game on the big-screen TV and gripe about their jobs to somebody other than "the wife." Pete felt comfortable enough here; at least he didn't feel threatened. And the ribs were good, just as the guy at the gas station up the road had said.

But Pete wasn't about to stick around, either. He'd picked up a sense of the place early on and knew that, with just a touch of the wrong ingredient, it could become trouble.

He was pretty sure the wrong ingredient was standing at the door now.

She didn't belong here. She was as polished as the chrome on a classic old Bentley. With her smooth-as-water natural blond hair and her peaches-and-cream complexion glowing only with health, she might as well have dropped in from Venus. The few other women in the joint looked thoroughly shellacked and frizzled.

Pete doubted any of them would've bought the outfit she was wearing, either. The neatly buttoned, maize-colored jacket and matching knee-skimming shorts, worn with tights and loafers, made her look like a model posing for a back-to-college spread in one of those wholesome fashion magazines his sisters used to read when they were teenagers.

His gaze returned to the young woman's hair, those soft gleaming waves that fell from a side part to just below her collarbone. It was a timeless look, as in style now as it had been in the forties or would be again in the next century.

He focused on her face, a collection of refined features arranged with perfect balance in a perfectly oval setting. She had a small, straight nose and delicately sculpted cheekbones. Her neck was long and thoroughbred, and her eye-brows arched with just the right amount of hauteur. He couldn't rightly judge her mouth—at the moment her lips were pressed too tight—but he thought it would be appropriately aristocratic. Yes, he decided, hers was unquestionably a face born of well-tended genes.

Pete watched her with more fascination than he usually allowed her type. She was on the prowl for something. A walk on the wild side? That was usually the case when a princess like her walked into a dive like this.

But Pete didn't think so. Even from clear across the smoke-filled room, he could see how scared she was. When her large, worried eyes fixed on the phone on the back wall over behind his right shoulder, he put two and two together and came up with car trouble. Probably out of gas, or maybe a flat tire.

Damn! Where was her God-given common sense? There was a service station just a mile up the road. Better yet, why hadn't she ever learned to change her own tires the way his sisters had?

His gaze swept over her fragile features and regal posture. But of course she wasn't the type to change tires. Probably never pumped her own gas, either.

Or, he thought on an unexpected wave of sympathy, maybe she didn't have any older brothers to teach her how. For a moment a picture flashed through his mind of his own sisters caught in a similar situation.

Pete shook his head fractionally. No, she was just a princess. Didn't pump gas. Didn't change tires. Thought she could sashay into any ol' place and not suffer the consequences. No one would dare give her trouble.

From under his lowered lashes, Pete scanned the room and winced. Someone was thinking of daring.

He'd noticed the guy earlier, a muscle-bound, muscle-shirted big-mouth with a taste for Scotch, sitting on the other side of the bar. Pete swore under his breath, glanced over his shoulder at the exit again and began to wipe his hands.

MARY ELIZABETH SERIOUSLY considered retreat, just backing out the door and fleeing up the road to her RV.

But that would mean walking three miles in the dark again, this time with a stitch in her side. And worse, now there was the added risk she might be followed. A few of the men were giving her some decidedly unsettling looks.

In addition, retreat would solve nothing. Even if she did arrive at her motor home safely, it would still be stuck in a ditch. Besides, on the far side of the dimly lit room, beyond the pool table and drifting veils of smoke, hung the solution to her problem—a public telephone. All she needed was the courage to get there.

She pulled in a long breath, gripped the strap of her shoulder bag, and with eyes trained on the floor, made her way through the nearly all-male clientele. It seemed a gauntlet, but eventually she reached her destination.

With her back to the room, she set her purse on the ledge under the phone and took out her wallet. While conversations rose to their natural volume again, she flipped through her credit cards and various forms of identification, searching for the AAA phone number she knew was in there.

It eluded her. A fine tremor of fear shivered over her skin. She started her search again, aware of a sweat breaking out on her neck. Driver's license, social security card, Visa, American Express...

Suddenly, the room dimmed to the degree where she couldn't see the contents of her wallet at all. She turned and, with a jolt, realized it wasn't the room that had dimmed, but only her particular corner of it. An immense pair of shoulders was blocking the light.

"Hi, how ya doin'?" For someone so big, the man who'd spoken had a remarkably high voice.

Mary Elizabeth could barely catch her breath, so acute was her alarm. "I'm fine, thank you. How are you?" Her eyes flicked upward to a square red face made even blockier by a flat-topped buzz cut. There seemed to be no demarcation between his head and shoulders except a pale border where the hair had recently been trimmed.

"I never seen you in here before." The man inched closer, causing her to back up.

He wasn't really bad-looking. He didn't wear a leather vest or have sinister tattoos like those bikers playing pool, yet she still found him threatening. Something in his depthless, slitty eyes . . . and he smelled of hard liquor.

"Excuse me, I just need to make a phone call." She attempted to turn and resume searching her wallet.

"And I just come over to help," he said. "This isn't the sort of place a pretty little lady like yourself ought to be wandering into alone."

Mary Elizabeth eyed him guardedly, trying to decide if his offer of help was sincere, wondering if she had perhaps misjudged him. "I . . . uh . . . it's car trouble." *Finally,* she found the card. "RV trouble, actually. Nothing mechanical. I just need a tow."

He leaned his beefy shoulder against the wall, hemming her in. The odor of liquor and smoke, combined with toosweet after-shave, nearly made her gag. "Well, how about that." He chuckled. "You're lookin' at the answer to your prayers, darlin'. I just happen to have a tow rig on the back of my truck."

She stood in horrified numbness as he lifted one hand and ran his moist fingertips down her cheek. "Excuse me," she said, shaking him off and stepping aside. In the process, however, the AAA card slipped from her fingers and fluttered to the floor between them. Swallowing, she bent to retrieve it, but just as she was reaching, his big sneakered foot landed squarely on top.

Heart hammering, she looked up the towering length of him.

With a dry chuckle, he removed his foot, but not until he'd made it clear he was playing a game of cat and mouse, a game he obviously enjoyed and wasn't about to give up.

She retrieved the card and glanced around the room. A few men were watching them, but they didn't seem inclined to interfere. The rest were oblivious, playing pool or pinball or watching a baseball game on TV. Mary Elizabeth glanced toward the bar for help, but as luck would have it, the bartender was female.

"How about a drink?" her unwanted companion asked, wrapping his sausagelike fingers around her upper arm. "Let me buy you a drink, huh? I'm in the mood for another myself."

"Thanks, but I'm not thirsty. All I want is to be left alone so I can call for a tow, then I'll be on my way. So if you'll excuse me..."

"Hell, we can have you towed in no time. I told you that already. Come on, relax." He gave her arm a little shake. "Take a load off."

Mary Elizabeth tried to stay calm, at least on the surface, but inside she was growing frantic. No way was she going to get in a truck with this gorilla and drive off down a dark, isolated road.

"Excuse me. I...I have to go to the ladies' room."

Her friend tilted his thick, squared-off head. "Whatsa matter? Am I bad company?"

She wanted to say yes but had been raised to be impeccably polite. "Excuse me." Surprisingly, he let her go.

Once she was inside the tiny washroom, she knew why he'd been so agreeable. The window was five feet up the wall and so narrow she doubted even her leg would fit through. Mary Elizabeth sighed aloud and would've leaned her weary self against the stall except that it was probably crawling with germs that science hadn't heard of yet.

What am I going to do? she implored her reflection as she patted a wet paper towel to her flushed cheeks. Inside her open purse, set on the rim of the sink, lay the plastic gun Mrs. Pidgin had given her. Mary Elizabeth smiled wanly. Perhaps she could fill the gun with water and squirt the brute to death.

Ah, well, Mrs. P.'s intentions had been good.

Her newfound friend was waiting outside the washroom door, patient as a puppy. "Missed you." He grinned. "Hope you like rum and coke." He held up a glass.

"No, thanks." Trying to ignore him, she headed for the bar. Another female was sure to sympathize. "Excuse me," she called, leaning over an unoccupied stool.

"Wait a sec," the bartender, busy at the cash register, answered distractedly.

"You know," came the high, now nightmarish voice close at Mary Elizabeth's side, "if I didn't have such a sweet, forgiving nature, I'd be mighty ticked off by now. Here I offer to give you a free tow, something worth fifty, sixty bucks..."

The bartender finally headed in Mary Elizabeth's direction.

"Please, could you do me a favor?" Mary Elizabeth's voice wobbled noticeably now, but at least she'd been able to fend off tears.

The young woman, who looked to be about her own age, glanced up from the tap where she was filling three glass mugs.

"Would you be so kind as to call Triple A for me? All I need is a tow. Here's the number...."

The bartender's left eyebrow arched. "And there's a pay phone, right there." She pointed with her chin.

"I know, but..." Mary Elizabeth rolled her eyes toward the man still crowding her, his breath on her neck.

The young woman huffed. "Sonny, leave 'er alone, huh? You're being a jerk." Then she walked away, delivering the three beers to the far end of the bar. It was apparent *she* didn't consider him a threat. Also apparent was the fact that she'd be of no help.

Mary Elizabeth slipped onto the stool, planted her elbows on the bar and dropped her head into her hands.

"So, what's your name?" Her friend, who was evidently named Sonny, placed the rum and coke under her nose.

Too weary even to look up, she said, "Will you please leave me alone? It's been a very long day." Now tears did flood her vision. "Damn," she spat, embarrassed by her weakness. On a spurt of anger she spun off the stool. This was a public place, and that, a public phone. No one had the right to stop her from going about her business.

"Hey, where you runnin' off to now?" Sonny gripped her arm and gave it a yank. "Here I'm tryin' to be nice... Whatsa matter? Don't you like me?"

Something must've happened behind her because she noticed Sonny's slitty eyes shift and refocus. Suddenly he went still, while a calm, deep voice with just a trace of a slow southern drawl said, "Why don't you give it a rest?"

Mary Elizabeth turned in surprise. A tall, dark-haired man was lounging back in his bar stool, his eyes fixed on the TV screen. He seemed relaxed, but looking at him, she got a sense of tightly coiled alertness.

For the first time since she'd wandered in here, she drew a clear and easy breath. She wasn't sure why; he certainly didn't look like anybody a woman ought to be breathing easily over.

Sonny released her arm and stepped aside. His eyes narrowed even further. "What did you say?"

"Leave her alone. Let her make her call." The stranger calmly took a sip of his beer and continued to watch the game.

Sonny shifted his considerable weight, one foot to the other. "And who's gonna make me?"

Slowly, the man at the bar set down his mug and carefully got to his feet.

Mary Elizabeth couldn't take her eyes off him. He was over six feet tall and powerfully built. Tough as the road he'd traveled in on, too, she'd bet. He had wind-tossed black hair, steely blue eyes, weathered skin and a jaw that was unrelenting. Dust burnished his black boots, and the edges of his pale denim jacket were frayed. Beneath the jacket, tucked into low-slung, well-worn jeans, he wore a plain black T-shirt.

But the thing about this man that mesmerized her so wasn't his clothing or eyes or build. She didn't know *what* it was, but it wasn't physical... although his physical aspect was certainly impressive, too.

Mary Elizabeth bit her lower lip while her eyes traveled over him, up, down, up and down again. In all her life she'd never met anyone quite like him. He was like a new, unexplored land, and though her stomach jumped with something akin to fright when she gazed at him, she didn't want to miss a single mile.

"Look, I don't want any trouble," he said with easy composure, raising his hands like a gunslinger showing he was unarmed.

Sonny snickered.

"But if you start it, I'll guarantee I won't run away."

"Oh, yeah?" Sonny replied with all the cleverness of a block of cement.

Mary Elizabeth's skin crawled with deepening dread. She'd never witnessed a fight before, but this situation seemed to have all the signs of one brewing.

"Go make your phone call, miss."

With a start, she realized the tall stranger was talking to her. The bright animal darkness of his eyes made her breath catch. She nodded.

But Sonny responded, "I already told her that isn't necessary."

The blue-eyed man impaled Sonny with an immobilizing stare. Then, still holding him in his sights, he took Mary Elizabeth by the arm. "Come on."

Relief flooded her as he began to escort her to the phone.

No sooner had he turned his back, however, than Sonny gave him a hard shove, sending him stumbling forward.

With a plummeting heart, Mary Elizabeth realized that the fight had not been averted, but rather it had just begun.

The stranger who'd come to her aid rebounded quickly and shoved Sonny in return. "Back off," he warned, blue eyes blazing.

"Go to hell," Sonny replied.

And then fists did fly. Mary Elizabeth let out a faint "Yi," the only sound she was capable of, as the two men crashed into bar stools and people retreated.

"I don't believe this!" she whispered, retreating with them.

A table went over, glasses sliding and smashing to the floor. The room resounded with the smack of fists, with grunts and fabric ripping, and like in a movie, it was all set to music—"Welcome to Earth, Third Rock from the Sun"—thumping from the jukebox.

At least they seemed evenly matched, Mary Elizabeth thought, watching them go at it—though she did sense a quickness in the taller man that Sonny lacked.

What Sonny had was a mean streak. She watched in horrified silence as he grabbed a beer bottle off the bar, smashed it against the brass rail and lunged at her tall dark stranger.

"Get out of here," he called to her just before the jagged bottle came down on the side of his forehead. Immediately blood beaded along the gash.

Rather than rattle him, the cut seemed to deepen his anger and resolve. He picked up a chair and slammed it against Sonny's arm, dislodging the broken bottle from his grip. Then he pushed Sonny against the bar where he kept him pinned until Sonny looked ready to give up.

Mary Elizabeth had no idea where the third guy came from, but suddenly there he was, gripping the dark stranger's shoulder, swinging him around and landing a blow to his midsection that made her nauseated.

Logic told her she should use the diversion to slip away. Nobody was interested in her anymore. Yet she couldn't leave. It was clear that the man who'd come to her aid was as much a stranger in this bar as she was, while Sonny was a local, and if she abandoned him, he'd probably get pulverized by Sonny's friends.

She shouldn't care, she told herself. She didn't know this man, she'd never see him again, and if he was in a bar like this he was probably accustomed to fighting, anyway. Besides, she had a responsibility to the tiny life inside her. That especially had her concerned.

But if she slunk away now, what sort of person would that make her? How would she ever face herself in a mirror?

Without another second's thought, she dug into her purse for the plastic gun. Tossing her bag onto a nearby table, she gripped the gun in two hands and flexed her knees. "All right, everybody freeze!" she called out.

Nobody heard. The debacle continued.

"Hey!" she hollered, affronted. This time a few onlookers turned. She heard someone say, "She's got a gun," and was pleased that the person sounded at least somewhat alarmed.

Within seconds the word passed. Attention turned on her like a tide. Those nearby backed away. A few people slipped out the door.

"Stop fighting," she shouted. "Stop!" To her utter amazement, they did. The three men turned and looked at her, then each of them swore, different epithets, but all at the same time.

"Now...get against the wall there," she ordered as she searched her memory for anything else she could borrow from the police movies she'd seen.

The three men moved, amazing her once again. A hush had fallen over the place. Even the jukebox had obediently shut down.

"Good." She straightened, feeling a heady sense of power. "Now, you..." She waved the gun at the bartender. "I want you to call the police, and this time don't tell me there's a pay phone."

In the dead silence, Mary Elizabeth became aware of sirens wailing in the distance. Confused, she glanced at the young woman behind the bar who made a face that said, *What do you think I am, an idiot?*

In no time flat, blue-and-red lights were throbbing against the windows, dueling with the neon. The doors banged open and six uniformed officers hurried in, straight to the heart of the fray.

"Thank God you got here so fast," Mary Elizabeth said, but the officers coming toward her didn't return her smile. In fact, every one of them had drawn his weapon.

"Drop the gun," one of them ordered.

She looked at each of the six faces, at each of the six guns pointed her way. "What...?" All at once, she realized what was happening. "Oh. You think..."

But before she could explain the gun was only a toy, three of the policemen had cocked their pistols. She dropped the gun.

A policewoman immediately lunged forward, grasped Mary Elizabeth's right wrist and twisted her arm up behind her back. Another officer, a serious young man with a dedicated, boyish face, carefully picked up the fallen gun.

After that, events swam together in a dreamlike sequence: across the room, the bartender talking excitedly, pointing this way and that; the odious Sonny saying, "But...but he...but..."; and the tall dark stranger scowling at *her*, Mary Elizabeth, where a moment ago he'd been duking it out on her behalf.

"Sonny, Sonny," a craggy-faced sergeant scolded, shaking his head. "It isn't even Saturday night."

Sonny returned a sheepish grin.

"Okay, let's go," the sergeant said. It was then that Mary Elizabeth noticed the handcuffs glinting on the three men's wrists. *No, that's a mistake,* she wanted to cry out. *The tall one is a good guy.* But just then she heard the officer who'd

picked up her gun reading her her rights. At the same time
something cold and metallic encircled her own wrists.

Mary Elizabeth's face drained of color. "You're hand-
cuffing *me?*"

"Yes, ma'am."

"But there's obviously been a misunderstanding."

"We'll straighten it out at the station. Do you have a
purse?"

"Uh, yes." Mary Elizabeth indicated a nearby table.

The officer picked up her bag and said, "Come with me,
please."

Mary Elizabeth was led through the gawking crowd, close
on the heels of her tall, dark stranger. "I don't believe this,"
she muttered, her eyes hot with humiliation.

"Why the hell not?" he snarled over his shoulder. "Acting as stupid as you just did, you must land in messes like
this all the time." His hard lips curled as he muttered something that sounded to her like "Liverpool." She frowned in
confusion until she reasoned he'd said "Little fool."

"Sorry," she said.

"You should be."

Outside, she was led to a cruiser, while the three men were
taken to a rescue van where medics waited to patch up their
injuries.

She was just slipping into the back seat of the cruiser
when it occurred to her that she hadn't gotten her hero's
name. She peered up at the serious young officer, and with
a giggle that rose from hysteria, asked, "Who *was* that
masked man?"

He frowned, staring at her oddly, then shut the door.

She sat back and surveyed her surroundings with combined interest and dread. "Oh, Lord, I'm riding in a cage!"
she moaned. The next moment, the full significance of what

was happening to her hit home, and two hot tears trickled down her cheeks.

After that, events really blurred. She was taken to the station and booked, only vaguely aware that the three men involved in the fight had been brought in, as well. Her possessions got handed over; she was escorted down a corridor to a cell; handcuffs came off, toilet facilities were pointed out, and then, with a sound that cut right through her, the iron-barred door clanged shut.

And so ended Mary Elizabeth Drummond's first day of independence.

CHAPTER THREE

THE FIRST THING on Pete's mind when he opened his eyes the next morning was his bike. Where the hell was it, and if it had even one scratch, how did the fool who'd scratched it want to die?

The second thing he thought about was Mary Elizabeth Drummond, that preppy little pain in the butt who was trying to wreck his vacation—and doing a pretty good job of it, too. He'd never met anyone so fly-brained in his life, and why he'd stuck his neck out for her was still a mystery.

Pete eased onto his back and scowled at the water-stained ceiling of his cell, recalling the previous night. If she just hadn't walked into that bar, none of this would've happened. He was familiar with places like that, knew the type of guy who frequented them. For the most part, just your ordinary, law-abiding Joe. But add a woman to the equation—an unattached woman, he amended, thinking of the few who'd been there with their husbands or boyfriends—and your ordinary Joe suddenly transmuted into King Kong. She should have known that, too—although, to be fair, he doubted she'd spent much time in bars.

Pete's mouth tightened in a rueful grimace. Of all the gin joints in all the towns in all the world...

Last night after being brought in, they'd sat at adjacent desks while being booked. That's when he'd first heard her name. Mary Elizabeth Drummond. Even in his thoughts he put a spin of mockery on it. He wasn't sure why, except that the name struck him as sort of stuffy and tedious. It had no... give.

Sitting where he was, he'd been able to hear the reluctance in her voice when the officer asked her name, a reluctance that had deepened when she was asked her address, birth date and social security number. Pete got the feeling she didn't want the police to know who she was. For a while, in fact, she'd actually *refused* to give her address. Said she was in transit, moving from one state to another, and at present didn't really have an address. Pete had noted her amazement and dismay when all her vital statistics came up on the computer screen, anyway, just on the cue of her social security number.

What really roused Pete's curiosity, though, was the anxiety he'd detected when she'd been asked if there was anyone she wanted to call. No, there was no one, she'd said, an answer that had compelled him to turn and take a new, harder look at her. A princess like that, you'd think she'd be on the phone right away, a dozen people she wanted to complain to.

Another thing about her that didn't jibe was her voice. It was husky and deep-throated, a Scotch-and-soda voice that belonged more to a torch singer in a smoky piano bar than to someone wearing Bass Weeguns loafers.

Pete winced reflexively when he remembered the turnaround in her attitude after she was asked to explain what had happened at the Starlight Lounge. Suddenly she was a fountain of information. A damn Niagara Falls of information. And she was angry.

Well, maybe *indignant* was a more appropriate word. She didn't seem capable of really ripping loose. He'd noticed that about her last night, first with Sonny and then at the station. Terminally polite, that was her problem.

But Pete knew she'd been angry inside. Her cheeks had been a feverish pink, her sentences rushed and tumbled, and her slender frame never really stopped shaking. She reminded him of a bottle of carbonated soda, shaken to a froth, but all sealed up.

She was convinced her arrest was a mistake, even after the officer patiently explained the charge against her for the third time. She seemed to think that if she kept yapping, eventually he'd see the error in his logic.

She kept repeating that the gun was only a toy. Couldn't quite grasp the concept that wielding even a toy in a public place was a serious, arrestable offense if that toy was perceived as real and dangerous by those it was pointed at.

Pete and the other two men were booked and on their way to their cells, and she was still sitting there yapping.

Pete swung his feet off the lumpy cot. *Get the broad out of your head,* he told himself. *You've got problems enough of your own.* He rubbed his eyes. "Augh," he said aloud, grimacing under a sudden pain. "Mean left hook you've got there, man," he grumbled to one of two snoring hulks in the cell across the aisle.

Pete watched with deepening disgust. He didn't like bullies. Never had. And if Sonny was anything, it was a bully. *That* was why he'd stuck his neck out for Mary Elizabeth Drummond.

Relieved that he'd finally found an acceptable rationale for his behavior, Pete got up stiffly and studied his face in the mirror over the small white sink. "Great," he said flatly. The area around his right eye had turned brownish purple overnight and his upper lip was puffed.

Ordinarily he wouldn't have cared. It wasn't the first fight he'd been in, or the worst, but he had his brother's wedding coming up in a week. He'd hoped to look at least halfway decent.

Peeling away the tape that held a gauze pad in place, Pete examined the two-inch gash that Sonny had carved into the side of his forehead. It could've been worse, he thought. He'd seen the swing coming in enough time to pull back and just be grazed.

That was seconds before Sonny's buddy had jumped into the fight. Could've been a lot worse, Pete thought, the lines of his face falling into a study of pensive concentration as he remembered—Mary Elizabeth Drummond pulling that gun from her purse. Fly-brained she might be, but she also had courage. He'd seen the gun shaking in her hands from twelve feet away, yet she'd stood her ground and gone out on a limb...for him?

Pete shook his head to knock away the nonsense and reached for the faucet. He splashed cold water on his face and, straightening, let it trickle down his neck. He couldn't start developing a soft spot for Ms. Drummond now. Because of her he'd been arrested. Because of her he'd spent the night on a cot that felt like a cobblestone road. Because of her he would be wasting a whole morning in court, when what he'd planned was to be riding his new bike.

He heard footsteps in the hall. Pete dried his face on a thin, scratchy towel. A young officer, new with the morning shift, banged on the bars of Sonny's cell, then unlocked Pete's cell and brought in breakfast.

"'Morning. Sleep okay?"

Pete nodded. He might be mad as hell, but the local constabulary would be the last to know it.

The young man set the tray down on the end of the cot. "Half an hour till we go over to the courthouse."

"I'll be ready." Pete reached for his coffee.

The officer paused. "We brought your bike in."

"What?"

"Your motorcycle. Last night you asked if we could remove it from the parking lot of the Starlight Lounge. I thought you'd like to know that we did and it's safe over at Bernie's Garage. That's on Third Street. You can pick it up after your court appearance."

"Thanks. I appreciate it. How much for moving it?"

"Thirty dollars."

Pete nodded agreeably. "I don't suppose you could tell me what the going rate is for a bar fight in this town?" He smiled—amiably he hoped.

"About a hundred, if you get any judge other than Collins. With Collins, oh, anywhere between one-fifty and three."

Careful to show no reaction, Pete took a sip of coffee. It was hot and surprisingly good, but didn't do much to lessen his irritation.

"How's the girl?" He wasn't sure why he asked, except that she was the source of that irritation.

The policeman grimaced. "Not too happy. Friend of yours?"

Pete cocked an eyebrow.

The officer laughed. "Didn't think so. She asked for tea this morning. Earl Gray, to be exact. With honey and lemon. That was after she insisted someone go feed her cat."

Pete shook his head, lips pressed tight to show he commiserated with the young man.

"Were you able to tow her RV?"

"Yep. It's at Bernie's, too."

"Is it going to be laid up long?" Somehow, the thought of her spending any significant time in this town, with Sonny on the loose, made Pete uneasy.

"Naw. Nothing wrong with it. She just got it stuck in a ditch."

Pete sipped his coffee, keeping his eyes down and his thoughts to himself. They weren't kind. They weren't too politically correct, either.

"Well, you go ahead and finish eating. I'll be back in half an hour."

The young officer was closing the door when Pete said, "So, did you get it for her? The Earl Gray, I mean?"

The officer's mouth twitched. "What do you think?"

"I think... I'm glad I won't be seeing her after today."

The lock slid shut to the sound of the officer's laughter. Then he said, "Hey, Sonny, rise and shine. Billy, get up, let's go."

THE DISTRICT COURTHOUSE was a three-minute cruiser ride from the police station. Mary Elizabeth was sitting with her police escort in the second row of folding chairs, chewing on her lower lip and wondering how her cat was, when the stranger from the night before walked in. Her whole body seemed to rise a little when he did.

She'd been waiting for him to make an appearance. The previous night, lying sleepless in her cell, she'd thought a lot about what he'd done for her, coming to her defense the way he had. It was enough to make the most hardened cynic have faith in mankind again. Yet she hadn't even had a chance to thank him.

She was reluctant to admit it, but there was another reason she'd been keeping an eye out for his arrival. She just wanted to get another look at him. Even last night, under the most stressful conditions, his looks had been distracting enough for her to take notice.

He walked with his police attendant down the aisle that divided the seats. When he got to Mary Elizabeth's row, he paused, his steely blue eyes meeting hers as if perhaps he'd been curious about her, too, this person he'd risked life and limb for. He didn't look any happier now than he had last night.

She knew she looked awful. She was frightened and embarrassed, and had been that way all night. Now her eyes were bleary and her skin was dull. Her clothes had seen better times, too. Instinctively, she ran her shackled hands along her linen walking shorts in a futile attempt to iron out the wrinkles.

But if she looked bad, the dark-haired stranger looked even worse. Noticing his bruises, her expression crumpled. *I'm sorry,* she wanted to say, and hoped her eyes conveyed the message.

If they did, her apology fell on stone. He merely scowled and turned his head.

Another time, another place, perhaps she wouldn't have minded. But here, today, it would've been nice to have a friend. She felt rather out of her element. Never having been arrested before, she didn't know what she was doing.

She'd thought of hiring a lawyer but had been told it wasn't necessary; her case was too small. Which was just as well since she couldn't afford a lawyer, anyway. Still, she felt vulnerable without defense, helpless without someone to negotiate this unfamiliar system with her.

What if she was found guilty? She'd have a criminal record then. What would that do to her future? To her chances of getting a job? Decent housing? And what if Charles found out? He'd never let her live it down.

With hands that shook visibly, she pressed at the wrinkled linen again as if doing so would iron away those problems. When her hands reached her knees, she surreptitiously tugged up her saggy tights. Just as surreptitiously, she glanced at the tall, loose-limbed stranger, slouched in his chair across the aisle.

He looked so calm, so capable and impregnable to injustice. She'd bet *he* would never allow anyone to pin a guilty verdict on him if he was innocent. Maybe she should take her cue from him. Maybe the time had come for her to accept that she was truly on her own and no one was going to watch out for her but herself.

Pulling in a deep breath, she squared her shoulders, lifted her chin and waited for her case to be called.

"Who's the judge today?" Pete asked the policeman sitting beside him.

"Gertrude Collins."

"Collins," Pete repeated. He sank lower in his seat, giving Mary Elizabeth a dark sidelong look. Nothing had gone right since running into that woman.

She was called first. Pete watched her walk up to the bench, her spine straight as a poker, her mouth tight with righteous indignation. Her charges were read and then the judge asked how she pleaded.

Lifting her chin, but not so high that her invisible crown slipped off her head, she said, "Not guilty." Pete exhaled a long breath through his teeth.

He watched the judge confer with her and the police prosecutor—explaining the options, he guessed. Cases as small as theirs were usually taken care of immediately and on the spot. Court dockets were too overloaded to make a production out of every case that came through. Besides, she was obviously guilty—they all were—and six policemen and a bar full of witnesses could testify to that fact.

But after a long deliberation, she still insisted she wanted to fight the charges. Pete heard the officer beside him sigh. He saw the judge sigh. Three people in front of him looked at their watches.

"Could I have the other defendants in this case?" The judge motioned for Mary Elizabeth to stay.

Pete was escorted up to the front of the courtroom, with Sonny and Billy close behind. Sonny and Billy were greatly subdued this morning. They stood before the judge as docile as lambs, like Pete, knowing that cooperation was the name of the game here, the key to getting out quickly.

Their charges were read: property damage, public intoxication, and assault and battery with dangerous weapons—the weapons being the broken bottle Sonny had wielded and the chair used by Pete. After spending a few minutes plea bargaining with the police prosecutor, who in turn conferred with the judge, they were each found guilty of simple assault and fined one hundred and fifty dollars. They paid their fines, along with the towing charges for their vehicles, and were told they were free to go.

The judge then looked at Mary Elizabeth, her expression seeming to say, *Got the picture?*

Mary Elizabeth swallowed.

Sonny and his buddy took off as soon as their fines were paid. Pete was pocketing his wallet and thinking of doing the same when Mary Elizabeth turned her eyes on him. He'd noticed they were an unusual shade of warm coffee-brown, and right now they were very large and very lost.

He tried to look away. He didn't like her kind, he told himself. He'd dated a few princesses in his day and found them dull and patronizing. The dull part he could excuse...

Still, there was a bruised look in those eyes that appeared too real, a vulnerability he never would've associated with her.

He caught himself up short, just as he was sliding into sympathy. Aw, no. He wasn't going to fall for that trap again. That's the way things had started with Cindy. He gave his shoulders a flexing roll and set off for the door.

But halfway there he paused. Behind him, Mary Elizabeth was asking the judge to clarify the trial process she'd have to face if she contested the charges. Pete didn't really care what happened, but he was curious enough to want to listen in. He made his way to the side of the courtroom and stood against the wall.

Mary Elizabeth spoke quietly. He couldn't hear everything she said, but he got the sense of it. Capitulation.

The judge sighed in relief. She found Mary Elizabeth not guilty, but fined her two-hundred-and-fifty dollars.

It was a reasonable sum, but Pete could see—could almost feel—Mary Elizabeth's indignation picking up a new head of steam. Why was her fine higher than the men's? she wanted to know. Pete squinched his eyes shut. The men, she said as her handcuffs came off, had smacked each other black and blue while she had done nothing except stop the fight, which you'd think she'd be commended for instead of punished. Furthermore, why was she being fined at all if she was innocent?

Before he could think, Pete cleared his throat, loudly. She glanced over and he shook his head, hoping she understood.

She was breathing hard, conflicting emotions warring in her eyes. Something in their depths made him think that maybe her reaction to her fine wasn't really indignation at all, but fear. Fear of what, he didn't know.

Finally he saw her give in—a slow exhalation of breath, a slumping of her shoulders.

"Sorry, Your Honor," she mumbled, and reached into her bag for her wallet.

Pete stood away from the wall and once again turned to leave. He didn't like what just happened, that small communication between him and her.

He was halfway to the door again when something caught in his peripheral vision: Mary Elizabeth searching through her purse. Dread crawled over him.

"It's not here," she said, no longer speaking in that Scotch-and-soda voice that so intrigued him. She was practically squeaking now. "I...I can't find my wallet." She searched again, taking several items out. Her face had gone crimson.

"Are you sure it was in your bag?" the judge inquired.

"Positive. I had it last night at the bar." She kept rummaging through the purse, swallowing, turning redder. Finally she looked up, her eyes slightly wild. "I think it was stolen."

"Stolen?" the judge repeated.

Mary Elizabeth nodded. "At the Starlight. After I pulled out the water pistol, I threw my purse onto a table. I don't even remember doing it. I just remember that's where I found it when I left. While it was lying there, somebody must've helped himself to the contents."

"I see." The judge dragged a hand down her face. "Officer Wilson," she called, addressing the policewoman who'd been part of the arresting team at the Starlight, "as soon as Ms. Drummond's business with the court is concluded, take the information regarding her wallet."

The policewoman gave a short nod.

Mary Elizabeth looked up at the judge, dazed. "Your Honor? How am I supposed to pay my fine?"

"Did your wallet contain *all* your money?"

Coffee-brown eyes shimmered with tears. She nodded. "Seven hundred and twenty dollars."

The judge cast her a stern look. "It isn't wise to carry so much money on your person, Ms. Drummond, especially when you're traveling. Better to divide it and put it away in several locations."

Mary Elizabeth lowered her eyes and said nothing, all her uppity self-righteousness gone. Pete was beginning to think it hadn't been very real to begin with.

"Well, I suggest you call your bank and have the money wired to you."

"I'm afraid I can't do that, Your Honor. I closed all my accounts before I set out on this trip."

Standing a few feet away, Pete scowled. Closed all her accounts? And she had only seven hundred bucks? Mary Elizabeth was becoming more of a puzzle every minute.

Then it hit. *That* was why she'd reacted to her fine. She'd been worried about the amount of money she'd have to hand over.

The judge said, "Then I suggest you contact a relative or a friend."

Again, Mary Elizabeth shook her head. "I . . . I can't do that, either."

The judge was growing impatient. "Unless you want to work out an alternative, I think you had better, young lady."

"May I ask what the alternative is?" Mary Elizabeth inquired, squeezing and twisting the strap of her purse.

"Fifteen days in the county jail."

Mary Elizabeth's eyes went a few degrees wilder.

Pete clasped the nape of his neck. *Don't do it, Mitchell. Get yourself the hell out of here,* he thought, even as he stepped forward and said, "Your Honor, I'll loan Ms. Drummond the money. That way you can get this train moving again." He could've sworn the formidable woman on the bench mouthed the words "Thank you." He didn't say "You're welcome." He was angry at her for assuming Mary Elizabeth had money readily available, an assumption based on the style of her hair and the quality of her clothes.

Mary Elizabeth turned in surprise. Her gaze traveled over him in quick assessment, taking in his black eye, two-day-old beard, faded jacket and jeans whose knee had finally popped a tear.

"That's very generous of you, but I couldn't possibly accept your money."

Instantly he rued his generosity, not knowing whether to laugh at her mistaken assumptions about him or shove her condescension down her throat.

"Fifteen days," he reminded her, half hoping she'd go for the time.

"But . . . are you sure you can spare it?" she asked.

"For you? Anything." He winked, but there was no mistaking his sarcasm.

She looked confused. "I'll repay you. Just as soon as I reach where I'm going."

"Of course you will. I didn't say it was a gift."

The judge asked, "Are you willing to pay her tow charge as well?"

"Yes. How much?"

"Sixty-five dollars."

Mary Elizabeth's face dropped. "I don't believe this," she muttered, but only loud enough for Pete to hear. He nudged her with his elbow, using restraint to just nudge and not ram. Her muttering ceased.

Pete handed over the cash, making a mental note to stop at the first ATM he came to.

"That's it? I'm free to go?" Mary Elizabeth asked, a conflicted mixture of incredulity and relief.

"Yes. Next case," the judge said quickly.

Mary Elizabeth couldn't shake the feeling she was caught in a nightmare. She felt almost sick from exhaustion and fear, and knew, as she walked away from the bench, her steps were weavy. All she wanted to do was crawl under a rock somewhere and sleep. Instead, Officer Wilson was waiting for her, pad and pen poised.

"The wallet's beige, cowhide, monogrammed in gold with my initials," Mary Elizabeth said.

"Credit cards?"

"Yes. Three." She fought off a tightening in her throat. "And a gasoline card, and four department store cards." Her sense of being caught in a dream world deepened. What was she to do now? No money, no plastic...

"Where would you like us to send the wallet, if it turns up?"

"Oh." Mary Elizabeth passed an unsteady hand over her brow. "My friend's in Sarasota. Yes, definitely my friend's." If it ever went back to Charles, she'd die of humiliation. She could almost hear him saying it now, "I told you you'd never make it on your own."

Unexpectedly, thoughts of home rushed over her, and with them came remembrance of her mother's affair, her shock at learning she was illegitimate, her distress over her pregnancy... so many problems that had somehow gotten relegated to a back burner since last evening.

Having procured all the necessary information, the officer pocketed her pen, wished Mary Elizabeth well, and walked off, leaving her standing alone with the weight of her remembered troubles. Feeling vague and quite disoriented, she turned to go. "Oh," she said in surprise. Peter Mitchell, whose name she'd learned just this hour, was still in the courtroom, standing right behind her.

He had the clearest blue eyes she'd ever seen. The fact that one of them was bruised didn't detract from their impact one bit. Right now those eyes were narrowed under a lowered brow, studying her. She guessed she looked pretty bewildered.

"Yes?" she asked uncertainly.

"Do you want to take my address?"

She blinked, uncomprehending.

"So you'll know where to send the money I lent you."

"Oh, yes, of course." She opened her purse and withdrew a pen and a small notebook. He took them from her and began to write. He had nice hands, she thought distractedly. Strong, broad hands that were cut and callused yet imbued with a certain masculine grace.

He wrote his address on the top sheet of paper, along with the amount she owed him. Then he flipped to the next sheet and wrote out an IOU, to which Mary Elizabeth added her signature and Chloe's address.

"That should do it," Pete said, pocketing the IOU.

"Yes." She glanced down at the address he'd written in a surprisingly neat but firm hand and felt a kick of adrenaline. "You live in Tampa?"

But he had already turned and was heading for the exit. She hurried to catch up. Her head had cleared remarkably. Moreover, her spirits were lifting, probably because it had just begun to sink in that she'd been found not guilty. She would have no criminal record, no impediments standing in the way of establishing herself in a new location.

"This is really a coincidence. I'm going to Florida myself."

Peter opened the courtroom door and made his way through the crowded corridor, his eyes fixed on the exit ahead.

"I'm going to Sarasota," she persisted, following. "That's on the Gulf Coast too, not very far from Tampa, right?"

"No," he said, hurrying on. "It's miles away. Many, many miles."

Mary Elizabeth would've contested his claim, but just then she spotted the policeman with the sincere, youthful face who'd arrested her the previous night. He was standing by the main door, just ending a conversation with someone who looked like a lawyer.

"Excuse me," she said. "Do you know if there's a phone at the garage where my RV was taken?"

"Yes, ma'am, there is."

"Great. Thanks." She'd call the credit card companies from there to notify them that her cards had been stolen. She continued out the door, Peter Mitchell a few brisk paces ahead of her. She'd thought perhaps they'd walk to the garage together or maybe take a cab, but apparently he wanted to go his own way, alone. She drooped with mild disappointment.

"Can I give you a lift?" the policeman asked, jogging down the courthouse steps after them. "I'm on my way to the garage myself. Got to take my vehicle in for a tune-up."

Mary Elizabeth looked toward Peter Mitchell, already chugging along the sidewalk, and her smile returned. "That would be great."

Pete didn't intend to stop. His instincts told him it was time to break away, go find a diner or a bookstore until Mary Elizabeth Drummond was out of town and safely gone from his life. He had no desire to get to know her better, especially if she was going to be living in Sarasota!

"Peter?" she called, and when he didn't respond, she said, "Mr. Mitchell." Damn. She spoke his name in that deep, dusky voice that had the ability to rise and fall and float around a man's imagination like a dancer's silk veil. He glanced over his shoulder.

"Come on." She beckoned him toward the open door of the squad car with a bright, wide-eyed smile. You'd think she'd just copped a ride on a twelve-horse coach. The earnest young officer was looking at him, too, waiting. Pete rolled his eyes heavenward, wondering who had it in for him now.

Bernie's Garage, a five-stall cinderblock building, sat on a quarter acre of asphalt enclosed by an eight-foot-high chain-link fence. Several impounded vehicles, as well as a few police cars under repair, were parked to one side of the garage. Civilian vehicles occupied the rest of the lot.

Pete spotted his bike as soon as they drove through the gate. His heart kicked over, lovesick. It seemed okay, but he wouldn't breathe easy until he'd had a closer look.

The officer twisted his wiry torso to glance at his passengers through the safety grate. "I hope you have a safe trip from here on."

"I'll certainly try," Mary Elizabeth said, "although it won't be easy."

Pete wished the guy would open the damn door and let him out.

"That wallet contained everything I needed to get by. My money, my credit cards..."

Dread crawled over Pete's skin again. That had been happening a lot lately.

"...My health insurance card..."

He cleared his throat, as he had in court, but she didn't look at him.

"...Important phone numbers..."

Pete nudged her loafer with his boot, and when she finally glanced his way he gave her the blackest warning look he could muster.

"Everything," she said, frowning in vexation at him. "It even contained my driver's license."

Mary Elizabeth watched Pete close his eyes and slap a hand to his brow. The next moment she understood what he had been trying to head off.

Her gaze shot to the police officer, who looked pretty disheartened himself. He looked away, pulled at his nose a few times, looked back.

She winced and slipped low in her seat. The officer had to have known that her license had been stolen along with her wallet. Would he have let her drive off if she hadn't mentioned it? She felt the irrational urge to apologize for complicating his life.

"Do you have four forms of identification? That's what you'll need to apply for a new license."

Mary Elizabeth thought hard. She'd brought along a birth certificate. And her RV registration was in the glove compartment. But that was all she could come up with. Anything else usable as ID had been stolen.

She supposed she could have her social security card reprocessed and mailed to her here.

Here? She didn't exactly have an address. A tremor of panic ran through her. *Think, Drummond. Concentrate.*

She could rent a post office box, then. She could have her new credit cards mailed here, as well. But the process would take days. Maybe a week or more.

"It might take a while," she replied, her voice unsteady.

The officer flattened his lips. "I'm really sorry about this, but I can't let you drive without a license."

"I understand." She understood, all right. She'd bungled things again. At the rate she was going, she'd never make it to Florida.

The officer stepped out of the squad car and opened the back door, almost being knocked over as Pete shot past. "Well, maybe it's a good thing you've got a camper, ma'am."

"Yes." She gulped, wondering if she'd have to stay here in this fenced-in lot until she got all her paperwork together.

She slid out of the cruiser. Peter Mitchell was crouched alongside a motorcycle, his pale denim jacket pulled taut across his wide back. She should have guessed he'd be riding a motorcycle, though that one looked sort of strange. Although it gleamed in the sunlight as if it were new, it was an older model than the ones she was used to seeing. Much older.

Hmm.

She'd overheard him report that he was self-employed. Was that his way of saying he was *un*employed? Was Peter Mitchell on the road looking for work? And how much of a sacrifice had he made paying her fine? Had she thanked him? She couldn't even remember.

"The phone is inside the garage," the policeman reminded her.

"I'll be along in a minute. I have to check on my cat first."

He nodded and walked off.

Mary Elizabeth did want to check on Monet, but first she turned her attention to Peter Mitchell. He was straddling his rumbling bike, ready to leave. She crossed the lot at a run. "Peter," she called, waving her arms in case he didn't hear.

The bike took a little lurch before stopping. "What's the matter?" he asked, looking at her from behind dark glasses.

"I haven't had a chance to thank you for everything you've done."

He lifted one shoulder in a scant shrug and revved the engine.

"I mean it," she said, placing a staying hand on his upper arm. Even through a layer of heavy denim, she felt the vibrancy of his muscled flesh. Her palm warmed with an unsettling tingle. "Not many people would've done what you did last night," she said, removing her hand. "And then paying my fine today... I want you to know I really, *really* appreciate it. I can't imagine how I could ever repay you.''

''Three-hundred-and-fifteen dollars will do,'' he said. He had a Clint Eastwood kind of voice, she thought, momentarily bemused. Soft as a prayer. Dark as sin. ''And as far as last night goes,'' he added, ''consider us even, all debts squared away.''

She tilted her head. ''How do you figure that?''

''You came to my rescue, too, by pulling that gun. You stopped the fight and kept me from getting the tar knocked out of me. It was a stupid stunt—it got you arrested—but it worked, and as I see it, repaid me in full for whatever I did for you.'' He shifted his balance and looked toward the open gate.

Mary Elizabeth knew there was nothing left to say. She ought to step aside and let him go. She shouldn't want to hold him back. She knew nothing about this man. And yet...

She reached for his arm again. ''Wait.''

''What now?'' His mouth was so serious it was almost grim. She noticed the upper lip was cracked and slightly swollen. A nice mouth, though, firm but warm-looking, and beautifully shaped.

''What is it?'' he repeated.

Her pulse raced. Was she out of her mind? She'd met the man in a *bar,* for heaven's sake. An unquestionably seedy bar, at that. He was no stranger to fighting, no stranger to being jailed. He was tough and huge and dangerous-looking, and he scared her half to death. And yet...

''I don't suppose you'd care to open the ledger again.''

He took off his dark glasses and squinted at her. The hard blue energy in his eyes seemed to compress. ''What do you mean?''

"Well, I was thinking… " She wondered if he could hear her heart thumping. "It's another crazy idea, but…"

"Spit it out, Mary Elizabeth." He drawled her name with almost singsong mockery.

"Would you consider driving me and my RV out of town? We could say that you've offered to drive me all the way to Florida, but once we're safely away from here…"

"Mary Elizabeth!" he said, clutching his chest in feigned shock. "That's illegal."

"Yeah, well…" she tried not to grin. "It's the company I've been keeping lately."

His beautifully shaped mouth twitched, and twitched again, before he brought it under proper control.

"To repay you, I could fix you some lunch. How's that?"

He looked off into the distance, seemingly considering the offer. But then he said, "Sorry, it wouldn't work. For one thing, what would I do with my bike? For another, well, I just prefer traveling alone."

Mary Elizabeth rubbed her arms, nodding, lips pressed tight. "It was just a thought."

"Yeah." He slipped on his sunglasses again, looked to the road, looked back. She thought she felt his gaze traveling over her, but wasn't sure. Then, with a nod and a hot blast of exhaust against her shins, he sped away.

She continued to stand there, clutching her elbows and listening to the sound of his bike growing fainter. When it finally faded altogether, the lot seemed unnaturally quiet. She could hear the tiniest metallic clank of a tool being placed or picked up from the cement floor in the garage. In all her life, she thought she'd never heard such a lonely sound.

She didn't have time to dwell on the phenomenon, however, because just then she spotted Sonny and his friend plodding along the sidewalk, heading for the entrance to this very lot. Within a matter of seconds she was inside her RV with every door and window locked.

She was relieved to see that Monet was all right and that someone had refilled his food and water bowls, but after the briefest of pats on the head, she dashed to the bathroom where Sonny couldn't possibly see her if he happened to look through a window.

She knew her behavior was bizarre. What could he possibly do to her here, with a policeman just yards away? Why would he want to do anything?

Nevertheless, she remained flat against the closed bathroom door, her breathing shallow, her heart galloping away. She heard Sonny's distinctively high voice, heard the young officer talking to him, then, after what seemed an eternity, a car engine starting up.

Only when it faded in the distance did she allow herself to relax. When she did, though, she realized she felt wretched. Far too much had happened within the past couple of days. It was finally backing up on her. But for once in her life she was in exactly the right place at the right time. She simply sank to her knees and let herself be sick.

When she finally felt better, she washed her face and lowered her shaky self to the toilet lid. Leaning forward, she dangled the wet washcloth between her knees and stared at the brown linoleum. Her ribs ached.

Maybe Mrs. Pidgin was right; this wasn't such a good idea. She couldn't even make the three-day journey, which she'd thought would be the easiest part of leaving home. How, then, would she start a new life, make new friends, find a job, a place to live? And how in heaven's name would she do all that *and* have a baby?

Maybe she ought to go back. Maybe there was no other way than to tell Roger about her pregnancy and marry him. So what if they didn't love each other? So what if they'd already broken up before she discovered she was pregnant? As Charles had said, it was the right thing to do.

The only question was, right for whom?

She closed her eyes, longing for the sweet oblivion of sleep. Unfortunately, there were things that demanded her attention—calling the credit card companies, for instance.

She hauled herself to her feet, brushed her teeth, combed her hair and unlocked the bathroom door, preoccupied with thoughts of finding her financial records. She was surprised to find the interior of the RV had darkened. Evidently, the sky had lowered while she'd been closeted in the windowless bathroom.

But she wasn't nearly as surprised by the darkness as by the fact that a light had been turned on in the kitchen. On a rising tide of curiosity and inexplicable hope, she hurried forward.

She was right. A light *had* been turned on, over the table, casting a warm cozy glow over her mother's Battenburg lace.

It also cast its warmth on a man who, after all, had not gone away. When he heard her come forward, he put down the book he was reading, and with one booted foot pushed out the chair opposite him.

It was then she noticed the cup of tea waiting for her. Earl Gray, to be exact. With honey and lemon.

CHAPTER FOUR

I OUGHT TO HAVE MY HEAD examined, Pete thought, putting down his book.

He'd gone five blocks, successfully ignoring his conscience, but then he'd noticed Sonny and his sidekick walking along the street in the direction of the garage. They'd be crazy to start trouble with Mary Elizabeth today, he'd thought; the consequences would be a lot more serious than a simple fine. On the other hand, they just might be vindictive enough not to care. By the time he'd reached the highway Pete had been racked with concern and guilt. So he'd returned, driven all the way back to Bernie's, only to find no trace of Sonny—but Mary Elizabeth in need of assistance anyway.

Mary Elizabeth seated herself opposite him. She looked pale, tired and humiliated, probably at having somebody hear her throw up. "What are you doing here?" she asked weakly. "How did you get in?"

"First things first. Would you like something to eat with that. Toast? Crackers?"

Her smile was faint. "Crackers would be nice."

Pete slid out of the bench and opened the cupboard where he'd found the tea. He returned with the entire box, and then realized maybe he ought to bring her a plate.

"That's fine," she said, reading his thoughts.

He set the box in front of her, slid into the bench and said, "Now, to answer your question, I came in through the door. How did you think?"

Her eyes widened. "But it was locked."

"No, it wasn't."

Mary Elizabeth dropped her head to one hand and groaned, "Oh, God. I thought I'd locked it. I thought . . ."

"Eat," he said. "Get something in your stomach."

She pulled a cracker from the box with two fingers, the others crooked daintily, and nibbled off a small bite. Pete watched as she took a sip of tea, turned the cracker and took another tiny bite. It looked like this might take a while. He settled more comfortably into the banquette and gazed around the RV.

As a general principle, he held motor homes in abject contempt. With their microwave ovens and color TVs, they made an utter mockery of camping. But when he'd entered Mary Elizabeth's cluttered motor home, his purist sensibilities had gone into something like sugar-shock.

He was used to traveling light. Even on trips that lasted several weeks, he managed to fit all the necessities of survival into a few well-planned saddlebags.

Trying to be charitable, he reminded himself that Mary Elizabeth wasn't on a camping trip. If what she'd told the police was true, she was moving. Having lots of cartons stacked around was only to be expected.

Cartons he could overlook. He could overlook the rocking chair that obstructed the living space, as well. What he couldn't quite get over, though, was the fancy lace on this table. And the stained-glass dingle-dangles hanging in the windows. And that vanilla-and-cinnamon smell he associated with expensive gift shops. There was a wreath of dry weeds on the door, a huge snoring cat overhanging the edge of the bunk above the cab, and framed embroidery every-where. He'd never seen a motor home quite like it.

Then again, he'd never met a traveler quite like Mary Elizabeth, either, a woman who'd chosen to set out on a sixteen-hundred-mile journey dressed in an outfit that he'd bet cost hundreds of dollars and could only be dry-cleaned.

"How are you feeling?" he asked her.

"Better." She finished off another cracker. "I really hate being sick. I'm usually not. Usually I have the constitution of a workhorse."

"Do you have the flu?"

"No." She looked aside and said no again, quietly. "A lot's happened to me lately. That's all."

He studied her sidecast eyes and closed expression. The words "Tell me about it" were almost on his lips, when he caught them back. Dammit, he didn't like women with se-crets, especially secrets that hinted at problems he didn't want to deal with. He preferred the straightforward kind, women who were undemanding, easy to please, easy to take pleasure from in return. Mary Elizabeth Drummond was none of the above, and he had no desire to get to know her better.

She drained her teacup. Her color was coming back, all peaches and cream. "You answered only one of my ques-tions," she reminded him. "You still haven't told me why you're here."

Pete didn't let himself rethink what he was about to do. Without preamble he said, "I changed my mind."

She closed her eyes and sat very still. "About what?"

"If you'll add the use of your shower to the lunch you offered earlier, I'll accept your deal."

Pent-up anxiety escaped on an explosive breath. "Thank you," she said, opening those big coffee-brown eyes and letting their warmth pour over him.

"Hey, don't get too grateful on me now. It's only until we're safely away from this town."

She nodded vigorously. "Of course. I understand. But what about your motorcycle?" She took another cracker out of the box and popped it into her mouth whole.

"I think I can work something out."

"Really?" Her delicate oval face brightened. Her whole *body* brightened, making him think it might be nice to just sit there and watch her for two or three hours.

"Hold on." Pete raised his hands, trying to stem her too-ready optimism—and maybe his reaction to it, as well. The last thing he wanted was to start liking this woman or finding her attractive. "I might work something out *if* you're willing to add a few bucks to what you already owe me."

Her smooth brow puckered. "What for?"

"I'll have to buy one of those trailers out there, if Bernie will sell one, that is."

"Oh. Oh, well, sure," she agreed, smiling again. "There's already a hitch at the rear of the motor home. The former owners used to tow a small car."

"Yes. I noticed." Pete had known towing his bike wouldn't be a problem even when he'd used it earlier as an excuse.

"Well, let's go ask." She popped out of her seat, combing her fingers through her hair.

"The policeman who gave us a ride is still here," Pete said, following. "You'd better tell him about this setup before he thinks you've skipped town and there's an APB out on you."

Her smile widened, showing off a set of remarkably white and even teeth. "Wouldn't that be something!" Then she opened the door and practically skipped down the RV's two metal steps.

Oh, great, Pete thought miserably. She was the bouncy kind, chirping cheerily just minutes after being sick. He hated bouncy, chirpy people.

The policeman, whose name was Riley, was standing just inside the garage. Pete knew he'd been watching the RV ever since he'd gone into it. "What's up?" he inquired.

"Mr. Mitchell has offered to drive me to Florida."

The officer gave Pete a tight once-over. "That right?"

Pete nodded. "It doesn't make sense, her being stuck here, trying to get her old license renewed. By the time it comes through, she could already be in Sarasota with her new license in her pocket. And since we're both traveling in that direction, anyway..."

The officer looked at Mary Elizabeth. "Are you sure that arrangement's okay with you?"

She nodded spiritedly. "It was my idea to begin with."

"I thought you were on vacation, Mitchell?"

"I was, but those court expenses this morning kind of put a crimp in my plans. A free ride home looks pretty good right about now."

"Well, you watch your p's and q's," Riley warned. "Remember, we have everybody's address, we know where you're going, and I plan to add this latest development to your file."

Just then a mechanic in a gray jumpsuit shambled over. "Car's all set, Pat."

"Thanks, Bernie." The officer turned back to Mary Elizabeth. "Well, good luck to you, ma'am." He touched the visor of his cap and actually cracked a smile before getting into his vehicle and driving away.

As soon as he was gone, Mary Elizabeth shouldered her way around Pete and strode into the garage. "So, you're Bernie?"

"Yuh. Bernie Kearns." The mechanic wiped his hands on a grease-blackened rag.

"You're just the man I want to see, then."

Forty minutes later Mary Elizabeth had convinced the garage owner to sell them a small wooden trailer, Pete had hooked it to the RV and secured his bike, and she had phoned all the department stores and credit card companies she had needed to contact.

"I feel so much better," she said, leaving the garage at Pete's side. "Whoever stole my wallet went on a shopping spree. They've charged close to two thousand dollars in my name so far, but I'm not going to be held accountable for those charges."

"And are they sending you new cards?"

"Uh-huh. They're being mailed to my friend's in Florida. So, how's your motorcycle?"

Pete led her to the trailer at the rear of the motor home. The Triumph's wheels were locked within deep wooden blocks, its body secured with enough chain and cord to hold down a mad Brahma bull.

"Are you sure it's secure enough?" she asked.

Pete frowned at his handiwork, genuinely concerned for several long seconds before realizing she was joking. He didn't laugh. He'd grown increasingly disgruntled as he'd worked. It was a jury-rigged job and it hadn't been easy. Thoughts of how much vacation time he'd already lost because of Mary Elizabeth had begun to eat away at him, too. On top of that he was starving.

Emitting a low grumble, he grabbed up his duffel bag and said, "Let's get this show on the road."

Inside, Pete tried to get into a better frame of mind, but when he took the front seat, his mood only darkened. He'd driven all sorts of vehicles in his time, from megaton backhoes to powerful sports cars, but never in his life had he expected to one day be sitting at the wheel of a motor home, with a lace potpourri ball swinging from the radio knob and a wind chime of ceramic geese jangling above his left ear.

"Is anything wrong?" Mary Elizabeth's bourbon-over-ice voice drew him out of his thoughts.

"Uh—no. Got a road map?"

She reached for a neatly folded map on the dashboard. Pete took it from her and opened it out over the steering wheel. Interstate 95, from Maine to Florida, had been highlighted with an orange marker.

"Okay. This is where we are," he said, moving the map between them and pointing. She leaned in. Pete picked up her scent, something fresh and floral—orange blossoms?

"Are you sure?"

"Uh-hmm. Northwest of the Tappan Zee Bridge." He smiled fractionally. "Why? Where'd you think you were?"

"Not there." Her lips stretched in a comic grimace. "I thought I was on my way back to Connecticut. Instead, I must've gotten on the Bronx River Parkway or maybe Route 87 and headed north."

"How did that happen?"

Her cheeks warmed to a soft pink. "I sort of got turned around in the Bronx." Quickly she added, "So, Peter, how do I get back to I-95?"

Pete studied the map and all its possibilities. "This way." But instead of drawing his finger due south, backtracking to the Bronx, he inscribed a loop that crossed the Hudson via the Tappan Zee Bridge and came down along the western bank of the river, in New Jersey.

"Isn't that kind of indirect?"

He noticed she had a distracting way of wrinkling her nose when she questioned him.

"Only a little. We're not far from the bridge now. Besides, that route is a little more pleasant. I'll leave you off...

let's see, somewhere in here, around Ridgefield. I don't think you'll have much trouble from there."

"That's very kind of you, taking me all that way."

Pete folded the map into a bulging package that began to swell as soon as it hit the dash. "That's me, all right," he mumbled in self-disgust. "Old Mr. Kind."

The orange cat roused itself from sleep and leapt down from the bunk, landing with a thud. He lumbered forward, sat at Mary Elizabeth's feet and looked up at her with an exhausted expression. Apparently, the vault into her lap was too much to expect so soon after his leap from the bunk.

"Come on, Monet." Mary Elizabeth patted her lap.

Pete's left eyebrow curled. *Monet?*

Mary Elizabeth sighed and finally heaved the lazy bundle off the floor. "I hope you don't mind if I sit for a minute. I haven't forgotten that lunch I promised you. I just feel so exhausted all of a sudden."

Pete's stomach was so empty it hurt. "No rush," he said. He turned the ignition. "All right, we're out of here."

The motor home eased its way through Bernie's lot, out the gate and down the street. Mary Elizabeth sank more comfortably into the contoured seat, experiencing the first release from tension she'd felt in days.

She looked out the side window. Commercial buildings flickered by, lamp poles, car lots, trees. She wanted to ask Peter about himself but didn't want to irk him any more than she already had. Obviously, he wasn't happy about this arrangement, but then she couldn't blame him. It was a tremendous imposition.

"By the way—" He spoke so unexpectedly she jumped. "It's Pete, not Peter. Nobody ever calls me Peter."

"Oh." She gave his hard profile a considering study. "How sad."

Frowning, he leaned away from her. She thought she heard his breath hissing like a slow tire leak.

On the outskirts of town, they passed a series of small strip malls, a vague familiarity making her think she'd come this way in the squad car last night. She saw a gas station, a two-story motel, a green highway sign—and sat up abruptly. She knew this place. This was where her adventure had begun.

Her head swiveled. Behind her the motel was just disappearing around a bend, the very motel she'd come off the highway seeking last night. She swiveled forward, and with sickening clarity the Starlight Lounge came into view. Across the road, under the sighing pines that shielded the cottage she'd been so afraid of, two young children were playing with a spaniel.

She sank back, pressed by the weight of irony. If only she'd started eeny-meenying on the opposite side of the road. If only she'd decided to try the house instead of the lounge.

But then she wouldn't have met Peter Mitchell, she thought unexpectedly, and somehow, on some level she didn't quite comprehend, he seemed worth the trouble.

They took the on ramp to the highway. Mary Elizabeth adjusted the cat to a more comfortable position and watched the trees sail by under a rain-threatening sky. A languorous warmth flowed through her, calming her overwrought nerves, quieting her mind. Not even the oldies station Peter had tuned in to disturbed her lassitude. She turned her body, tucked up her left leg and watched him through her lowered lashes. Even in such a large vehicle he seemed sizable. Though it was unfamiliar to him, he looked competent and in control.

He'd taken off his jacket, revealing a T-shirt-clad body that was solid and well-muscled. But his build wasn't grotesquely bulky like Sonny's. There was fluidity of line to his body, a naturalness to his strength.

Her languorous gaze lifted to his profile. She studied the hard, down-curving set of his mouth, the cynical squint lines carved into his sun-hammered skin. The heavy shadow along his unshaven jaw, coupled with the black eye and cut lip, gave him a sinister cast. But Mary Elizabeth doubted there was a sinister bone in his entire body. He might be rough and raucous, like the song "Great Balls of Fire" that was playing on the radio. But sinister? No. Anyone who'd come to the aid of a stranger to the extent he'd come to hers had to be honorable right to the core.

From the expressions that flashed across his face, she also sensed he was a considerably intelligent man, which made her wonder why he rode an ancient motorcycle, dressed in ratty denim and habituated country bars. And why, above all, hadn't he risen higher in life?

Perhaps she *should* be concerned about this driving arrangement. Peter Mitchell was a package of contradictions, a package that, when all was said and done, she really didn't know. She just thought she did because they'd been through so much together since last evening. For all she actually knew, she might be riding merrily along with another Jeffrey Dahmer.

She opened her heavy eyes a fluttery crack and took in his profile again. No, he wasn't a Jeffrey Dahmer. He was a good man, an honorable man, tall and quiet, like an old-time cowboy. Peter Mitchell, she thought groggily as sleep overtook her, king of chivalry and rock 'n' roll...

THE MOTOR HOME ROCKED gently over an unevenness in the road. Pete glanced at Mary Elizabeth's slumped form, turned at an angle to face him. The motion of the vehicle must have lulled her to sleep. She looked as zonked as the cat in her arms.

He was surprised. He'd expected her to bend his ear, ask him nosy questions, chirp all the way to Ridgefield. She mustn't have slept too well last night in her jail cell. Pete smiled faintly. Served her right, the little brat.

She was a pretty little brat, though; you couldn't deny her that. The waves in her hair had drooped somewhat overnight, but it still looked nice, better in fact, falling like silk across her face. He liked the color, too, the soft striations of honey and ash.

And then there was that peaches-and-cream complexion. He glanced again as if to confirm his memory of it. Flawless, still.

His glance cut to her mouth. In repose, it looked softer than it usually did. Wider and fuller, too. Awake, she was usually so tense, her lips all but disappeared.

She did have a great smile, though. Great teeth. *Rich* teeth. Probably fluoridated, polished, braced and capped since the first one poked through.

On impulse, Pete flipped down the visor and bared his own teeth in the attached mirror. They weren't as white as hers—he drank too much coffee—but they were strong and straight and all his own, which was saying a lot for someone who hadn't been taken to a dentist...ever. He'd had to take himself, when he was sixteen and becoming self-conscious about such things.

He heard Mary Elizabeth sigh and quickly flipped up the visor, his face warming. What the hell was he doing?

He slanted a look her way, but she continued to sleep. Her left arm had slipped off the cat and come to rest on her leg, her hand hanging limply over the bent knee. Pete gazed at her hand, a hand with long graceful fingers and nails modestly filed and buffed.

It was also a hand with a pale band of skin on its ring finger. He scowled, sensing trouble. She'd told the police she was single, but that telltale ring mark indicated otherwise. What was Mary Elizabeth trying to hide? Was she on the run from something? From some*one?* For a second Pete felt the urge to check his sideview mirror, expecting to find an irate husband trailing in the motor home's wake.

But, no, Mary Elizabeth didn't strike him as anyone's wife. It could've simply been a piece of meaningless jewelry, he told himself.

Then why the evasive answers when she was being booked? Why the anxiety?

And why, he wondered irritably, was he wasting his time puzzling over an up-town girl who'd gotten his face busted, his police record lengthened, and his wallet drained of three hundred and sixty bucks? He was never going to see her after today.

He drove two miles before he caved in and looked at her again. She was still wearing her jacket, all three buttons fastened, but the lapels had folded open, exposing the silky shell she wore underneath. Because of the way she was sitting, it pulled across her front, revealing a figure that was slim, graceful and feminine.

Too feminine.

And there she was, trusting him so blindly and completely that she'd fallen asleep. In a motor home, no less. With a bed in back where visibility from passing motorists would be virtually nonexistent. How vulnerable could a woman get? *Ah, Ms. Drummond, you have a lot to learn.* The question was, why did he feel it was up to him to do the teaching?

"Mary Elizabeth," he called softly. "Hey. Wake up." She continued to sleep. "I want to talk to you." *No, I don't. But, you see, I have these two sisters.* "Yo, princess." He finally poked her arm.

Mary Elizabeth woke with a start. "Wha'za matter?" She turned her head, confused. "Oh. Peter." She exhaled a sigh as she reoriented herself.

"It's Pete," he reminded her. "Sorry to wake you, but we've got to talk." Slowing the RV, he eased it into a roadside rest area.

"We do? About what?"

He parked the vehicle under trees that were dripping with gathered mist. "The facts of life."

She cast him a wry look. "The facts of life?"

"Yes. On the road. The first rule of which is, you've got to be careful. Very, very careful. And I'm afraid you've flunked that one big time."

"By going into the Starlight? I already know that."

"Yeah, that was pretty dumb. But what I'm referring to now is the way you invited me onboard here. You shouldn't have done that. I could've been anybody for all you knew. A maniac, an escaped convict..."

Mary Elizabeth chafed under his criticism. "What's your point, Peter?"

"Pete," he corrected her. "My point is, disaster can happen anytime, anyplace, just like that." He snapped his fingers. "And you were courting disaster—robbery, rape, murder."

"I was not. I trusted you. I wouldn't have invited someone onboard I didn't trust."

"But that's my point. These days you can't tell who's trustworthy and who's not. Appearances are deceiving, and the world is full of creeps waiting to take advantage of the unwary."

"And that's *my* point," she insisted. He apparently thought she had fluff for brains. "I was not vulnerable. I didn't invite just anybody." A tiny part of her also knew he was right, but she didn't want to admit to herself she'd been so careless.

"Yeah? So, what do you know about me?"

She met his challenge with one of her own. "Well, are you or are you not a trustworthy man?"

He studied her a long, silent while. Finally he sniffed and looked away. "You were just lucky it was me."

"I wasn't lucky. I *knew*. And I didn't judge you by appearances only. In fact, not by appearances at all."

His gaze slid back to her. A raised eyebrow seemed to ask the question he refused to voice.

She said, "If you can't judge a person by his actions, how *can* you judge him?"

His penetrating blue eyes, fringed with indecently thick lashes, swept over her with deepening interest. "Yeah, well, just don't do it again. The next guy might not be so 'trustworthy,' and I won't be around to pull your bacon out of the fire."

Although she rarely even raised her voice, she suddenly wanted to hit him. Just haul back and wham that arrogant male superiority complex down his throat. Instead, she removed the cat from her lap and undid her seat belt.

"Where are you going?"

"To make you lunch." The sooner their obligations to each other were paid, the better. Why had she thought she liked this person?

"Well—" he looked out the wet windshield to the quiet rest area "—this is as good a place as any to take a shower. How about I do that first?"

"It makes no difference to me."

When Pete stepped out of the steamy bathroom ten minutes later, he found the table had been set with a platinum-rimmed white plate, a linen napkin and a cut-glass tumbler.

Upon the plate lay a sandwich and a pickle. A *thin* sandwich and a pickle. A thin sandwich *with the crusts cut off*, and a pickle. His empty stomach growled.

Mary Elizabeth was sitting in the passenger seat up front, with her feet resting on the driver's seat. Bathed in the watery green light that poured through the wide front windows, she seemed to be sitting in a strange underwater cave. She didn't bother to look up from the book she was reading when he said, "Aren't you going to eat, too?"

She shook her head, eyes still fixed on the page. "The tea and crackers will hold me for a while." Apparently she was still miffed about his advice concerning her trust in strangers. Fine, let her sulk, he told himself. He didn't want to talk to her, either.

Yet something about her kept Pete rooted to the spot and staring at her. Was it her complete and utter disdain of him? Or was it something else? The aloneness he felt surrounding her? The tragic beauty he read in her delicate features bathed in that strange, green, other-worldly light? *Who are you?* he wanted to ask. *What are you running from? Where are you going?*

She finally looked up and just for a heartbeat he thought he saw an unguarded reaction, the slightest widening of those coffee-brown eyes. But then shutters came down and she said, "Is there something else?" The orange cat in her lap lifted his head and cast him the same disdainful look.

"Do you mind if I get something to drink?"

"Of course not." She flicked back her hair, a minimal gesture that nonetheless conveyed a wealth of pride. Then she went back to her reading, as chilling as any ice princess he'd ever met.

CHAPTER FIVE

MARY ELIZABETH WAS burning up. In spite of his bruises and days-old beard, she had already concluded that Peter Mitchell was an uncommonly handsome man. But when she'd looked up just now, the realization had hit on a purely visceral level. With his thick, still-damp hair combed back from his face, and the rugged planes of that face freshly shaven, he was truly a sight to behold.

He'd changed into a fresh pair of jeans—these were not torn—and an ordinary navy polo shirt that was respectable enough to have come straight from her brother's closet. Unfortunately, she'd never seen anyone looking quite so virile in an ordinary knit shirt before.

In that unguarded moment, she'd found herself responding to him in a frankly feminine way, her body rising to an elemental physical pull. It was bizarre. Showering and shaving hadn't changed his appearance that much, but the changes were sufficient to make her uncomfortably aware of him in a physical way.

She was appalled. What was she doing feeling sexual stirrings for this man? She was pregnant, for heaven's sake. That part of her life had shut down, at least for the foreseeable future. In addition, she didn't think she even liked him anymore.

She heard Pete take a seat at the table. Cautiously she looked up. He was staring at the sandwich she'd prepared, a curious expression on his face. She couldn't imagine what was wrong now.

The next moment he picked up one of the triangular halves, popped the entire thing in his mouth, chewed three times and swallowed. She was so amazed she didn't even try to pretend she wasn't gaping when he met her eyes.

She watched him pick up the other half of the sandwich, demolish it with the same quick ease, and then polish off a ten-ounce glass of milk. He left the pickle.

"Thanks for lunch," he said flatly.

Heat slid up her cheeks. What a dope she was to have thought a man as large as Pete would be satisfied by a meal so insubstantial.

Almost instantly her embarrassment was replaced by anger. At least she'd tried. He didn't have to be so sarcastic.

He went to the sink with his dishes. "Should I wash these?"

Her eyebrows arched. "Should I?"

"What?" He turned from the sink, frowning.

"Are you trying to tell me you're the sort of man who wouldn't be caught dead in a kitchen?"

He placed the glass in the sink with extreme care. "No," he said calmly, but irritation grated just under the surface. "What I'm trying to ask is, are you restricting your water usage?"

Mary Elizabeth swiveled the bucket seat forward, and when she was sure he couldn't see her, winced. "No, there's enough water. I have an extra-large tank." Behind her she heard mutters of exasperation.

Before long they were on the road again, crossing the long Tappan Zee Bridge. On the approaching side of the Hudson rose the steep, picturesque banks known as the Palisades. In the distance to the south shimmered the concrete spires of Manhattan, barely visible today in the mist shrouding the area.

Halfway across the river Pete turned on the wipers. He also sneezed and, pulling a clean handkerchief from his jeans pocket, sneezed again.

"Bless you," Mary Elizabeth responded out of habit. "Catching a cold?"

Turning off the wipers, he grumbled, "No such luck."

"What do you mean, no such luck? You *like* catching colds?"

"Better than I like being allergic to cats." He gave Monet, lounging across her lap, an evil scowl.

"Oh." She folded the cat closer. "Well, you'll only be bothered a little while longer."

"Amen to that." He hung his left wrist over the steering wheel, slouched a little and sneezed.

Mary Elizabeth decided she didn't like the way he drove. He appeared careless, inattentive . . . and she didn't like the way he looked at her cat.

What she didn't mind so much, though, was his scent. Was it his soap? His after-shave or shampoo? *Something* smelled awfully good. Warm. Outdoorsy. A cross between sandalwood and pine. Nothing like the sweet fruity fragrance that Roger used to ooze.

At the unexpected intrusion of Roger on her thoughts Mary Elizabeth felt a weight press down on her. Guilt again? She turned her head and watched the low gray clouds skulking across the sky. She felt like one of those clouds, slinking away from responsibility, and emitted a sigh.

"What's the matter?" Pete asked.

"Nothing."

After a minute or so, he said, "If it's all the same with you, I'm going to turn off at the first town we come to."

"How come?"

"I have some shopping to do."

"Peter, I'm rather in a hurry. Couldn't you wait until after we've parted company?"

"It's Pete," he bit out, "and, no, I can't wait."

Mary Elizabeth's lips parted on a mute protest.

"What's your hurry?" he inquired.

"Not that it's any business of yours, but I have a job interview waiting for me in Sarasota."

Pete gave her a reassessing once-over. "Important position?"

"Important in the sense that I need it."

His gaze returned to the line of traffic ahead, moving across the long bridge. He turned the wipers on and off again.

"What sort of job is it?"

"It's a temporary clerical position in a dentist's office, just until I can find something in my field."

"Which is?"

She was reluctant to go on. In her continued silence he asked, "What's the matter? Are you in a line of work you can't talk about?"

"Of course not. It's just that I get the feeling you consider my talk of a job trivial. I work, Peter. I always have. Nothing's ever been handed to me."

He cast her a doubtful glance. "So what do you do?"

"Well, for the past five years I've served as curator of a small local-history museum in my home town."

Pete cocked his head, his dark eyebrows lifting. "Really?"

His surprise annoyed her. She derived an unholy amount of satisfaction when he sneezed again, three times in a row, and his eyes began to water.

"Yes, really."

"How'd you get a job like that?" he asked as they left the bridge behind.

"I slept with the entire board of directors."

He choked on a laugh. She rather liked what laughter did to his hard-bitten face.

"I do have a degree in art history, you know," she said.

"Oh? From where?" he asked in nasally interest.

"Smith."

"Figures."

She turned offended eyes on him. "What's wrong with Smith?"

"Other than it's one of the Seven Sisters? Nothing."

"I suppose the college you went to is better."

He turned a probing frown on her, making her realize her remark had been unkind, meant to underscore the fact he didn't have a degree.

"I didn't exactly go to college, Mary Elizabeth. I got most of my training in the army. I finished off my degree nights at a university extension near my home."

Her head swiveled. "You have a degree?"

"Jeez, what a snob!"

"I am not."

"Ha!"

She ignored his derision. "What's it in?"

"Electrical engineering."

Her eyes widened. "Is that what you do for a living?"

"Yes. And no." He paused to blow his nose. "I run my own construction company. I build houses."

Her perception of him fractured, flew apart and reassembled like the colorful chips of a kaleidoscope design.

"Are you really on vacation, then?"

"Yeah. What did you think?"

She knew her color was heightening. She shrugged.

"I saw an ad in a magazine for that bike we're towing," he explained. "A guy up in New Hampshire was selling it, so I said to myself, 'Mitchell, take some time off and go check it out.'"

Her confusion deepened. "Is that motorcycle something special?"

"It's a '53 Triumph."

"What does that mean?"

"To me it means Marlon Brando in *The Wild One*, James Dean in *Rebel Without a Cause....*" His left eyebrow arched.

She shook her head. "Never saw them."

"Steve McQueen in *The Great Escape*?"

Again she made a helpless gesture. But suddenly she perked. "Ever see Miss Piggy on *The Muppet Show*?"

"Miss Piggy?" Disbelief opened his expression.

"Yes. She did a motorcycle number once to the song 'I Get Around.'"

Pete pulled on his lower lip. "Uh, gee, no. I missed that one."

"She was great."

"Right up there with Brando, was she?"

"Absolutely." Mary Elizabeth found herself grinning and unable to stop. She noticed he was smiling, too. They rode on in companionable ease for several minutes.

"So, what does being curator of a local museum entail?"

"Well, when I took over, our collection was in pretty sad shape—a few Revolutionary War uniforms, a room dedicated to the logging industry." She raised her index finger and gave it a few sardonic twirls. To her utter delight, Pete smiled again.

"So the first thing I did was study local history. Can you wait a sec?"

She got up, took two steps into the kitchen and returned with a large bowl of M&Ms. "Want some?"

He shook his head, horrified. She'd been sick only a short time ago and had nothing solid in her but crackers.

She deliberated over the bowl and then chose a brown. "I read everything I could get my hands on—books, diaries, old maps, photographs...." With her index finger she stirred the contents of the bowl, found another brown, and popped it into her mouth. "Then I scoured the region—auctions, antiques shops, old estates—looking for artifacts."

Pete watched her picking through the candy, moving it around, popping another brown.

"I also pleaded for bequests through regional newspapers and magazines. And soon stuff was pouring in."

"Mary Elizabeth, what are you doing?"

She raised her head to find him frowning at her. "Pardon?"

"You eat M&Ms by color group?"

She looked from his incredulous face to her bowl and up again. She suspected her smile was rather sheepish.

Pete slapped a hand to his forehead. "What am I doing with this woman?" he muttered.

She popped another brown and placed the offending bowl on the floor.

"Why did you leave your job?" Pete braked carefully and directed the motor home into the parking lot of a shopping mall. The mist was so heavy he hadn't bothered to turn off the wipers for several miles. "You obviously enjoyed it."

Mary Elizabeth tried to keep thoughts of her argument with Charles from telegraphing. "I did, but I'd exhausted it. There wasn't much left for me to do."

"Sounds like you enjoyed the process of pulling the museum together more than the final product."

She thought awhile, then slowly nodded. "I guess I did."

"I can understand that. Not much different from building a house. I love seeing the structure taking shape, but I sure as hell don't want to stick around after the sod is down and the owners have moved in."

She smiled softly, liking the comparison he'd drawn, enjoying the connection they shared.

"I don't imagine there's much money in local museum work, though," he probed.

"No. But it was never an issue—" she grimaced "—until today. I lived at home and didn't have the expenses that most people have. Even though I paid my father for room and board, I was still able to save money."

"Seven hundred dollars?" he asked doubtfully.

She shook her head. "That's just what I've put aside since I bought this RV."

Of course, Pete thought. The RV. That's why she didn't have much money. She'd recently made a huge purchase.

But something else she'd said was now puzzling him. "You still lived at home?" Inadvertently his eyes flicked over her.

"Yes." She gazed at her tightly interlaced hands. "Moving out isn't a high priority with my... um, father. He has fairly old-fashioned standards, and the only satisfactory reason for a daughter to move out is marriage."

"Ah, I see." Satisfied that he had a clearer bead on her, he uncoiled himself from his seat. "I'll be back in a few minutes. Don't go 'way."

By the time Pete emerged from the mall, the mist had turned to unabashed rain. He jogged across the slick parking lot with his purchases tucked into his jacket. His stride was strong and sure. Mary Elizabeth had no trouble picturing him walking a scaffold or balancing on a roof peak.

He bounded up the two metal steps, closed the door and shook his head, wet hair sticking to his forehead. His presence immediately filled the RV. "Getting nasty out there," he muttered right before sneezing.

He went to the sink, drew a glass of water, opened a box of allergy medication and swallowed two tablets.

Mary Elizabeth suppressed a grin. She didn't know why she found his allergy so amusing. The man was obviously in agony. But he was so big, so strong and arrogant, that she couldn't help feeling tickled by the thought of him being done in by a fat, lazy cat.

"Come here."

She huffed. The man certainly loved to give orders.

She got up and stepped closer, but not too close. Dampened by the rain, his scent seemed to have intensified in a disturbingly alluring way.

He slipped his wallet out of his back pocket and thumbed out several twenty dollar bills. "Here." He pushed the bills at her, and when she only stared at them, uncomprehending, he dropped them on the counter. "You won't get far without gas money."

The extent of his generosity brought a tightness to her throat. "I can't let you do this. You've already done too much."

"How do you expect to get this boat to Sarasota then? Wishful thinking?"

She swallowed. "No, I thought I'd find a pawn shop. I have lots of things I can sell—earrings, a pearl necklace that was my moth—"

Pete clamped a swift hand over her mouth and muttered a choice expletive. "Don't tell me what you've got that's valuable, lady!"

"But..." Her lips moved against his warm, rough palm.

"No 'buts,' Mary Elizabeth. Dammit, you've got to be more careful. I mean it." He removed his hand slowly, his eyes traveling over her features and finally coming to rest at her still-parted lips. For a moment they were both quiet, a current of awareness buzzing between them, stirring their blood.

Shaken, Mary Elizabeth stepped back. No, not *between* them, she thought. She was the only one experiencing these inappropriate feelings, she was sure. Why would a man like Peter Mitchell be interested in a woman like her? She was clearly not his type.

But then, he wasn't her type, either. So what was she doing?

She made herself relax, telling herself she'd done nothing to get upset over. He hadn't picked up on what she'd been feeling, and even if he had, they'd be parting soon, never to see each other again.

Turning to the counter, Pete opened a waxed-paper bag. "No offense to the lunch you made me," he said, unwrapping a thick meatball grinder and taking a healthy bite.

Remembering the sandwich she'd made him, her cheeks warmed. "No offense taken," she returned with difficulty.

Pete popped open a can of cola. "Come on. I can eat while I'm driving."

The windshield wipers beat a steady thwock-thwock as they traveled along the Palisades Parkway heading south. To the left, below the cliffs, the Hudson rolled on, slow and gray. Ahead, across the river, the towers of Manhattan grew sharper.

Mary Elizabeth turned down the volume on the radio, interrupting the Flamingos in mid doo-op. "Is that thunder I hear?"

Pete opened his window and listened. "Oh, hell." He reached for the radio and raised the volume. She was about to object—she'd heard just about all the oldies she could take for one day—but then realized he was searching for a local weather report.

"...At times heavy," a female voice chirped liltingly, "with a late afternoon thunderstorm in the Hudson Valley and scattered squalls inland as far south as Trenton. But cheer up, folks. Skies will be clearing by morning and the weekend looks great."

Pete punched a radio button and the Flamingos returned. Mary Elizabeth rolled her eyes. "What's your fascination with this music?"

He thought awhile. "I have absolutely no idea, Mary Elizabeth."

She shook her head, accepted Monet into her lap again and gazed out the rain-streaked windshield. In her peripheral vision she could see that Peter had finished his sandwich but not his drink. He'd wedged the can between his thighs. Without realizing it, she soon became mesmerized by the way his strong hands curled around the aluminum can and lifted it to his lips, by the way he tipped back his head, took a long thirsty pull, then wedged the container between his thighs again.

"Don't hesitate to tell me if you see anything you like," he drawled.

Her gaze shot upward to a pair of laughing blue eyes. Her cheeks flushed, yet she was able to say, "I will. When I see it."

Pete coughed on a sharp laugh.

Mary Elizabeth sat back, smiling. She rather liked this banter they engaged in. It was something new for her. Her father would've thought it common. Roger would've taken offense.

They rode on for another mile. "Tragedy" was playing now, and Mary Elizabeth was paying closer attention to the lyrics than she cared to admit, when she became aware of something rustling. Turning, she noticed Peter unwrapping the cellophane from a thin cigar. He clamped it between his strong even teeth, deftly struck a match one-handedly and lit the end, puffing clouds of foul-smelling smoke into the close air. Her throat closed up in reflexive self-defense.

He held the cigar under a crooked index finger as he steered around a cloverleaf and blew a thin stream of foulness in the general direction of the slightly opened window to his left. Most of the smoke hit the glass and swirled right back in.

Mary Elizabeth cleared her throat. "Do you mind?"

He clamped the cigar between his teeth and shot her a wide, waggish grin. "We're almost there, princess. A few more miles. If I can put up with that fat fur ball, I'm sure you can put up with the aroma of a fine cigarillo."

"Payback. Is that what this is?"

His grin broadened. He chewed on the cigar, closed his gorgeous lips around it and drew in a mouthful of smoke which he released in playful little puffs.

A short time later Peter moved the RV into the breakdown lane and let it slow to a lazy roll before stopping under an overpass.

Mary Elizabeth sat up. "Anything wrong?"

"We're here. There's your ramp onto I-95. I told you it wasn't far."

"Oh." Even to herself she sounded surprised and disappointed.

Attractive lines crinkled outward from the corners of his eyes. "Miss me already?"

She tried to think of a comeback, but her lightheartedness had fled. She merely stared at the highway. Rain fell so hard it was smoking off the asphalt. Vehicles, all with their lights on, had slowed to a crawl.

"Do you think I'll have any trouble from here on—you know, with the police?"

"Hard to say. I'd advise you to keep to the speed limit, don't drive too late at night and, well, just be careful. The rest is up to dumb luck."

Mary Elizabeth nodded. "What about you? Are you going to be all right in this rain?"

He puffed thoughtfully for a minute. "Are you really in such a hurry to get where you're going?"

Her blood began to rush. "Well, um, yes."

"Doesn't your schedule allow for sitting out the occasional monsoon?"

She ran the tip of her tongue over lips that were suddenly paper-dry. "Is that what you'd like to do? Sit here until the storm has passed?"

He squinted ahead. "Rain riding's not my all-time favorite way to spend an afternoon. I'll do it if it's necessary but..."

"No, I wouldn't want you to get wet or anything."

"Wet?" He laughed. "Hell, that's the least of it."

"Oh?"

"Not much traction on wet pavement." He puffed on his cigar, letting her imagination paint a running list of horrors. "And then there's always the chance of being hit by lightning," he added.

"That happens?"

"Well, sure, Mary Elizabeth." He swiveled to face her, filling her eyes with his casually charismatic presence. "Tell you what we could do." He glanced at his watch. "Check-in time at most motels is three o'clock, and it's past that now."

Mary Elizabeth felt an uncomfortable heat crawling up her neck.

"My God, Mary Elizabeth." He chuckled. "You are so easy to get a rise out of. I didn't even *mean* that as a tease."

She struggled to look innocent and baffled.

"All I was suggesting was you drop me off at a motel somewhere and then be on your way. This rain's not going to let up until morning, so I might as well find a hole to crawl into for the night."

"I could do that," she said in a falsely light voice, not looking at him. "Where's the nearest motel?"

"I'd guess off the next exit." He turned the ignition key, put the RV in gear and carefully eased into traffic.

Just as he'd predicted, they found a motel a few miles ahead. Pete parked in front of the office. "Let me get a room and detach my bike, then you can be going."

Mary Elizabeth didn't move. She felt weighted down by the realization that this was it; the time to separate had come. Until now she hadn't fully acknowledged how secure she felt traveling with him.

"Are you sure this is what you want to do?" she asked. "What I mean is, if you'd like, you can ride with me the entire way."

"I can, can I?" His smile was wry, making it clear he knew exactly who'd be doing whom the favor.

"I'd pay you, of course," she added. "I might have to do it in installments, but I would."

"Thanks, but it isn't a matter of money. I have a week of vacation time ahead of me and you've got to get to Florida pronto. Right?"

She smiled diffidently.

"Well then, this is where we say adios."

After registering, Pete drove the RV around to the rear wing of the motel where his room was located. Although he worked quickly to unchain his bike, the rain soaked through his clothes in no time. Mary Elizabeth watched from the open doorway of the RV in stunned disbelief as he hauled the dripping bike right into his first-floor, disabled-access room.

He loped back to the RV to get his duffel bag. "You know how to get back to the highway?" His hair was wet, a puddle forming on the floor at his feet.

For a long bemused moment, Mary Elizabeth stood transfixed. The rain, penetrating his clothes and washing over his skin, intensified his physical presence until she almost couldn't breathe. With an effort, she nodded. "I know the way."

He fit the strap of his bag over his shoulder. "Well, you take care of yourself, Mary Elizabeth," he said, his tone soft and dark. "And stay out of bars."

She fought the urge to touch him, just one brief touch to that hard, vibrant cheek before he left. "You, too, Peter." She noticed he didn't correct her this time.

He swung out of the RV, went a few steps and turned again. She was still standing in the open door, watching him.

"You know, driving an RV in this weather isn't too much fun, either." He blinked futilely at the rain, which continued to pour down, gathering and spilling off his lashes. "If you'd rather cool your heels till it lets up, you could park outside my room. I put your license plate number on my registration form."

"Thanks. That was kind of you. I'll consider it." Why was he still standing there talking? she wondered. Why didn't he have the good sense to get in out of the rain?

"Well then, I guess I'll be seeing you around, princess." He turned and this time sprinted all the way to his room.

Mary Elizabeth continued to stand in the doorway, staring through the sheets of rain. She felt mysteriously let down.

A close clap of thunder brought her to her senses. She closed the door and decided maybe she *would* stay a while. She got behind the wheel and drove the motor home to the far end of the parking lot near the woods where it wouldn't be in anyone's way. There, she sat, staring at the rain washing down the windshield, wondering if the gods were trying to tell her something—like maybe this trip wasn't meant to be?

She was just tired, that was her problem. Tired, it was easy to start thinking hopeless thoughts. What she should do was take a hot shower and grab a bite to eat. That would wake her up and make her feel more cheerful. With renewed conviction she got to her feet.

The rain continued into the evening, drumming on the metal roof of the motor home, creating what should have been a lulling white noise. Unfortunately, the thunder and lightning continued as well, keeping Mary Elizabeth on edge in spite of her exhaustion.

It was too early to sleep, anyway, she reasoned, watching TV and sipping yet another cup of after-dinner tea.

Inadvertently, her mind wandered to Peter. She wondered what he was doing, if he'd gone to a restaurant, if he'd eaten at all. Maybe she should've invited him over.

But they'd already said their goodbyes. What was the point of inviting him back? In fact, why would she *want* to?

To emphasize her point, she slipped out of the banquette, found a can of room deodorizer, and went through the RV spraying away the faint, lingering odor of his cigar.

The sweet cloying scent of jasmine caught in the dampness of the closed-up camper and almost made her gag. She hurried to open windows and flapped her arms.

When the air was breathable again, she decided to call it a night. Although her body was still going, her brain had evidently shut down. Besides, if she got to sleep now, she could be on the road before dawn.

She retired to the bedroom, got into pajamas and crawled into bed. There, she lay against her propped pillows, knees bent, and listened to the storm. Light from the parking lot streamed palely into the room through the narrow slats of the window blinds, casting bars of light and shadow over familiar objects that in this setting looked new and strange.

Spying her Walkman amid the jumbled contents of a carton on the adjacent bed, she reached across the light-slatted darkness. Resettling herself, she untangled the cord, fit the earphones over her head and adjusted the switch to "radio." Lord only knew where her cassette tapes were.

The radio came on at a station playing jazz, something dense and screechy. She moved to another station where a full-throated country-rocker was singing about wanting "a real man."

From her position, Mary Elizabeth had a clear view out the window alongside her bed to the room where Peter was staying. The drapes were drawn but his light was still on.

She really was exhausted, tired right to the bone. Then again, wasn't she always now that she was pregnant? But this was nice, being propped in this soft nest of pillows, earphones drowning out the rain and too-frequent thunder. And although she was reluctant to admit it, it was comforting to watch the light from Peter's room and know he was there.

She found a different station. "Oh, brother," she complained when the deep, plaintive crooning of Elvis Presley filled her ears. She'd probably stumbled onto the station Peter had tormented her with all afternoon.

Although this song wasn't half bad.

All right, admit it, Drummond. You really like the song. She closed her eyes, opened them drowsily to take one more look at the motel, and closed them again, while Elvis's anguished voice pleaded for just one night with her, a voice she occasionally mistook for Peter's as she glided off to sleep.

INSIDE HIS ROOM, Pete bent over his king-size bed, folding his freshly laundered clothes. Luckily, he'd landed in a motel with a washer and dryer. In the background the TV flickered and droned. By the door stood his drip-dried bike. On the dresser lay an empty pizza box and two beer cans, also empty.

He'd thought of inviting Mary Elizabeth over. For all his claims to being a loner, he wouldn't have minded company tonight. But then, she'd probably turn up her nose at pepperoni pizza or eat it with a knife and fork. So in the end he'd eaten alone, watching "Wheel of Fortune" while his laundry spun in a dryer down the hall.

He packed his folded, still-warm clothes into his bag and buckled the flap. Maybe he'd read to pass the time. Or maybe he'd see if there was something more interesting on the tube. Propping himself on the bed, remote control in hand, he surfed his way through the channels. When he stumbled upon an X-rated movie, he reared back, his head bonging the hollow wall in surprise. What if he'd been a kid innocently looking for a cartoon show? he thought with the proper amount of indignation.

But in spite of that indignation, he lingered awhile.

Growing uncomfortably warm, he snapped the set off. No, he didn't need to watch that sort of stuff, either. He turned on the radio instead, and the room filled with the sounds of Bonnie Raitt singing "Real Man." Her husky voice reminded him of Mary Elizabeth.

He eased off the bed and meandered toward the window, turning off lights before drawing aside the drape. It was still raining.

And she was still parked out there by the trees.

He wiped a hand over his mouth where a smile wanted to form. He hadn't been sure she'd stay.

Pete watched the rain, the lightning bursts in the distance, and thought of the frequent electrical storms that rode in off the Gulf at home. He wondered if Mary Elizabeth knew what sort of weather she was moving to.

Abruptly, he became annoyed. Why did every thought turn inevitably to Mary Elizabeth Drummond? He tried to put his special spin of mockery on her name, but strangely he couldn't find it anymore. It was gone.

And *that* was why he hadn't invited her over for pizza, he finally admitted—not because she'd turn up her nose, but because he'd stopped seeing her as someone he could easily slot and label.

That, and the spark of attraction he'd been fighting all day. There, he admitted it, and it only hurt a little.

It was crazy; he didn't know when he'd stopped wanting to run from her and when he'd started enjoying her company. He only knew it had happened, and if he asked her over, he'd be begging for trouble. Their night might not end with the last slice of pizza.

He couldn't risk that. She was moving to Florida, to a town that was less than a two-hour drive from his place, and he had to ask himself if he really wanted to start something here. She had a gift for landing herself in trouble and then getting him to help her out of it. Now she wanted him to drive the entire distance, and if he invited her over, he just might end up agreeing. It would only be one more favor, but one that would ruin his vacation. And, dammit, he had needs, too.

With a conscious effort he banished Mary Elizabeth from his mind and thought instead of his brother getting married....

And of Sue Ellen getting divorced. It was hard not to. He and Sue Ellen had shared something good at one time. They'd been one of those high school couples who seem like an institution, dating forever, always together. Pete and Sue Ellen. You could hardly say one name without saying the other.

She'd wanted to get married right after graduation, but he'd convinced her that was out of the question. For one thing, she was already enrolled in college, and her parents damn well expected her to go. For another, what would they live on? The few extra dollars he made painting houses with his father? The paycheck he brought home from his part-time job at the gas station? Sue Ellen said money didn't matter, but that was only because she didn't know what it was like to go without it.

Pete did. Although his family never went hungry or lacked a roof over their heads, he knew the quality of their lives could've been better. A lot better.

Not that his parents didn't try. They worked as hard as they could, both of them, but the small backwater town where they lived didn't offer much opportunity for employment. His mother went from one menial job to another, the only type available to a woman who wasn't a secretary, a nurse or a teacher. In addition, his father suffered chronic back pain from a construction accident, and that limited the types of jobs he could take on.

Pete didn't want to repeat his parents' life, and although he sorely wanted to marry Sue Ellen, he knew that in the end they'd be far better off if she went to college and he got the training he needed to build a solid career.

Going into the army was one of those ideas that had been with him so long he didn't even question it by the time he was eighteen. An older cousin had gone in and done well, and Pete never forgot it. It was the most efficient way of earning and saving a decent wage, that cousin had said, since life in the military provided everything a person would normally spend money on. Equally important was the lure of getting some valuable training on the side, free.

Pete wasn't concerned merely about his own future with Sue Ellen. He was worried about his brother and sisters, too. What sort of livelihood would they eke out if he didn't do something? As the oldest and the one who'd always had to watch out for everyone else, Pete felt their future was riding on his coattails.

He wanted to go into business for himself, and he wanted that business to be prosperous enough to employ them all, the entire Mitchell clan, if need be.

When Pete's mother died unexpectedly a month after his graduation, leaving his increasingly disabled father with three children still in school, the pressure on Pete to provide intensified.

So he'd entered the army, sure that his and Sue Ellen's love would endure. Of course it would endure. They were meant to be together, weren't they?

But two years into his hitch, while Pete was slogging his way through the jungles of Central America, Sue Ellen decided she'd waited long enough and married some northern boy she'd met at college.

Pete's slow exhalation fogged the rain-rippled window. Now she was divorced. Calling him three times a week. Driving down to his office in Tampa. Prompting his sisters to rhapsodize about a reunion at Brad's wedding. Causing him to wonder if maybe they weren't on to something . . .

He breathed out a sardonic laugh. What the hell was he thinking? There was nothing between him and Sue Ellen anymore. Less than nothing. He suspected she was coming around only because his business was doing so well these days. But even if there were something, he had no intention of ever getting married again.

He sighed. It was the rain. That was what was causing these sentimental thoughts. Just the rain. It brought out the romantic in him every time.

Pete stood back from the window and reached for the remote control. He wanted to change the radio station, find something to divert his attention. He only hoped that in the dark he didn't accidentally click on the TV and tune in the orgy again. It had been too damn long.

Ah! *That* was it! he thought, smiling in relief. *That* was why he'd found himself being drawn to Mary Elizabeth Drummond today.

His smile thinned. How long *had* it been since he'd slept with a woman? A year? Eighteen months? It wasn't just that he was being more careful these days; relationships simply didn't seem worth the hassle.

I'm getting old, he thought, his shoulders slumping. Here he was, pushing thirty-seven, the only Mitchell offspring not married or about to be, and thinking of relationships as hassles. *What's even worse, I'm sleeping in a damn motel instead of a tent the way I used to, and I'm liking it!*

The radio suddenly came in clear, The King begging some woman for just one night with her, that's all he was praying for, the need conveyed by his voice almost painfully desperate. Pete knew the feeling.

He gazed out the window. The motor home across the lot was glazed with rain. All the lights were out, which meant Mary Elizabeth was probably getting some sleep. That was good. She'd looked awfully tired when he'd left her.

He groaned and looked aside, vexed by his continuing preoccupation with her. She'd probably exhausted herself with all that reaching for the radio dial today and turning down the volume on his oldies station.

Actually, he'd heard enough oldies himself for one day. He tuned in a classical station instead. "Opera night," he muttered with automatic derision.

But something in the music caught his attention, something in the expressive soprano voice that cut through preconceived notions of what was listenable and what was not. The sound was lush, full of passion and longing, and although Pete didn't understand a word that was sung, he still felt a tightness in his chest. Outside, the rain continued to pour down, and he thought, *Here finally is music made for a night such as this.*

I'm really getting old, he thought defensively. But the aria continued to flow through him, anyway, carrying him off. And he continued to stand in the darkness of his room, gazing out the window, thinking about romance and fate, youth and heartache and Sue Ellen Carlisle....

...But picturing Mary Elizabeth's delicate face on the rain.

CHAPTER SIX

MARY ELIZABETH WOKE shortly after 5:00 a.m. For several seconds she didn't know where she was. Startled, she gazed around the small bedroom, still dark at that predawn hour. Somewhere nearby a whispery voice was asking, "Who's sor-ry now?" Groping over the coverlet, her hand fell upon the source of the whispering, the headphones to her Walkman, and in a flash of remembrance, she knew where she was, and why.

Cool, fresh air was drifting through the open window over her bed. She propped up on an elbow and gazed across the parking lot toward the motel. The rain had stopped, but the world was still soaked and dripping. She sank back into the pillows.

It was then that she became aware of the discomfort in her lower body, a discomfort that felt like indigestion, menstrual cramps and nausea all rolled into one. Was that the reason she'd awakened so early? she wondered, running a light hand over her stomach.

Warily, she sat up, lowering her feet to the floor and clutching the edge of the thin mattress in two tense fists. In the process of sitting up, the tightness in her abdomen seemed to have risen right to her diaphragm, pressing the air out of her lungs and causing perspiration to bead on her upper lip. She took a slow breath, but it brought no relief.

A cup of ginger tea, she thought. That's what she needed. There was nothing like ginger tea to soothe an ailing stomach. Carefully, she got to her feet and shuffled to the kitchen.

But twenty minutes later, as she sat doubled over at the table with a half-drained cup under her nose, Mary Elizabeth felt worse than ever. The tea she'd swallowed seemed to be sitting right on top of that hard ball of cramps, just under her rib cage, with no place to go. Groaning in agony, she curled up in the corner of the banquette that Peter seemed to favor and hugged her arms.

Peter. How she wished he was here.

She lifted aside the lace window curtain and stared across the parking lot to his room. He'd be leaving today, going his own way while she went hers. She didn't know why that thought bothered her so much. She hadn't planned on having him drop into her life, so what difference did it now make if they parted company?

The difference, replied an impatient voice inside her head, was that she'd experienced the sense of security that came from being in the company of a strong, seasoned traveler. She felt there was no calamity Peter couldn't handle, and, quite frankly, after the events of the past two days, she was beginning to feel rather like Chicken Little. If the sky wasn't falling at this precise moment, just wait. Open your umbrella while you were at it, too.

Mary Elizabeth huddled into her bathrobe, feeling increasingly wretched. What was happening to her? she wondered in deepening anxiety, flinching under another cramp.

Suddenly her eyes snapped wide open. Was this the start of a miscarriage? Her strength drained out of her.

The clock on the cooking stove read only 5:35. Outside, the sky was still dark. "Oh, God," she moaned, pressing a hand to her slightly rounded belly. She was alone, sitting in the parking lot of a strange motel somewhere in New Jersey, without money, without identification, without family—and she was having a miscarriage.

She levered herself to her feet, and on legs that trembled, shuffled back to bed.

PETE DIDN'T KNOW WHY he couldn't sleep. It was only 6:30 and he didn't have to be out of the room till eleven. Yet for the past hour he'd been wide awake, staring at the ceiling, thinking about where he'd go today, what he'd see and do. Occasionally his mind wandered to Mary Elizabeth, to whether she'd get to Florida without being stopped by the police, if her RV would make it without giving her trouble, whether she'd run into any more creeps like Sonny.

All right, so maybe his mind wandered to her a lot. It was understandable, considering all they'd been through together.

Pete finally gave up the idea of sleep. He hauled himself out of his rumpled bed, took a shower and dressed.

Seven o'clock, and the RV was still there, all the curtains drawn.

She'd been tired last night, he conceded, but if she planned to cover any decent amount of road today, she really ought to get moving.

Against his better judgment, Pete crossed the puddled parking lot and tapped at her door. There was no answer. He tapped again, louder, and waited. Tapped again on the rear window.

Finally he heard movement within, saw a curtain lift, and then the door opened.

"Hey, there," he began. "I hope I didn't wake you, but I thought..." His words slowed as her appearance registered—the uncharacteristically hunched posture, the sunken eyes, the tension around her mouth. He bounded up the steps and pulled the door closed behind him. "What's wrong?" he asked, gripping her arms.

She made a valiant effort to straighten her spine. "I'm just feeling a bit indisposed this morning." She smiled wanly. Her face was pale.

"Have you taken anything for it, for whatever's bothering you?"

She nodded. "Some tea, a few antacid tablets..."

"Any relief?"

"Not much." Again she attempted to smile, to appear in control of the situation. "Peter?" Her voice was small and tentative.

Pete found himself stroking her arms, kneading them, feeling them quivering under his fingers. "What is it, princess?" he said in almost a whisper.

"Could I prevail upon you for just one more favor before we say goodbye?"

Pete lifted a hand to her head, cradling it, petting. She was obviously scared to death. "Go ahead, I'm listening."

"Could you drive me to the nearest hospital?"

He worked at keeping his expression set. "Is it that bad? Are you sure a walk-in clinic...?"

She was already shaking her head. "Those places aren't always equipped for..." She paused, her eyes going a little wild.

"For what?" Pete leaned closer.

She swallowed, avoiding his gaze. "Well, you know, they're just not as good as hospitals."

"Can you tell me what's wrong?" He tried to keep his voice calm even though adrenaline was dumping into his system like water from a busted hydrant.

"I...I'm not sure."

"Well, is it a sharp pain or a dull pressure?"

"Both."

"Is it around your appendix?"

She shrugged. She was being vague and evasive. He knew it, but he didn't think it wise to press. Time was passing and apparently she didn't *want* to tell him.

How many secrets do you have, Mary Elizabeth? Pete wondered, frowning down at the top of her mussed blond head.

"Okay. Let me go lock up my room and talk to whoever's at the front desk. I'll ask where the nearest hospital is. Do you feel you can get into some street clothes?"

She nodded. Her eyes were closed, her body rigid.

"What?" Pete asked, tensing. "What's happening?"

She smiled fragilely. "Go. I'm fine. The sooner we get this over with, the sooner you can be on your way."

The hospital emergency room was small but busy. Mary Elizabeth was relieved Pete had come with her. While she continued to battle cramps, he made short order of explaining her missing health insurance card. He was calm and articulate and unexpectedly charming, while still conveying unbending assertiveness. The admissions clerk *would* find Mary Elizabeth in the mammoth computerized system, and she *would* be cleared for coverage.

Although Mary Elizabeth was deeply grateful for Pete's help in tackling the financial bureaucracy, she prayed he wouldn't be around when she had to explain what was wrong with her. No one knew she was pregnant except Charles and Mrs. Pidgin, not even Chloe. For one thing, she'd promised Charles not to tell anyone else. For another, she was simply too embarrassed. She certainly didn't want Peter Mitchell to know.

Unfortunately, her current luck held true and Pete never left her side. While one clerk was handling her admission, another was asking how she felt, if she was in pain, *what was wrong with her.*

"I'm not sure," she said. "I'm having abdominal pain."

"Is it localized, one side or the other?"

"It's hard to say. Will I be able to see a doctor soon?" Unwittingly she pressed a hand to her stomach as another spasm assailed her.

The woman shuffled together forms, fastened them on a clipboard and scooted around her desk. "Charlene," she called to a passing nurse, "take these people down to room three." She then jammed the clipboard into Pete's midsection. "Here, you can finish filling these out while you're waiting for the doctor."

Pete nodded brusquely, took Mary Elizabeth's arm and followed the nurse named Charlene.

Mary Elizabeth balked. "You can wait here. I'll be fine alone. Really I will."

Pete continued to propel her down the corridor. "I've come this far...." he said, leading her into room three.

The nurse handed Mary Elizabeth a blue hospital gown and closed the curtain around the bed. Left alone inside the enclosure, Mary Elizabeth worked herself out of her clothes.

"Are you decent?" Peter's quiet voice, just beyond the curtain, sent her scurrying for the nearest chair, grabbing at the back of the gown as she went.

"Uh-huh."

He stepped inside, gave her a sweeping glance and winked. In spite of her discomfort, she smiled.

"Do you feel up to filling this out?"

"Sure." She took the clipboard from him.

She was almost done with the forms when the doctor came in. He was a tall, thin, stoop-shouldered man with gray hair and a kind face.

"Good morning." He smiled. "What seems to be the problem?"

Mary Elizabeth glanced at Peter, standing at the foot of the bed. "Would you mind?" She tilted her head toward the door.

He hesitated. "Are you sure?"

"Yes."

With lingering reluctance, he drew aside the curtain and ducked out.

"Was that your husband?"

"No, just a friend."

The doctor skimmed her chart, puzzlement etched on his brow.

"I'm moving to Florida. He's keeping me company, helping with the driving," she temporized.

She knew exactly when the doctor reached the line that asked if she was pregnant. The furrows on his forehead deepened.

"Is he the father of the baby you're carrying?" When he looked up she was relieved to see his smile was still kind.

"No. We're just, as I said, friends." She was grateful he didn't pursue the issue.

Instead, he asked her to lie on the bed and proceeded to examine her, while she told him about the nature of her discomfort and her fear that she was having a miscarriage. His movements quickened noticeably.

Standing outside the room, Pete tried to rouse a few pangs of guilt for keeping his heel in the door, but he failed. He was too curious about the mysteries in Mary Elizabeth's eyes and more than a little worried about the pain he read in her body language.

Suddenly he felt he'd been hit with a brick. She was pregnant? Mary Elizabeth Drummond? Impossible. Not the Mary Elizabeth he knew.

He was still grappling with that revelation when the rest of her words took hold. Pete pushed a hand through his hair and clutched his pounding skull. She was having a miscarriage? Right now? In there?

His pulse skyrocketed. He didn't want to know about this. Enough was enough, goddammit. He was on vacation!

He eased the door closed, looked toward the exit and began to walk away.

"CONSTIPATION?" Mary Elizabeth repeated, sitting up. Her face was red-hot, her eyes incredulous.

"That's my guess." The doctor lowered himself into a vinyl chair.

"You mean, I'm not having a miscarriage?"

"I see no indication of that."

Mary Elizabeth's eyes welled up so fast she didn't have time to check her reaction. "Thank you," she whispered to a deity she couldn't remember praying to.

"Constipation is a common malady during pregnancy," the doctor said. His clinical detachment helped her rein in her billowing emotions. "Surely your physician has told you."

"I haven't seen a physician yet," she explained. "I didn't want to start up with one, knowing I'd be moving."

"Ah, well, let me be the first to tell you, then. Constipation can be a devil of a problem when you're pregnant. In your case I'd guess it's been complicated by the stress of moving. Stress can foul up the plumbing of the healthiest person." He fingered his stethoscope. "Have you found yourself unusually troubled lately? This move, this pregnancy... are they worrying you?"

"Oh, sure," she said, trying to sound intelligently realistic, yet upbeat. If only he knew what else she'd been through lately!

"And you say you haven't had any morning sickness?"

"That's right, but I have been nauseous the past couple of days. Is it possible I'm just starting to have morning sickness now?"

"I doubt it. Not at three months. My guess is your nausea, like your constipation, is tied in with stress. Does that make sense to you?"

"It certainly does."

The doctor chuckled. "Don't look so glum. Constipation can be dealt with easily enough. Morning sickness can't. You're one of the lucky ones."

Mary Elizabeth rubbed her aching stomach and tried to feel lucky. "So, what now?"

"Time to call roto-rooter."

She rolled her eyes.

"Don't worry, it's a very gentle process, quite safe for the baby. There's a mild sedative I could prescribe for you, as well, to ease your anxiety, but quite frankly I'd prefer not to. I'd prefer you try to alleviate your anxiety by more natural means."

Mary Elizabeth nodded. "I can do that. I took a yoga class once, in college."

"Good. Now, until you engage a physician, I recommend a diet high in fiber. Eat lots of fruit and vegetables...." The attending nurse handed him a folder stuffed with pamphlets on pregnancy.

"Think you know everything, don't you, Charlene."

"I do," she parried dryly.

"Ah, nurses. Was a time they knew their place." The good-natured doctor got to his feet, chuckling. "Unfortunately, I have to leave you in this know-it-all's hands and go see another patient. But I'll be back before you're released."

"Thank you, Doctor. Oh, and could you not say anything about this to my friend?"

The doctor frowned at her but agreed, anyway.

Forty minutes later, Mary Elizabeth was feeling infinitely better and ready to leave. The nurse stood at the examining room door while she gathered up her belongings.

"Good luck to you now."

"Thanks. I'll need it."

"What are you hoping for?" The nurse opened the door. "A boy or a girl?"

Mary Elizabeth blanched when she noticed Pete waiting for her out in the hall. Had he heard?

"Yes, one or the other," she said distractedly. The nurse laughed.

Pete slouched against the wall, arms folded high on his chest, Bad Attitude written all over his sullen face. Their eyes met, and in that instant she realized he knew she was pregnant. Moreover, he'd known for a while. Had the doctor told him?

He pushed away from the wall. "How're you doing?"

She pressed her lips together, chagrined. "Okay."

He turned to the nurse. "Is she really?"

"She's tired but otherwise fine."

His eyes darted from one woman to the other. He wore the look of a man who thought something was being put over on him.

"Take care now," the nurse called, walking away.

Pete stared after her, grim and dissatisfied.

"Come on, Peter." Mary Elizabeth poked his chest with the folder of pamphlets and started for the exit.

They weren't even through the entry when he gripped her arm and unloaded the question. "What happened in there?"

Heat slid up her neck. "Not much."

His face grew dark and forbidding. "Did you... miscarry?"

Mary Elizabeth stared at the left pocket of his blue chambray shirt. "No."

His grip tightened. "Are you sure?"

"Of course I'm sure. Now I'd like to ask you something, mister. How did you . . . ?"

"I listened in at the door."

"You've got a nerve. I asked you to leave."

"Why? Why are you hiding your pregnancy?"

"I'm not hiding it. It's simply none of your business." She gathered her indignation around her like a protective cloak, stepped around him and rammed open the glass door. Outside, the clear September sun had dried the pavement and soaked up all but the largest puddles.

Pete overtook her in a few easy strides. "So, what was wrong with you?"

Walking by his side, eyes fixed on her motor home parked in the lot reserved for emergency room patients, Mary Elizabeth felt embarrassment spill over her again. "I had cramps."

"Cramps. What kind of cramps?" he inquired impatiently. "Are they going to come back? Are they the sort associated with miscarriage? Were you spotting? Did you pass any clots?"

Mary Elizabeth stopped in her tracks. "Do you have children, Peter?" He didn't wear a ring, but that didn't mean he wasn't married, or divorced, or a father. She was shaken by the fact that even after everything they'd been through she still knew so little about him.

"No. Five nieces and nephews."

"Ah." Nieces. Nephews. She was dismayed by how easily her equanimity returned.

"My youngest sister had trouble with both her pregnancies."

She resumed walking. His *sister* had had trouble, and *he* had taken such an interest that he knew things about female physiology that even she didn't?

He must have seen her puzzlement because he explained, "Lindy's husband hasn't been the most responsible of guys. There have been times during their marriage when she's...well—" he looked aside "—come to stay with me."

"During her pregnancies?"

"Yeah. I even went to a few Lamaze classes with her, so do you want to try telling me again what was wrong with you?"

Mary Elizabeth bit her lower lip. "It...it was nothing like that, nothing to do with miscarrying."

They'd reached the RV. Pete unlocked the door and held it open for her. "So, why did you have me rush you to the hospital?"

Tired of being badgered, she spun to face him. "I've never been pregnant before. How was I supposed to know I wasn't aborting? It felt pretty bad."

"*What* did?" He tossed the keys onto the dashboard, the clatter startling the cat, who was sleeping a few inches away.

"All right." She tossed up her hands and, feeling trapped, began to pace. "You want to know? Okay, I'll tell you. Here it is."

Pete folded his arms and leaned against the kitchen counter. "Anytime, Mary Elizabeth."

"Oh, God, this is so undignified."

"Have you ever been strangled?" he asked impatiently.

She glared at him. "I was constipated. There, are you happy?"

As soon as she'd said it, she wished she hadn't. She hurried down the hall and closed herself in the bedroom. In the mirror behind the door, her face glowed redder than a valentine.

The door flew open. "Constipated?" Pete loomed over her, hands on his hips, disbelief written all over his handsome face.

"Get *out* of here. Did I ask you in here?" She pushed at his unmoving chest. "Get out."

"You had me rush you to the hospital," he went on, ignoring her outrage, "you left me out in the hall, worried half to death for more than an hour, and now all you can say is you were constipated?"

Mary Elizabeth wrapped her arms around her head and emitted a moan. She wanted to die. Just slip under the covers of her unmade bed and die.

Pete began to chuckle. She wanted to smack him.

"It isn't funny, Peter," she mumbled, still hiding like an ostrich.

"Yes, it is," he said, his amusement building.

She dropped her arms and glowered. "You have the sense of humor of a ten-year-old."

He cleared his throat and made an attempt to compose himself. "I'm just relieved you're all right. That's partially why I'm laughing."

Her glower softened. "And the other part of you is laughing because it finds me ridiculous."

To her utter amazement, the laughter left his eyes completely. "No. Occasionally I find the things you do funny, but not ridiculous. Never that." His long fingers closed around her shoulders and drew her to him. She stiffened instinctively when their bodies met.

But in spite of the vague impropriety she felt being held in this man's arms, Mary Elizabeth began to relax. Being held with such tender care felt wonderful. So did hearing his strong, reassuring heartbeat under her ear. She sighed, shuddering as she sank further into his comforting warmth and strength.

He moved his hand under her hair and slowly stroked her neck. She closed her eyes, drifting on the delightful, tingly sensations his touch set off.

They both felt the change in their embrace at the same time. His fingers were moving up her neck into her hair when the shift occurred, away from mere friendly consolation toward an unsettling sensual awareness—awareness of the warmth of his breath on her cheek, the lush press of her breasts against his chest, the bracketing fit of his hip bones just above hers, and a flash-fire surge of arousal that was undeniably reciprocal.

I must be imagining things, he thought, his body freezing into position.

And holding her breath, she said to herself, *I must be dreaming.*

But it is happening, he admitted miserably.

He is feeling it, too, she thought, embarrassed.

Maybe if we feign ignorance, it'll just go away, they both decided.

Pete loosened his hold and she immediately stepped back. Neither of them met the other's eyes.

"Sit down, Mary Elizabeth." He guided her to her rumpled bed, then pushed aside a carton on the bed opposite and sat. "Tell me what happened. What did the doctor say?"

Mary Elizabeth looked past him, out the window to the small brick hospital. She continued to feel self-conscious, but she gave Pete a full and honest account of her examination, anyway. He deserved one.

"I'm sorry I got you involved in a false alarm," she murmured when she was done. "Poor Peter, you could've been miles away by now."

"Don't apologize. When you're pregnant it's always better to err on the side of caution."

"I suppose you're right."

"Sure I'm right. Now, will you smile, dammit? Everything turned out fine."

She smiled, but only to please him. Inwardly she'd felt a vague sense of dissatisfaction building all morning, a sadness, a something that weighed on her like guilt. But of course, it *was* guilt. Wasn't it always?

The touch of Pete's hand on her knee startled her. "What's the matter now?" His eyes were too intent.

She forced another smile. "Nothing," she said while a small voice inside her heart nagged, *Why did you wait so long, Mary Elizabeth? Why did you go back to bed instead of calling for help immediately?*

Pete's eyes narrowed, boring into her.

"Honestly, I'm fine."

He dropped his hand. "If you say so."

She nodded and then yawned. In mid-yawn she laughed. "Sorry. Sleepiness is apparently another joy of being pregnant."

Pete smiled with gentle sympathy. "I know. I once saw my sister Pam conk out right at the supper table. Don't worry. Second trimester you'll feel more energetic." He got to his feet. "Look, I've got to get back to the motel to check out. Why don't you just curl up there and catch yourself a nap."

She nodded, already dropping to her side. Pete lifted her feet, pried off her loafers and drew the blanket up to her chin.

"Wake me when you're ready to part company," she said drowsily. "I don't want to be left sleeping in a parking lot."

"No one will bother you."

"I know. I'd just feel, I don't know, creepy."

He stroked her hair. "Okay. Don't worry. Get some sleep now."

Mary Elizabeth drew the blanket up over her ear, imagining that by doing so she'd capture forever the warmth of his touch. By the time the engine started she was soundly asleep.

Pete looked in on Mary Elizabeth after returning his room key. She was still asleep, her honey-and-ash-colored hair fanned out across the pillow like a length of silk, her lips slightly parted, her thick lashes fluttering with a dream.

He sat on the other bed and watched her. He was ready to leave. He'd examined his bike, strapped on his pack and reviewed his road map. It was clearly time to resume his vacation. Time was passing. He'd wasted Thursday night in jail, Friday morning in court, Friday afternoon driving this boat through the rain, and here it was already halfway through Saturday...

So why didn't he just wake her up like she'd asked, say goodbye and leave?

He rose off the bed, and then sat right back down again.

Good Lord! Mary Elizabeth was pregnant. The thought still had the power to knock the wind out of him. Pregnancy usually did. The mere idea of a whole new person being created, cell by cell, within a woman's body never failed to put him in a state of awe. But Mary Elizabeth's being pregnant set off feelings that went beyond that, feelings that were complex and unsettling.

He glanced again at her ringless left hand lying gracefully on the pillow. It wasn't so much the fact that she was pregnant and unmarried, although, in his opinion, that wasn't exactly the best way to bring a new person into the world. It was rather that being pregnant and unmarried *and Mary Elizabeth* just didn't go together. She struck him as a woman for whom there was a proper time and place for everything—and this wasn't it.

His image of her would never be the same. Apparently she wasn't the "princess" he'd dubbed her, but a woman struggling with more problems than he had imagined, and doing so with more dignity than he'd given her credit for, as well.

Pete's mind teemed with questions. Who was the father? Why did they split? Did he leave her? She, him? Had he been abusive? Was he out searching for her, gaining ground even as Pete sat here musing? Was that why she was so tense and eager to reach her friend in Florida?

Pete closed his eyes and pinched the bridge of his nose. He was jumping to wild conclusions. He had to chill out.

He got up and, bracing a hand on the dresser under the rear window, gazed at his bike parked outside his motel room, whispering to him of sun and wind and the open road. Today he planned to ride through rural New Jersey, go someplace he'd never been. He needed to let the white lines soothe his brain, wipe out the emotional garbage that had accumulated with work and family responsibilities. He especially needed to let the vibrations of the engine shake loose those feelings of confinement he got when people tried to set him up, tie him down and marry him off. After a week of white-line tomorrows, he'd be okay. He'd return to Tampa reassured of his autonomy, stronger in himself, and ready to handle whatever came his way.

He stepped back from the window and gazed down at Mary Elizabeth, a sunbeam pouring a diagonal ray of gold across her curved cheek.

He hadn't liked the idea of her traveling alone even before he knew she was pregnant. Now he hated it. His sisters would probably get on his case about his attitude. Mary Elizabeth was pregnant, they'd say, not incapacitated. But he couldn't help feeling extra-protective toward her now. Lots of unforeseen problems could arise—today's problem, for instance.

Pete frowned. The doctor had told her that stress was making her ill, the stress of moving. Pete didn't doubt it, especially when you threw in getting stuck on a dark country road, running into a creep like Sonny, being arrested, having her wallet stolen and spending a night in jail.

And being pregnant, besides! Suddenly Pete felt like a jackass for giving her such a dressing down when they first met. Granted, he was being hauled off to jail because of her at the time, but he still felt bad now.

He lowered himself to the bed again and watched her sleep. He could alleviate that stress. He could drive her all the way to her friend's.

But then he'd be cutting his vacation short. Cutting it short? Hell, he'd be ending it. Getting her to Sarasota as soon as possible didn't include the sort of casual touring he meant to do.

And what about afterward, when she was settled? They'd know each other then, be able to call and visit. But did he really want her in his life? Did he want to know a pregnant woman who was apparently alone in the world except for one old college friend? A woman who was moving to a place she'd never been?

But mostly he worried about the physical pull he felt toward her. If he traveled with her, that pull would have to be denied, no question about it. And just how hard would that be? Would it plague him throughout the drive, turn their time together into a marathon test of willpower?

"What am I going to do with you, Mary Elizabeth?" he whispered on a troubled sigh. "What am I going to do?"

MARY ELIZABETH WOKE slowly to the familiar hum and rock of her motor home. Drifting in the muzzy land halfway between sleep and full wakefulness, she was aware nonetheless that something wasn't quite right.

Pushing back her hair, she squinted at her watch. Twelve forty-two. She sat up abruptly. They should have reached Peter's motel hours ago.

She slipped out of bed and peered out the high rear window. His motorcycle was once again secured to the trailer, rattling like Marley's ghost under its shroud of cord and chain. With a sudden leap in her pulse, she lifted her gaze. Gone was the dense urban sprawl of the New York City area. In its place were hills, wooded hills, and a twisty two-lane road!

"Peter Mitchell, where the devil are we?" She scooped a sleeping Monet out of the passenger seat and set him down in the kitchen. He stood there for a moment, bug-eyed, disoriented, then simply collapsed where he'd landed and went back to sleep.

Pete gave Mary Elizabeth a grin so confident it bordered on arrogance. His teeth gleamed around a cigar. This one, fortunately, was unlit.

"Well, hello there, Mary Elizabeth. Feeling better?"

She plopped into the passenger seat. "Where's the motel? Where's I-95? Why are you still driving?"

"You *sound* better. Look like hell though, if you don't mind my saying."

Mary Elizabeth combed her fingers through her hair. "I suppose you look like a prince when you first roll out of bed."

Not bothering to remove the cigar, he tipped back his head and laughed. He had a wonderful laugh, she admitted through her agitation. Rich, expressive and contagious.

"These here are the hills of northwestern New Jersey, Mary Elizabeth."

"Northwestern New Jersey," she repeated in a flat, dazed tone. "You mean, you've taken me even farther off course than I was before?"

"Well, not by much."

"Did it ever occur to you that I might not want to be in the hills of northwestern New Jersey?"

"Oh, it occurred to me, all right, but I figured you wouldn't mind once you thought about it. You're obviously in need of a little R and R before moving on."

Mary Elizabeth covered her face with her hands and moaned, "I'm on a schedule."

Just then the RV slowed and made a wide turn. Curious, she peeked through her fingers. Pete was nosing the vehicle through a stone gate into a campground.

She dropped her hands. A campground, she thought in a continuing daze. In northwest New Jersey. On Saturday afternoon. When she'd figured to be somewhere in Georgia by now, her trip almost over.

Mary Elizabeth kept her mutters to a minimum, however, while Pete registered them at a rustic cabin and received a site number and a map of the grounds.

By the time he set the RV in motion again, she felt considerably more sanguine. After the clamorous, exhaust-filled air of the New York region, this was really sort of nice, this refreshing scent of pine, the soft swish of a breeze through the trees. Maybe it wouldn't hurt to stop for just a few hours.

Their site was nestled under a canopy of trees on a rise overlooking a lake. A picnic table and a fire pit came with the space, as well as electric, sewer and water hookups. Mary Elizabeth sat at the picnic table—Pete's orders—watching him move around the campsite, engaging hoses and lines with an efficiency that amazed her.

He scrambled up the ladder at the rear of the RV, lithely stepped along the roof, and squatted to do something mysterious to the air-conditioning unit.

She sighed. These were the responsibilities that had scared her into not venturing far from home on her few weekend outings. She fully intended to read all the instruction manuals that came with the camper—she'd have to if she was going to make it her home—but so far she knew only the basics about the mechanical systems.

Swinging off the ladder, Pete gave her a cavalier grin. "There, all set. Feel like taking a walk?"

She glanced toward the lake, a lake almost as blue and deep as his eyes. Shrugging, she got to her feet and fell into step by his side. All around them families were enjoying a last warm weekend of summer, tossing Frisbees, paddling canoes, cooking over campfires. Mary Elizabeth felt distinctly out of place.

Walking at the water's edge, she finally asked him the question that had been troubling her since she'd awakened. "So, what are we doing here, Peter?"

"I already told you. I thought you needed—"

"To rest? I could've done that back in the parking lot of the motel. You know, the one just a mile off I-95?" she said pointedly.

His arm bumped hers companionably. "But could you go fishing for your supper back at that motel?"

"I don't need to go fishing. I have enough food to get me through a Valley Forge winter."

"Not the way *I* eat. Besides I don't like quiche, and I noticed you have so *much* of it."

Mary Elizabeth opened her mouth, words of protest ready to spill, when all at once his remark took on strange new meaning. Her footsteps slowed, then stopped completely.

"What did you say?" she asked softly.

Pete picked up a flat stone and skimmed it across the surface of the lake. "I've decided to take you up on your suggestion," he replied, giving her a casual over-the-shoulder glance.

She held her breath. "Which one?"

"I'll go the distance with you...."

Her breath escaped on a burst of relief.

"Wait. Hold it. You haven't heard my half of the deal yet. Before we do anything, we have to get a few ground rules straight, the most important being, I'm not making the trip in three days. You have to understand that. I have almost a week's vacation left and I intend to take every minute of it."

Her momentary elation tumbled. "I can't do that. I told my friend I'd be at her place by tonight."

"Sweetheart, I don't think you're going to make it."

She battled a grin. "I know that, but I thought I'd at least make it by Monday."

Pete shook his head. "With me driving, a week. Take it or leave it."

Mary Elizabeth chewed on her bottom lip.

"Another thing," he went on, "I get to stop the bus any time the spirit moves me and go off side-tripping on my bike."

Her lip-chewing picked up fervor. "Anything else?"

"I get to sleep inside. It'll save me a bundle on motel fees."

Mary Elizabeth tried not to react. After all, the idea of having him drive had originally been hers, so of course he must have assumed she'd thought through all the details. *This* detail had gotten by her.

"Oh, one more thing," he added. "After you're settled in Sarasota, I don't expect us to keep in touch."

A tight ache filled her chest. He didn't *expect?* Wasn't it rather he didn't *want?*

They resumed walking. Eventually he said, "You're awfully quiet, Mary Elizabeth. What are you thinking?"

"I'm thinking there's no free lunch. If you're ready to do me this favor, how do you expect me to repay you?"

He began to smile. "Funny you should ask."

CHAPTER SEVEN

"YOU WANT ME TO *what?*"

"Go to my brother's wedding with me next Saturday. Pretend to be my date."

After a taut span of silence, Mary Elizabeth laughed. "I don't think so, Peter."

Pete skipped another stone, the movement from shoulder to wrist fluid and compact. "Why not?"

"Why not?" She planted her spread-fingered hands on her hips and gaped at him. "I'm pregnant!"

"What does that have to do with the price of bananas? You hardly show." His glance swept the green chino jacket she was wearing today which, as usual, was buttoned. "Wear something loose like that and nobody'll notice."

"That's not the point. It's... I don't know. It just feels wrong. Besides, we hardly know each other."

He shrugged nonchalantly. "A week can solve that."

She chewed on her lip, considering the proposition. It was crazy.

It was also tempting... and because it was she replied, "No, thanks," and resumed walking.

"Ah, well." Pete pulled the RV keys from his jeans pocket and dangled them in front of her. "Have it your way, princess."

Her steps slowed. "But why would you want me to pretend I'm your... your date? It doesn't make sense."

"Yes, it does. I have a solid, rational explanation. But before we start swapping war stories, let's go up to the clubhouse and see if we can rent us a boat and some fishing gear." Without waiting to hear what she thought of the idea, he started off, calling over his shoulder, "And we *will* swap, story for story. That's another stipulation. I'm not going anywhere with you until I find out about that little bombshell you're carrying and the guy who's responsible."

Mary Elizabeth caught up beside him. "I don't see how that's any of your business."

"It will be, if I happen to wake up some night looking up the barrel of a twelve-gauge shotgun."

Mary Elizabeth rolled her eyes. "That happen to you often, Peter?"

He chuckled, a down-and-dirty sound that brought on a smile she had trouble suppressing.

"I'll tell you right now," she assured him, "nobody's following me." At least she hoped not. She hoped Mrs. Pidgin was able to keep her destination a secret.

"I still want to hear about it."

Mary Elizabeth walked along, puzzled by her reaction to his proposal, by her reluctance to accept it. After all, having him drive had originally been her idea, hadn't it? And it would be to her advantage if she agreed.

Was she balking because, if she complied with his agenda, she'd be arriving at Chloe's a week late? That certainly was a serious consideration. But, oddly, she wasn't nearly as bothered by that as by the idea of spending a week with Peter Mitchell in an eighteen-foot motor home. And that, she knew, was because of the fascination she'd felt for him from the moment she'd laid eyes on him, a fascination that had quickly turned into something more.

She gave him a sidelong glance, taking in the chiseled perfection of his rugged profile. She really didn't know why she was worried. Acting on an attraction was no longer an option open to her. She was pregnant. Her social life had temporarily shut down. Remembering that, surely she could keep these stirrings under control.

Likewise, she shouldn't be concerned about Peter, either. Why would he want to get involved with a woman who was pregnant, a woman carrying another man's child? If anything, her condition should drive him away. She ought to feel safe traveling with him. Her pregnancy acted as a shield.

"When did you say this wedding's supposed to take place?" They'd reached the clubhouse. She paused on the dirt path.

"Next Saturday. I'm Brad's best man, so you'll have to sit with the family during the ceremony, but afterward, at the reception, I'll be all yours."

"Oh, joy."

"So, is that a yes?"

"No! Let me think about it. I still want to hear your reasons."

"Fine. But first, the gear."

"Peter," she called, following him up the porch steps. "I've never fished before."

Opening the wooden screen door, he turned. "You're kidding."

"No."

"You grew up in Maine, and you never fished?"

"No!"

He shook his head. "You've got more to learn than I thought, Mary Elizabeth."

"So," PETE SAID, WATCHING a dragonfly scissor across the surface of the lake, "are you ready?" The dinghy was designed with two benches. He sat on one, Mary Elizabeth on the other, their poles reaching out over the water in opposite directions.

"For what?" she asked.

"For shoes and ships and sealing wax . . ."

"Oh."

"Want me to go first?" he offered.

"No, no. I don't mind." She pulled in a breath that lifted her shoulders almost to her ears, then expelled it in a shuddery gust. "Okay, here it is. About a year ago I started seeing this guy named Roger. My . . . um . . . father set us up."

"A blind date?"

"Not exactly. Roger works at . . . with my father, so I already knew him. My . . . father simply persuaded me to attend a company dinner as Roger's date. We had a good time, he asked me out again, and things progressed from there."

Pete noted the hesitation in her voice, the awkward pauses and leaps over detail, but he didn't interrupt. She'd relaxed significantly in the short time they'd been rocking on the lake. He didn't want to tamper with a good thing.

"Unfortunately," she continued, "there was never any real spark between us. I liked Roger well enough, but I wasn't crazy about him, you know?" Her nose wrinkled with familiar predictability as she reached the end of her sentence.

"Yet everyone seemed to think we were an ideal couple. My . . . father, especially. He was always talking about our future together, always hyping Roger's virtues, always telling me how lucky I was to be dating him."

Pete's eyes narrowed. Just for a second there, he thought Mary Elizabeth sounded bitter.

"So," she said on a sigh, "we became engaged."

Pete's scowl deepened.

"I know." Two spots of color emerged on her cheeks. "It was a terribly passive thing to do. I'm not proud of it."

Pete returned his gaze to his side of the lake. "I'm not criticizing. God knows I've done plenty of things simply because momentum carried me along."

"Momentum. That's a good way of explaining it." She paused, then abruptly sat up. "Oh!" She swung her leg over the bench to face the water directly. "Peter, something just tugged on my line."

Pete put down his pole and carefully moved from his bench to hers. "I think you're right." He sat behind her, with his thighs bracketing her hips and his hands reaching around to cover hers. Then together, they began to reel in whatever she'd lured.

Positioned as he was, Pete caught the orange blossom fragrance of her hair, felt the supple warmth of her back against his chest, and his body coiled with a purely sexual reaction.

He reminded himself that Mary Elizabeth was not someone he wanted to think about in those terms. He also reminded himself of the multitude of reasons—not least of which was her pregnancy. With a determined effort, he concentrated on the rod and reel, and put his easy responsiveness to this unlikely woman out of his mind.

"It *is* a fish!" She laughed when a silvery walleye splashed through the surface.

"Not a bad size, either. Ah, beginner's luck." Pete deftly unhooked the fish and lowered it into a bucket.

"This is so neat!" she exclaimed, admiring her catch.

Baiting her hook again, Pete glimpsed the sparkle in her soft brown eyes and tried not to feel too pleased that she was having a good time.

"Continue," he said gruffly. "You and Roger became engaged...."

"Yes. That was last May." She took her pole from him and cast the line clumsily but with obvious delight. "About that time, I also began to give our relationship serious thought—you know, the fact that it was so lukewarm?" Pete watched her nose wrinkle and wondered why he'd ever thought of the quirk as anything but adorable.

She continued, "I came to the conclusion that maybe it was my fault. Maybe I hadn't given our relationship all I could. Before that time, Roger and I hadn't, you know, been intimate?"

Pete was glad her embarrassed gaze was fixed on the water and not his face. Dating all that time, and not intimate?

"But with marriage on the horizon, thoughts of making love occupied my mind more and more. Maybe that would change things between us, I thought. That would add the spark that was missing. And so..." She shrugged and fell broodingly silent.

Finally Pete asked, "Did it work?"

She shook her head. "I don't know why I ever thought it would. I was never really attracted to Roger in that way," she said dismally. "Actually, I'd always found kissing him rather distasteful." She paused. "All right, to be totally honest, it usually felt like I was kissing a plate of wet pasta."

Pete couldn't help laughing and was glad to see Mary Elizabeth smiling, too. He got the feeling this was the first time she'd looked at her relationship with Roger in anything but a tragic light.

"The ironic thing about it was, Roger felt the same way I did. I just didn't know it."

Pete wondered what kind of blood ran in Roger's veins, not to be attracted to this long-legged, blond-haired beauty with a voice that could liquify stone.

"But finally," she continued, "the night my father suggested we start making arrangements for a Christmas wedding, we both came clean and confessed we were unhappy. We broke off our engagement that very night. That was seven weeks ago. Right now I'm about eleven weeks along."

Pete calculated quickly. "You didn't know you were pregnant when you broke up?"

"No. It was too soon for me to miss my...um...monthly cycle. Besides, we'd taken precautions."

Pete turned his gaze on her, one eyebrow raised.

"Condoms are usually reliable," she explained, "but occasionally you hear about an accident happening. I guess it was just my dumb luck to have one of those accidents happen to me."

A flock of geese in V-formation honked their way across the blue sky heading south. Watching them, Pete said, "Does Roger know?"

Mary Elizabeth sighed, frowning. "No."

Pete let his breath hiss through his teeth. This didn't sound like it was going anywhere good. "Do you intend to tell him?"

She gulped. "No."

Pete hesitated, wondering if he really wanted to poke his nose any further into Mary Elizabeth's life, which only got messier the better he knew her.

Curiosity won out over prudence.

"Don't you think he has a right to know?" he asked.

Her mouth hardened, but her voice was surprisingly thin and uncertain when she said, "What about my right to be married to someone I love?"

"Who said anything about marriage?"

She sighed. "Roger is a decent guy. We might not love each other, but he'd want to marry me. He'd think it was the right thing to do."

"But you wouldn't have to agree."

"Yes, I would. I come from a small town, Peter. Everyone would know I was the one who'd denied the child a proper home."

"Jeez, Mary Elizabeth! Coming from a small town may be tough, but it doesn't mean you have to roll over and play dead."

"How would you know?"

"I didn't always live in Tampa."

"Oh." She hunched forward, her momentary boldness deflated. "It isn't just that. Good Lord, I'd like to think I have more backbone than that."

He had suspected she was dancing around the issue, avoiding the heart of it. "What is it, then?"

She gnawed on her bottom lip. "I didn't tell Roger because I just don't want him to know."

"Why? If he's such a decent guy..."

"The child, that's why. I don't want to raise a child who's unwanted and resented by its own father."

Pete sat quietly for a while, unsure what to make of the rancor he'd picked up in her voice. He was also puzzled by the erratic leaps and zigzags in her logic.

Eventually he said, "Have you ever considered the possibility that Roger would love the child?"

She shook her head, sending blond hair swirling. "No. Whether we got married or not, Roger would begrudge the child, I'm sure of it. Maybe not outwardly. Outwardly he might claim to want visitation rights and even insist on paying child support because that's the proper thing to do. But inside I know he'd feel trapped in a situation that embarrassed him and burdened him financially and socially."

Pete was intrigued by the strength of conviction in her voice, by the depth of sadness in her eyes. Was there something about this Roger she wasn't letting on?

She held the forgotten fishing pole at a heedless angle and said, "I don't want that, Peter. I don't want any baby I've brought into the world growing up like that, resented and unwanted. There's got to be a better way."

"Like running off to Florida?" he said with more sympathy than she apparently heard.

She lifted her chin as if challenged. "Yes."

He studied her tensed face, the delicate blue veins throbbing at her temple. "I don't know, kid," he drawled. "In my experience, honesty has usually proved to be the best policy. Keeps things simple, you know?"

She kept her eyes trained on the water, her jaw set with conviction. "It's what's best for the baby."

"But leaving home, quitting a job you liked—that's really a drastic step."

He waited through an interminable silence. During the entire time, her eyes stayed fixed on the water, long lashes hooding whatever was in their depths. Pete had a hunch it was more secrets.

"Your family must be upset by your decision to leave home." Her mouth hardened and he sensed he'd hit a raw nerve.

"Yes," she replied, but her expression told him no. "But I'm leaving for their benefit, too."

"I don't follow...."

"Well, my father is sort of a public figure." She paused. "I guess it doesn't matter, my telling you. He's president of a bank. It's a local bank, but still quite prestigious. He's also head of the chamber of commerce and a deacon in our church. His reputation would be seriously tarnished if I remained in the area—you know, pregnant and unmarried?"

Pete scrubbed at the back of his head. Her *father's* reputation would be tarnished because *she* was pregnant? What kind of crazy logic was that? Come to think of it, what kind of *father* was that? Where was the familial support she needed at this difficult time in her life? Where was the love?

"What about your mother?"

"Died when I was twelve."

Pete's heart contracted. "I'm sorry." He really was. He already had a bad feeling about this father of hers and didn't like the idea of her being left in his care. "Do you have any brothers or sisters?"

"One brother, one sister, but they don't know I'm pregnant. Susan is married and busy with her own life. Charlie's in London." Layers of loneliness darkened her eyes, yet she smiled, briefly, hollowly. She was a paradox, and becoming more of one the more he knew about her.

Pete thought of his own family, how involved they were in one another's lives. Although they often exasperated one another, he couldn't imagine any of them not sharing news as important as a pregnancy.

"What are you going to do when you go back home to visit? Do you plan to leave the baby in Florida, pretend it doesn't exist?"

She began peeling away at some tape wrapped around the grip of her pole. "Lately," she said, concentrating on the tape, "I've been thinking that the best thing I can do for everyone concerned, especially the baby, is give it up for adoption. I mean, what sort of life can *I* offer a child, living in an RV, pawning him off on day-care while I go to work."

To someone who liked his women uncomplicated, Pete thought, Mary Elizabeth Drummond could easily become a nightmare.

"You plan to live in your RV when you get to Florida?"

"Yes."

"I'd wondered why someone like you was traveling in something like that. Is that why you bought it?"

"No. I got it a year ago." She gazed across the lake to the far shore. "I've always wanted to travel," she said simply, but in her eyes he saw emotions that complicated her response, emotions that echoed in his own chest in a way that made him feel they had a lot more in common than they knew.

"And giving up the baby... is that what you really want to do?"

She coughed nervously. "Yes. A husband and wife looking to adopt would give it a much better home than I could. Sometimes those couples have been through excruciating medical problems. They'd cherish my baby."

Pete's glance shot to her face. Her eyes were glassy, her expression set in an effort not to cry.

Just then, however, his line began to whir. He gripped the pole and braced himself, grateful for the diversion. He didn't think he wanted to pursue the reasons for those tears. No, he *knew* he didn't.

BY THE TIME HIS CATCH was flapping around in the bucket with its hapless mate, Mary Elizabeth felt she'd regained an admirable grip on her composure. She hadn't intended to divulge quite so much about her personal life, but Peter had been surprisingly easy to talk to, probably because he was a stranger, she reasoned—although he didn't feel like a stranger anymore. He felt like a friend.

"Okay," she said, "you know my story, now let's hear yours. What's the reason behind your asking me to attend your brother's wedding?"

She watched him settle on the bench facing hers and cast his line. When the baited hook had sunk, he said, "All right. Here's the way it is. Someone I'd rather avoid is going to be at the wedding, a woman named Sue Ellen Carlisle." The rippling circles around his line widened outward. "She and

I used to be an item in high school, but you know how life is. After graduation she went her way, I went mine.''

Mary Elizabeth tried to read his expression, but it had gone blank. She hadn't a clue how *life was* with him, and evidently he didn't plan to tell her.

''Now Sue Ellen is divorced, and I've got a hunch people at the wedding are going to be trying to get us together again.''

''People?''

''Hmm. My brother. My two sisters. Friends who knew us back in high school.''

''Why would they want to do that?''

''Basically, because some folks don't know how to mind their own business.''

She sidestepped his cynicism. ''Were you and Sue Ellen really serious? Like, king and queen of the prom or something?''

The corner of his mouth lifted lazily. ''I wasn't exactly king-of-the-prom material back in high school, Mary Elizabeth.'' His smile faded. ''But, yeah, we were serious.''

She wasn't sure she was glad she'd asked. She'd finally picked up a reaction, a thread of sadness in his voice, a hint of remembered heartache that, illogical as it was, made her jealous. Apparently, breaking up hadn't been his idea, and this Sue Ellen was a person capable of hurting the inviolable Peter Mitchell.

Mary Elizabeth murmured, ''And now she's divorced.''

''Yep. Fifteen years later she's divorced, and people are saying dumb things like, 'Hey, Pete, why don't you ask her out?''' He shook his head in disgust. ''Especially my sisters. They're married, so they think the whole world should be. They're always trying to fix me up with somebody. I think it's really just a case of misery-loves-company.''

The slap of the water softly lapping the boat filled the ensuing silence. Mary Elizabeth wanted to probe deeper. Each new thing she learned about him only made her hunger to learn more. But she wasn't sure she should.

"What do you have against marriage?" she asked hesitantly.

"Nothing, as long as it doesn't involve me." He gazed out over the sun-shot water, again avoiding her question with flippancy, firming her suspicion there was more to his past than he was letting on.

"You don't intend to ever get married?"

"Nope. Not cut out for marital bliss."

"But how do you know unless you try it?"

His jaw hardened. "I don't have to eat mud to know it's not for me, either. Hell, Mary Elizabeth, lots of men are confirmed bachelors. Why are you having such a difficult time with the concept?"

He'd become prickly enough for her to back off the issue and not say what was on her mind, that she thought he'd carved out a terribly lonely existence for himself.

"Have you seen this Sue Ellen recently? Do you know how she'd react if people actually started matchmaking at the wedding?"

Pete clicked his tongue. "That's part of the problem. I've got a strong notion Sue Ellen wouldn't mind us getting back together herself."

"And you don't want to?"

"You got that right. She's half the reason I decided it was time to leave Tampa for a while, go on vacation."

"The other half being...?"

"That Triumph turning up for sale."

"Ah, now I get it. You want me to be your *date!*"

"Yes. I'll protect you on the road if you'll protect me at the wedding."

She smiled. That was an odd way of looking at the arrangement. "But surely you know other women. Why me?"

"To be perfectly honest, I haven't been seeing anyone special lately. Oh, I've dated, but my family and friends know who and how casual it's been. Now, if I show up with you, a complete stranger, I could say anything about you and nobody'd be the wiser. I could say we're practically engaged, or thinking of moving in together...."

"But won't your family want to know why you'd never mentioned me before?"

"Not really. I don't tell them all my business. But just to be safe I'll say I had a hunch our relationship was special but I didn't want to let them in on it before I was sure."

"But what happens after the wedding, when I'm suddenly not around anymore?"

Pete thought a moment. "Suppose we go with the truth, say you're moving to Sarasota. That way I can pretend we're still seeing each other, but Sarasota's enough of a distance that they wouldn't bother checking. Then, after a couple of months, I'll merely say we broke up."

Mary Elizabeth scowled at the half inch of water at the bottom of the boat sloshing around her shoes. "I don't know, Peter. There are still so many holes in your story. What if someone at the wedding asks me something about you that I should know?"

"We have a week to learn the details of each other's lives."

"But shouldn't we have a past, you and I—how we met, places we've been together?"

"Of course. We'll work on it. We'll come up with something believable."

"And all I have to do at the wedding is ... what?"

"Dance with me, sit and talk with me, go along with the pretense that we're crazy about each other—and keep Sue Ellen and my pushy relatives off my back."

Mary Elizabeth closed her eyes and made a sound that was half groan, half laugh. "Oh, Peter, I'm still not sure we can pull it off. Look at us. We're not exactly a made-to-order match."

They sat quietly in the gently rocking boat, faces serious, eyes exploring each other, searching for the reminders that they came from vastly different worlds. Those reminders were becoming increasingly difficult to find.

Finally Pete grinned carelessly and drawled, "You've got a lot of promise, Mary Elizabeth. I can fix you up, make you look almost as good as somebody I might take out."

"Oh? Why do I have to be the one with *promise?* What about you?"

"I'm perfect. Who'd want to change me?"

"Your arrogance, Mr. Mitchell, is second only to your impertinence."

Grinning, he ran his knuckles over his jutting chin. "I knew you'd like me once you got to know me better."

She moved to hit him, but he caught her wrist and laughed. "So, what's it gonna be, sweetheart? Two for the road, or adios, amigo?"

Clasped in his strong grip, with her arm pressed against his muscle-ridged chest, Mary Elizabeth experienced that pull of physical attraction that had plagued her much too often lately. She was sure he was feeling it, too. Everything inside her lifted with the sensation—and then fell.

"It's three for the road, Peter," she reminded him quietly. "Three."

She watched her point hit home. He swallowed, loosened his grip and moved away from her.

Mary Elizabeth glanced toward her camper tucked under the trees. She could be in Florida by Monday night if she left tomorrow morning and drove two ten-hour days.

But she'd be driving without a license. If she got caught, her license might be taken away from her for years. And given her streak of luck lately...

Just twenty hours on the road, she thought.

But what if she fell sick again? What if the RV broke down?

A mere two days.

"When did you say we'd be getting to Tampa?" she asked.

"Friday. And it won't be Tampa. It'll be Elmira, the small town where I grew up, about forty miles away. Brad's fiancée still lives there. So do most of the two families."

"I see. But I wouldn't be free to continue on to my friend's until when, Saturday night?"

"Better make that Sunday morning."

Hmm. Monday night. Sunday morning. Almost a whole week.

But did it really make a difference?

Of course it did, her conscience nagged. What about her job interview? She was supposed to be interviewed on Tuesday.

"I'll have to call my friend and see if my interview can be rescheduled."

"So, is that an answer?"

She shut her eyes and moaned, wondering what she was getting into. "I suppose it is."

PRODDING THE GLOWING coals in the fire pit late that afternoon, Pete thought about Mary Elizabeth's answer and felt a pang of guilt. She was up at the clubhouse now, phoning her friend to ask if the job interview could be put off. But what if it couldn't? What if she lost the position just because he insisted on taking his time getting to Florida?

He shook his head. Why was he feeling guilty? Taking his time was his right. It was a God-given prerogative of being on vacation. Besides, he hadn't forced her to agree to his terms. She could've said no. But she hadn't, and in his experience he'd found that people usually did what they really wanted, even when they claimed it wasn't. And he suspected that what Mary Elizabeth really wanted was to slow down and maybe lose herself on the road for a while. If she didn't, she should. She was wired pretty tight.

He wished he could rationalize his not telling her about his marriage as easily as he rationalized his guilt. But the plain truth was he just hated talking about Cindy and that part of his life. Would he be forced to before he and Mary Elizabeth got to Elmira? Maybe nobody would bring the subject up. If they were polite they wouldn't, but when had his family ever been polite?

He turned the potatoes, poked the coals again and sat back on his heels, his mind wandering to his afternoon on the lake with Mary Elizabeth. The corner of his mouth lifted. She'd looked so damn pretty sitting there in that boat, her silky blond hair gleaming with sunlight, her eyes dancing when she'd reeled in that skinny walleye.

Catching himself in mid-reverie, Pete swore under his breath. He had to stop thinking of her as a woman. Nothing could happen between them. It was a matter of principle with him that he didn't get involved with a woman if he knew he wasn't going to see her again, and he wasn't going to see Mary Elizabeth again after next Sunday.

Considering she was pregnant, a one-week-stand became even more taboo. A guy didn't start up with a woman who was pregnant unless he was ready to get serious and share his life with her and her baby. It just wasn't right, morally, psychologically, any way you looked at it.

Pete placed four ears of corn on the hot grate and scowled. All right, so he was aware Mary Elizabeth was planning to give up her baby. But so what? If he got involved with her, he'd still have to see her through the pregnancy, and the birth, and the emotional adjustment period afterward. What kind of heel would he be if he didn't? Those were pretty traumatic life events she was facing, and she was facing them alone. But that was a helluva lot for a woman to ask a guy to commit to after knowing her only a few days. It was certainly more than he was ready to commit to.

He'd just have to cool his engines while they were together. He'd be friendly enough—no sense in being miserable for a week—but Mary Elizabeth would know he meant nothing by it. He'd make sure she did.

Pete stood up, wiped his sooty hands on a bandanna and gazed toward the clubhouse through the trees. Mary Elizabeth was coming along the path, returning to the campsite, her pale hair swinging with each long stride she took. Without any warning his body betrayed him, responding to the merest sight of her with an involuntary flush of heat and need.

He jammed the bandanna into his back pocket and scowled at the fire. Something told him cooling his engines was going to be one of the hardest jobs he'd ever tackled.

CHAPTER EIGHT

MARY ELIZABETH'S CALL to Chloe wasn't the most honest of communications. She needed to tell her friend about her new travel plans, but not wanting to alarm her, she didn't mention Peter. She merely said she had decided to slow down, maybe visit Pennsylvania Dutch country or the Carolina coast, places she really had always wanted to see. Chloe seemed confused, but Mary Elizabeth didn't know how else to explain this strange new turn of events.

The job interview was another sticky matter. Chloe's husband had arranged the interview, and while it was only for a temporary position as a receptionist in a dentist's office, that dentist was a friend of his and the interview, a personal favor.

"I'm not sure it can be put off," Chloe said. "Dr. Taylor has already postponed hiring somebody because we asked him to wait for you."

"I'm sorry, Chloe."

"Oh, it's all right. I'll see what can be arranged."

Before hanging up, Mary Elizabeth remembered her wallet. She told Chloe not to be alarmed if it arrived in the mail. Skipping details, she merely said she'd lost it and had given Chloe's address to the police. She also asked Chloe to watch the mail for her new credit cards. Chloe was full of questions, but Mary Elizabeth dodged them by saying her supper was on the fire and needed tending.

And, in fact, it was. By the time she got back to the campsite, Peter had the fish cleaned, seasoned and wrapped in foil, and ready to place over the coals in the fire pit, alongside the three potatoes that were already baking there and the four ears of corn he'd bartered from the family camping next to them. In exchange, he'd given them three of her lovely little quiches. Looked mighty pleased with himself for doing so, too.

She sat at the picnic table, watching him. "You're very good at this," she commented.

He looked up from the fire, the angles and planes of his face emphasized by the warm glow. One corner of his mouth lifted. "Good at lots of things."

Although she didn't doubt it, she said, "You need a healthy dose of humility."

"Me?" He pretended to look offended.

"Yes, you." In the silence that followed, she questioned again the wisdom of agreeing to travel with this man for an entire week. How totally different from her original travel plan on leaving home. She tried to figure out how she'd reached this place in her life, but the chain of events eluded her. If her call to Chloe had accomplished anything, it was to underscore how truly bizarre her course had become. She wasn't a bizarre person. Things like this didn't normally happen to her.

She watched Peter move around the fire, the muscles of his thighs rippling and bunching as he reached for things, knelt, got up. It was because of him, she thought, feeling a quiver of indefinable fear shoot through her. She'd chosen this path because she'd wanted to remain with him.

The fear expanded and rose to her throat. Oh, Lord, what had she done? The answer came back to her in the stirring of her senses as she continued to watch him, this tall, forceful man who intrigued her more than any mystery.

Okay, this isn't a problem, she assured herself on a shaky sigh. All she had to do was remember her circumstances. She was pregnant. She needed a job, medical care, a semi-permanent place to park her RV. And those were only the physical problems. What about the emotional ones she was carrying—her myriad insecurities, the shock she still felt over her parentage? She had so many issues to deal with, no man in his right mind would *want* to touch her—if he knew about those issues. Pete didn't, not fully.

Okay, so she'd just have to be careful, make sure she didn't send out any signals that might give him the wrong idea. That might be difficult. There were times she caught herself just staring at the man. But she could do it if she set her mind to it. She knew she could. She'd always had good self-control.

She watched him peel away the foil from the fish, careful not to tear it—and she refused to think of those large rough hands being so capable.

"Have you done a lot of camping?" she asked with forced nonchalance.

He nodded. "Ever since I was a boy. Of course, back then I thought of it as running away from home."

She was relieved; here was something safe they could talk about. "You used to run away?"

"All the time." He chuckled. "Got my backside warmed every time I did, too."

"Why'd you run away?"

He came to sit beside her at the table, bringing along the long steel tongs he'd been using to turn the vegetables. "Is this our first session of getting to know each other?" He cast her a grin that was both playful and seductive. She didn't think he meant it to be; that was just the way he was.

She looked at the fire. "I suppose it could be."

He leaned forward, swinging the tongs between his knees. "I was a punk, that's why I ran away."

"Well, I assumed that. But why else?"

"I wanted to see the world." He laughed, a tight, self-conscious sound that told her he was uneasy with talking about his past.

"Where'd that ambition come from?"

His grin changed subtly at the edges, then gradually faded. "I was the oldest of four, both my parents worked, and I had the responsibility of taking care of the kids while they were gone. I had to get the girls' breakfast, walk them to school, entertain them afterward, pick up Brad from the baby-sitter's, start supper—" He broke off abruptly. "Let's just say I wasn't too happy about the situation, so occasionally I took off, just me and my Schwinn and the horizon."

Mary Elizabeth barely breathed. She hadn't expected him to open up to her like that.

"Somebody would always find me, though—a neighbor, the police." He shook his head, smiling faintly. "By the time I was twelve I had quite a reputation around town. That crazy Mitchell boy, people used to say. Gonna put his mama in the ground."

"This was all before you were *twelve?* Taking care of your siblings? The running away?"

"Well, sure, Mary Elizabeth. Kids grow up fast in small cracker towns. When I turned thirteen my sister Pam took my place, 'cause I was old enough to go to work with my daddy paintin' houses."

She noticed he'd slipped into a more pronounced southern drawl, a deliberate attempt at levity that nonetheless conveyed a heavy measure of derision.

"When was this, during summer vacations?"

"Yep, summer vacations, winter vacations, afternoons after school, too. If we were lucky enough to get a job, it didn't matter what time of year it was. We just worked."

How different from her own youth, she thought. She realized she must've been frowning because he said, "That's okay. I never wanted to be on the debate team, anyway."

Her frown deepened. Maybe he'd never wanted to be on the debate team, but given his size and strength and athletic grace, surely he must have wanted to go out for sports.

"It must've been awful," she commiserated.

"Awful?" He ran his knuckles along his jaw, thinking back. "No, not really. Sure, it was hard, but it taught me a lot about responsibility and survival. And there was no question that my parents loved us. I may have sometimes been angry as a kid, but I hold no grudges now. They did the best they could. My mother certainly didn't want to be away from us so much. She would've much preferred being a stay-at-home mom. I would've preferred it, too. I hated seeing her so tired, but there was simply no other way my parents could've made ends meet."

"Do your parents still work?"

Pete swallowed, then gave his head a brisk shake. "They're gone. My mother died young, only forty-one. My father passed away eight months ago."

"Oh, I'm sorry," Mary Elizabeth murmured. She wished she hadn't asked. Pete's voice had fallen into a monotone that betrayed a lingering sorrow. "Um, how did you learn to fight so well?" she asked to change the subject.

"The usual way. Got into lots of brawls." The tongs, she noticed, were swinging at a more agitated pace.

"Why was that?"

He exhaled a derisive laugh. "For a while, I had a chip on my shoulder the size of Ohio."

"From feeling trapped in a family situation you didn't like?"

"I guess. I was sick of just scraping by, angry at people who labeled us. And I didn't much like that tiny backwater town I was stuck in." He paused thoughtfully. "Hell, I don't know why I fought. I was just a punk, I guess." He reached forward and prodded the potatoes. "These are done," he said, getting up. She sensed him pulling away from her.

She tried to pull him back. "So, Peter, when did you get your first motorcycle?"

He wiped his hands on a red bandanna and grinned. "I was fifteen, too young to ride it, but that didn't matter. It was junkyard salvage. Needed major repair before I could put it on the road, anyway."

"And when you got it working, did you try to leave town on it the way you used to on your bicycle?"

His grin faded. "No, I started dating Sue Ellen then."

That knife twist of irrational jealousy returned to puncture Mary Elizabeth's sense of detachment. Her levity was forced when she said, "I see. Kicked the wheels out from under you, did she?"

"For a while," he admitted. "But I'd always planned on going into the army after high school, and I did. Come on, let's eat."

With a bit of nudging, Peter continued to talk about himself during the meal. Mary Elizabeth was especially curious about his stint in the military. At first he tried to pass it off simply as a way of escaping the small town of Elmira and the burden of watching over his siblings, who then had ranged in age from fifteen to eight. And while she didn't doubt those reasons were true, she felt they weren't the entire truth.

Sure enough, as he continued to talk, a far broader picture came into view. Peter had been consumed with the idea of starting his own business, a business substantial enough to employ his entire family and bring them financial independence and security. In short, he'd seen the military as the first and most vital step toward that end.

Apparently, he'd seen right. Brad now worked as his foreman. Pam did the books. Her husband and Lindy's were general laborers, and Lindy was studying carpentry. And that didn't take into account the smattering of second-rung relatives who were also on Pete's payroll.

"I'm not sure the military was the right decision," he said thoughtfully. "Maybe I would've been better off staying at home, working part-time, going to school nights. But back then, I didn't have much guidance in those matters. It seemed like a good idea."

"And you got to see the world."

He grimaced. "Yeah. The jungles of Central America." He paused, glancing at her plate. "Eat your corn, Mary Elizabeth. Lots of fibre in corn."

She made a face at him but followed his directive anyway.

"What made you decide to settle in Tampa?"

"Oh, it's a big city, lots of opportunity for a guy with ambition. If I'd stayed in Elmira, I'd be just one more guy with a pickup truck calling himself a contractor and scratching for work."

"But what about your family? They didn't move, did they?"

"Brad did, but the girls stayed. It's a long commute, but that doesn't seem to bother my relatives."

There was just enough derision in his tone for her to say, "I thought you liked your relatives."

"I do, most of the time," he admitted. "And most of the time I enjoy working with them. It's just that sometimes..." His voice thinned.

"Sometimes, what?"

"Nothing," he said, and concentrated on eating.

"Sometimes you feel you've never left home? That you're still twelve years old and forced to baby-sit everybody?"

He moved the food around on his plate, a slow grin forming those creases around his mouth and eyes that she was quickly coming to love. "You're a lot smarter than you look, Mary Elizabeth."

Her grin matched his. "And you, Mr. Mitchell, are a lot more complicated than you like to let on."

"Complicated? Uh-uh." He bit into his corn with his strong, even teeth.

"Yes, you are."

He shook his head. "What you see is what you get, a simple man with simple tastes. Beer, sports and rock 'n' roll—that's what makes me tick."

"A regular Renaissance man, by golly."

"I like my work, too. Add that to the list."

"And motorcycles," she teased dryly.

"Goes without saying. So, how are we doing? Think you know me yet?"

"I'm getting there."

"Jeez Louise! How much more do you want to know?"

Everything, her heart replied. She noticed him look at her strangely, and her breath seized up on her. Had she just telegraphed that thought?

Quickly, she drank the last of her milk, got to her feet and, mumbling something about just wanting to be prepared for the wedding, began clearing her place.

After she went inside, Pete sat at the table, smoking a cigarillo in the golden light of the lowering sun. Why had he told her so much about himself, all those stories about his childhood? His private life was usually off limits to outsiders. How had she gotten through his defenses? One minute she was asking him a simple question about camping, and the next he was telling her how he *felt*, explaining *reasons* for things, explaining . . . himself. Why?

He took a puff on his cigar, determined to shake off those bothersome questions. A guy could go crazy thinking too hard. He and Mary Elizabeth had just been talking, that's all, and he wasn't going to read anything more into it. Besides, they had a bigger problem. The sun was almost on the horizon, and night was coming on. It was nearly bedtime.

No, this isn't a problem, he assured himself. Mary Elizabeth might be an attractive woman, but he certainly didn't want to get involved with her. He knew that. He knew all the reasons, too. All he had to do was keep reminding himself of them and they'd get through this week with no trouble.

Feeling more at ease, he snuffed out his cigarillo and headed for the RV.

Mary Elizabeth was filling the dishpan when he came in. He placed his plate and cutlery on the counter and, without a word, wandered off to the bedroom. Puzzled, she perked her ears, trying to hear what he was doing.

"Where do you want me to put these boxes?" he called casually.

"What boxes?"

"The ones on my bed."

"*Your* bed? Your bed's out here."

Pete returned, his gaze combing the kitchen. When he saw she was motioning toward the bunk, his eyebrows almost disappeared under his hair. "You don't really expect me to sleep up there?"

"Why not?" She lowered their plates into the sudsy water.

"I'll show you why not." He climbed the short ladder, crawled onto the thin mattress and, lying down, rolled carefully onto his side.

Mary Elizabeth studied his cramped body in its boxlike quarters and abruptly burst out laughing. "You look like you're in a coffin."

"And we all know how comfy those things are. How about I move the stuff from the bedroom to here?"

She sobered. "No, don't bother. I'll sleep up there."

"You shouldn't be climbing ladders in your condition."

"I'm only three months along, Peter. I think I can manage."

"Yeah, well, what if you fall out?"

"I won't f—" In mid-sentence, Mary Elizabeth froze. Pete's shoulder dropped forward, the weight of his upper body carrying the rest of him along, over the side of the bunk. "Peter!"

All in one lithe move, he tumbled, rotated and landed soundly on his feet. "You're not sleeping up there," he declared flatly.

Puddles had formed where the soap dripped off her motionless hands. "Peter Mitchell," she swore, eyes narrowed, "you're going to be the death of me yet." She reached for a paper towel and made a hasty pass at the wet floor.

"Better me than a tumble from a bunk. Now, if you want those boxes someplace else, tell me now. Otherwise . . ." He started to walk off.

Mary Elizabeth dried her hands and followed him into the bedroom. Her heart was racing. "But we can't sleep in the same room."

"Why not? Do you snore?"

She shot him an impatient look. "I read late."

"Great. So do I."

She gazed at the paper towel she was absentmindedly wringing. "You know that's not the problem."

Looking amused and thoroughly self-possessed, he said, "I'd suggest we hang a rope between the beds and throw a blanket over it—you know, like in *It Happened One Night*? But this is the 1990s, sweetheart, not the 1930s."

"I don't care." She folded her arms.

"Question. Have you ever slept with a man?"

"What, are you deaf? I told you about me and Roger."

"You're not listening. I didn't ask if you'd had sex, I asked if you'd slept with a man."

She didn't know where to settle her uneasy gaze. Hesitantly she replied, "No."

"That college you went to... that was an all-female college, right?"

Again, her nod was slow in coming.

"You never took baths with your brother when you were a kid?"

"Don't be ridiculous."

"You never..."

"Stop." She cut the air with a wide motion of her hands. "Whether I bathed with my brother or didn't bathe with him has nothing to do with you and me now, sleeping in the same room."

"Sure it does. You're obviously uncomfortable around the opposite sex. I, on the other hand, couldn't care less."

Mary Elizabeth gave him a slightly startled once-over. She was amused to see the tips of his ears turn pink.

"That didn't come out quite right. What I mean is..." He paused and she got the idea he was searching his mind. "You and I have an agreement, sort of like a business contract, and I never mix business with sex. The complications just aren't worth it." He paused again as if reviewing what he'd said.

Apparently finding something lacking in his argument, he went on. "Secondly, I'm just not interested. That's not a reflection on you, Mary Elizabeth. God knows you're a desirable woman." He could've been saying *You're a tall woman* or *You have a nose and two eyes* for all the fervor he invested in his words. "But with this traveling arrangement lasting only a week, I'd feel like a heel getting involved with you. I'd feel I was using you, and, well, I just don't do that sort of thing." He paused a moment, looking at her, but not really meeting her eyes. "Have I made myself clear? Do you know where we stand?"

Yes, to both questions, she thought, surprised by his forthrightness. Paradoxically, she felt both relieved and let down. She lowered herself to the edge of her bed and looked across the way, testing the view, trying to imagine Peter stretched out there. Despite his avowals of disinterest, ribbons of discomfiting heat fluttered through her.

"We'll respect each other's privacy when we're dressing?"

His lips twitched. "Undressing, too."

"Well . . . I suppose we could give it a try."

"Atta girl." Pete hoisted an instrument case off the cluttered bed. "After the first night, you'll be looking at me like one of your old sorority sisters, you'll see."

Somehow Mary Elizabeth doubted that.

"Be careful with that thing."

"What is it?"

"My violin."

"Do you play?"

"Sort of."

"Will you promise not to while we're traveling together?"

"What do I get out of that?"

"I won't light up my cigars in your presence."

"Oh, yay," she replied vapidly—right before being hit with a pillow.

Mary Elizabeth got ready for bed first. By the time Pete was done using the bathroom she was under the covers with Monet curled up at her feet and her tiny book light glowing over a page of a hardcover novel. Spotting the cat, Pete groaned and returned to the bathroom to take his allergy medicine.

When he returned, she tried not to look up, tried not to feel his presence filling the small room. She failed. Pete had the body of a man who does physical labor for a living—strong and lean and solid. Just a glance at his thick, tanned forearms did more for her than all of Roger's lovemaking combined. When he peeled off his shirt, the sight of all that hair and chest muscle was almost her undoing.

"You might want to turn," he suggested matter-of-factly, unbuckling his belt.

"Oh." She rotated onto her side, eyes to the wall, her mind filled with images that refused to go away, no matter what grim thoughts she forced on herself. She waited until she heard his mattress sigh to ease onto her back again.

They read for several minutes without speaking.

"It isn't a question of modesty or prudishness," she said clear out of the blue.

"Really?" Uncannily, he knew exactly what she was talking about. "Is that why you're wearing pajamas *and* a robe to bed?"

"Oh. I...I was cold." Okay, so maybe she was a tad prudish, too. "It's the intimacy of this arrangement. I'm not used to intimacy. Growing up, I didn't even share a room with my sister."

Pete laid his book on his dark chest and stacked his hands under his head. "I understand."

She looked over. "Do you? What I'm referring to has more to do with talking and sharing what's in one's heart than with anything physical." *You know, like what we've been doing today.*

He caught her in his bright, knowing gaze and repeated more softly, "I understand. Intimacy is pretty scary business. It opens the door to our deepest vulnerabilities. Nobody likes to be seen as vulnerable."

She couldn't picture Peter feeling vulnerable about anything, not anything physical, anyway. Unlike her, he lay comfortably exposed, covers to his waist, pale underarms subjected to the scrutiny of anyone who wanted to look.

But emotional intimacy might be a different story. He'd let her into his life today, but only with trepidation and, at times, resistance. It had been a limited tour, too, whole rooms of his past closed off to her inspection. Oddly, she didn't mind that now. Knowing he wasn't invulnerable made him more human. Approachable.

She smiled and went back to her reading. He did the same. But within minutes, her mind had wandered again. "It's been quite a day, hasn't it." She spoke softly, almost to herself.

"I'll say. It's not every day that starts off with a run to the emergency room." He turned a page of his Tony Hillerman mystery. Outside, crickets sang a subdued September song. The breeze swished through the pines. Television sounds drifted from nearby campers.

She swallowed. "Peter?"

In the next bed, Pete felt a quickening of his pulse. Something in the way she said his name made him wary. It was a prelude to something he didn't think he wanted to explore.

"Mmm," he replied lazily.

"Can I tell you something?"

Keep it light, Mitchell. "You will, anyway, with or without my permission," he tossed off, "so shoot."

And she did. "I hate being pregnant."

Oh, man. This was going to be worse than he thought. He lay unmoving. He didn't want to even look over.

"I just hate it. It's complicated my life something awful." Her voice didn't wobble, but he didn't like the way it had thinned.

"The plain truth is I'm embarrassed by my condition. I'm disappointed and I'm angry." Pete listened to her swallow. "I keep asking myself why. Why did this have to happen to me?"

He looked over then, and the anguish he saw in her face tore at him. "Well, for cryin' out loud, Mary Elizabeth, that's perfectly understandable."

"Is it?" she said with bitter doubt, and then fell silent. She seemed hesitant to go any further.

Pete knew he could use that hesitancy as leverage to vault himself out of this little tête-à-tête. He *should* use it ... but he noticed a tear caught at the outer corner of her eye, hanging there, quivering.

"What is it, sweetheart?" he asked softly. "You can tell me. There isn't much I haven't heard already. I have very colorful friends."

She smiled faintly, but continued to stare up at the ceiling. "Life would be so much easier if I weren't pregnant. I could return to Maine, continue working at my job, remain a part of my family. And I'm afraid that's the reason I didn't go into the hospital right away when I thought I was having a miscarriage."

Pete braced himself up on one elbow. "What's this?"

"This morning, I woke around five, but instead of calling for help and going straight to the hospital, I went back to bed."

"Are you trying to tell me you *wanted* to lose the baby?"

Her lips trembled. "Yes. Maybe."

"But you could've terminated the pregnancy yourself, back home. Nobody would've even had to know—Roger, your father, anybody." Objectively, Pete marveled at himself. He sounded so calm, so wise, even while his heart was thumping in his chest like a car about to blow a rod.

"No, I couldn't have. That's the point I'm trying to make," she said, finally turning her head. The tear at the corner of her eye spilled into her hair.

"Why not?"

"I'm basically a coward. Abortion would've involved a conscious choice on my part, a decision I couldn't make. But a miscarriage is a different story. A miscarriage would remove the decision from my hands."

He thought of lying back, turning off his light, burying himself deep under the covers and forgetting any of this conversation had happened. Instead, he swung his bare feet to the floor, making sure to keep the sheet across his lap. "Would it make you feel any better if I told you you probably did the right thing, going back to bed? My sister Lindy had false labor during both her pregnancies, and her doctor's advice was to lie down. If the contractions didn't go away after a rest, *then* she should call him. But invariably they went away."

"Interesting . . . but, no, I don't feel better."

"How about the fact that when we're feeling sick, our first instinct is to crawl into bed?"

She rocked her head on the pillow.

"You couldn't have been positive it was a miscarriage. You probably had lots of other ideas swimming around in your head, clouding your judgment."

"Nope. Doesn't wash."

Pete got so frustrated he threw off the covers and moved to her bed. He didn't even care about his lack of clothing. At least he had his shorts on, and even if he hadn't, this was too important an issue for modesty to interfere.

Gripping her arms, he hauled her to a sitting position. "Will you give yourself a break, goddammit? You're so hard on yourself." His fingers pressed into her soft flesh. "I hate to disillusion you, Mary Elizabeth, but you're only human, and humans sometimes feel the way you do. If you got a kick out of being pregnant in your situation, then I'd really think you were nuts. But being disappointed and angry?" He shook his head. "Welcome to the human race, princess."

He watched relief enter her eyes, felt it wash through her body. For a moment he thought she was going to cry. It came out a laugh instead.

"That's better." He loosened his grip. "Now, about that cockeyed idea about subconsciously wanting to miscarry, I don't buy that. First of all, I was there, remember? I saw you leaving the examining room. I talked to you after. You were happy not to've lost the baby. Your feelings came out in ways you probably weren't even aware of. Sighs of relief. Smiles as you spoke."

The tension was melting visibly from her face, loosening her shoulders, steadying her breathing.

"And secondly," Pete continued, "you made your decision regarding the life of this baby a long time ago, back in Maine. You did," he insisted when he saw doubt momentarily darken her expression. "Remember that the next time you start feeling depressed or angry at yourself, will you? And while you're at it, give yourself a pat on the back. It took courage to do what you did. This going to Florida isn't just a running away. You deliberately chose to give up your home, your job and your family for this baby, and in my book, kid, a person can't get any more heroic."

Mary Elizabeth wanted to cry again. She also wanted to dance. She ended up just sitting there, enjoying how light Peter had made her feel. They were close enough for her to see the starburst of violet rays surrounding the dark pupils of his blue eyes. Such beautiful eyes, she thought. Such a beautiful man.

"How'd you get to be so nice?" Her smile trembled.

"Jeez, Mary Elizabeth—" he released her and pushed away "—I'm a lot of things, but nice isn't one of them."

"Stupendous, then."

Pete got to his feet. "That's more like it."

He noticed her eyes had lowered and spots of color had emerged on her cheeks. He looked down at his shorts, then quickly got back into bed and turned off his light.

Arranging the covers, he saw her reach for her book. "Get some sleep," he said gruffly. "Sleep's important when you're pregnant."

"I know." But she continued to lie there, staring at the book. He noticed her eyes weren't moving.

He finally reached across the distance that separated them, moved her book to the floor and turned off the tiny light. Darkness wrapped over them.

Unfortunately that's all the darkness did. Pete lay back, still hearing the soft rasp of her breathing, still catching the fragrance of her hair, knowing she was lying there as aware of him as he was of her.

He wished sleep would come. Wished he could drive out that last lingering image of her before he'd snapped off the light. Bathed in the intimate glow cast by the small bulb, she'd looked warm, mysterious and absolutely beautiful. He especially wished he could ignore how close he felt to her at this moment. That was something else you had to worry about with intimacy. He wished he had remembered.

He released a long breath through his teeth. Maybe this sleeping arrangement wasn't such a good idea after all. He hoped he knew what he was doing.

CHAPTER NINE

MORNING CAME as a surprise. Mary Elizabeth lay in the pearl gray light, listening to Peter's steady breathing, and realized the intimacy of falling asleep with a man couldn't begin to compare with the intimacy of waking up with him.

He lay facing her, his eyes closed, one arm draped atop the covers, his shoulder and part of his chest exposed. He looked younger in sleep, another surprise.

He stirred fractionally. The silence of the hour magnified the rustle of the bed linens out of all proportion. He made a sound in his throat, his eyelids twitched, and before Mary Elizabeth could turn away, he was looking at her.

She froze, breath suspended, body throbbing with self-consciousness at pulse points she hadn't even known existed before. She wondered how she looked, what he saw. Were there sleep lines on her cheeks? Sand in the corners of her eyes?

She felt his focus sharpen, his awareness of her deepening. Should she say good morning? For a confused moment she felt they already had. Should she get up and go to the bathroom? Ask if he needed to use the facilities first? And if he did, should she pretend indifference to his parading in his B.V.D.s? How did people *do* this?

He said nothing, did nothing. Just closed his sleepy eyes, opened them, and lay there watching her, a riveting connectedness riding on their gaze.

God, this wasn't good. What was she doing, sleeping bed-to-bed with a man she'd met only three days ago? They'd become much too familiar in too short a time.

But that didn't mean they couldn't back up. If they kept the mood between them light, surely they could reclaim some of their emotional distance—couldn't they?

Peter rolled away from her, a gesture of blatant indifference that made her feel foolish for thinking he shared her sharpened sensitivity. She had to relax. If she kept taking everything so seriously, she'd never survive the week.

She watched his back, measured the rise and fall of his breathing, and when she thought he was asleep, she eased out of bed, collected her clothing and tiptoed to the bathroom....

... Leaving Pete behind, staring at the wall and trying to calm his speeding heart. What a way to wake up, to open your eyes and have Mary Elizabeth filling your vision. What scared him, though, was that he hadn't been surprised or even disoriented. It had felt quite natural to find her there, looking all soft and warm just an arm's length away. For one wild moment he wondered if he had been dreaming about her. She'd seemed such a natural extension of his thoughts.

All at once Pete felt claustrophobic. He turned onto his back and wiped his wrist over his clammy brow. His heart was palpitating. Such a small room ... there wasn't enough air to breathe in here. He had to get outside. He had to have more space.

He threw off the covers, got out of bed, yanked on some clothes and reached for his helmet.

He didn't come back from his ride for an hour. He felt a lot better when he did. The sky today was a deep china blue, and the air sparkled with the crisp clarity of approaching autumn, a weather condition he just didn't get down in

Tampa. It cleared his mind and let him see he still had control of his life; he still had his freedom. He shouldn't let sexual urges or even dreams trick him into thinking he didn't.

The only detail that marred his ride was his concern about not leaving a note. Mary Elizabeth was going to be worried. She'd think he had cut out. His oversight bothered him so much that he returned sooner than he'd planned.

Vaulting off his bike, he bounded into the RV...and found she was still in the bathroom!

"Oh, hi!" she said with a blithe smile when she eventually stepped out. "I thought you'd still be asleep."

Pete slapped a hand to his forehead. The woman was going to drive him nuts.

She'd obviously been fussing with herself the entire time he'd been gone. Fresh, deep waves were back in her hair, every strand in place, and although he couldn't see any makeup, that didn't mean she wasn't wearing any. She'd probably just applied it with expert care. Today she was wearing brown corduroy pants, a beige tweed jacket with brown elbow patches, and a blouse with a flouncy tie, held down with a brooch in the shape of a horseshoe.

It was probably that brooch that made him say, "Where are you off to, a polo match?"

For a moment she looked confused, and then quietly embarrassed. Pete wanted to kick himself. He'd only meant to tease her, but apparently he'd caught her blindside.

Looking down at her outfit she murmured something almost incoherent about choosing it because the day was chilly. Then she made a quick cup of tea and some toast and took her breakfast into the bedroom.

Just as well, Pete thought, alone with his guilt in the kitchen. This was exactly what he wanted, a mutual respect for each other's right to space and privacy, and he hadn't even needed to bring up the issue with her. She'd agreed tacitly. He ought to be pleased. And he was. He was so damn pleased he'd be doing cartwheels soon if he didn't contain himself.

Restlessly, Pete walked outside. The sky didn't look quite so blue anymore. A few minutes later he walked back in. She was still in the bedroom. "Hi," he ventured, standing in the doorway. "What are you doing?" Yep, he sure was pleased they understood their need for space.

Mary Elizabeth didn't turn from the closet. She didn't want Peter to see the tears she knew were still clinging to her eyelashes. Damn, she'd thought she looked nice—until he made that sarcastic comment about her being dressed for a polo match.

Which only went to prove what a fool she was. She hadn't spent all that time in the bathroom, primping in front of a mirror, just to look nice. She'd done it to please him, a man who obviously couldn't be pleased. Not by her, anyway. She was clearly not his type. He found everything about her laughable.

And why not? She was laughable. Who in their right mind still curled their hair on rollers? Who wore tweed jackets with elbow patches?

The daughter of Charles Drummond, that's who. But she wasn't Charles Drummond's daughter anymore. She only owned the woman's wardrobe. And shared her habits. Walked like her and talked like her. Mary Elizabeth suddenly disliked everything about the daughter of Charles Drummond.

"Um...I'm looking for something to wear to your brother's wedding," she replied, surreptitiously wiping her eyes.

"Ah. Good idea. What've you got?"

"Oh, I don't know. I've just started looking." She still hadn't turned around. She hoped he got her message.

He did. "Well, I'll leave you to your task." Peter stood away from the door frame, but before leaving he added, "I'm sorry I made that comment before. I was only trying to crack a joke. I guess I haven't quite figured out yet when that's okay and when it's not."

She turned from the closet then, but he was already gone. A few minutes later the RV started up and they were on the road again.

For the next thirty miles, Mary Elizabeth plowed through her wardrobe, trying on clothes. She had several outfits she could wear to a wedding, several that she *had* worn, but none of them pleased her. Time and again she looked in the mirror and thought, *Would Peter Mitchell really be involved with that person?* The best she could say about her was she looked nice. Inoffensive. Ladylike. She lived up to the expected standard of propriety set by Charles Drummond.

Mary Elizabeth had another problem she hadn't counted on. Nothing fit right anymore. For the past couple of weeks she'd worn jackets or baggy sweaters that hid the fact that the skirt or pants beneath were unzipped and held in place with a loose belt. She couldn't do this with her wedding finery. The roomiest dresses either revealed her small pot belly or refused to zip.

She finally abandoned her search and went to sit up front. "I can't go to your brother's wedding," she announced glumly, slumping in her seat.

"Why not?" Pete moved an unlit cigar from one corner of his scowl to the other.

"None of my clothes fit right anymore."

He glanced over, down at her waist, up again. One eyebrow cocked.

"You don't believe me? Here, look." She lifted her tweed jacket to reveal the undone zipper of her trousers.

Both Pete's eyebrows shot up. He swallowed, and a strange look came into his eyes, something between terror and awe.

Mary Elizabeth tensed. "You don't think this means I'm having twins, do you?"

Pete removed his cigar. "No. You're slim. Light-boned. You were bound to show early."

Just when she was enjoying a moment of relief, embarrassment overtook her. What was she doing, showing this man her pregnant stomach? Such an intimate thing to do. No wonder he'd looked ready to swallow his tongue. She sank in her seat, convinced she could do absolutely nothing right.

"Tell you what," he said. "Tomorrow, we'll swing into Baltimore and get you something new to wear. How does that sound?"

It sounded wonderful, until she remembered she had no money. She shrugged and mumbled something gloomy about making do with what she had.

"Aren't you in a mood!" Pete chuckled. "Don't worry. It's only your hormones. During pregnancy, they don't know if they're coming or going."

She didn't find the insight amusing.

He brought the RV to an abrupt stop, swung out of his seat, went into the kitchen, then returned with her bowl of M&Ms, which he planted in her lap. "*That's* what's wrong. You haven't had your daily dose of sugar yet."

She glanced at him out of the corner of her eye, feeling a faint smile tugging at her lips. He started up the RV again and eased onto the quiet country road. For the next couple of miles the only sound between them was the ticking tumble of candy being stirred and picked over.

Pete was fiddling with the radio, trying to find another oldies station, when she said clear out of the blue, "What about my hair?"

"Huh?" His head swiveled.

"My hair. Do you think I should change it for the wedding?"

He glanced at her, frowning. "It looks okay to me."

"High praise, indeed," she said, still in a snappish mood.

Pete huffed. "Look, Mary Elizabeth, that remark I made yesterday about changing you into somebody I'd be more likely to date . . . I was only kidding."

"No, you weren't."

"Now you're telling me what I was thinking?"

"Yes."

He slouched away from her, grumbling. "All right, you want a small suggestion?"

"Yes. That's why I asked."

"Now, remember, I think you have beautiful hair. I love the color and the way it shines. But maybe . . ." He hesitated. "Maybe you could find a more casual style. Something, I don't know, swingier, looser, less Laura Petrie."

Mary Elizabeth gasped audibly.

Pete suddenly looked as if he'd been hit with a two-by-four. "Oh, hell! Did I just say what I think I said? I'm sorry, Mary Elizabeth. I'm really . . . Honest, I didn't mean it."

"Laura Petrie? The sixties? Is that what you think of my hair?" Without thinking, she beaned him with an M&M. It felt so good, she beaned him with another. After firing off at least a dozen shots, she sat back with a contented sigh and said, "You're right. I fuss way too much with my appearance. Actually, I'm obsessive. A more casual look is exactly what I want, too. I only wanted your stamp of approval."

Looking at Monet sprawled on the warm dash, Pete muttered, "We're riding with a bona fide crazy lady, did you know that?"

They rolled on another mile.

"What about my makeup?"

"It's fine. Perfect," Pete said quickly. "I'll tell you one thing I *would* like to change."

She sat up straighter. "What?"

"Your name."

"My name? You don't like my name?"

"Well, it is sort of long, don't you think? By the time I finish saying it, I've usually forgotten what I wanted to say in the first place. I also find it—" he paused "—sort of starchy."

She refused to be hurt. After all, she wanted to change, didn't she? "What do you want to call me?"

He shrugged. "Doesn't anybody call you by a nickname? Beth? Liz? Marybeth?"

"No. I've always been Mary Elizabeth."

"Hmm. Let's see, then. Besides those options, there's Liza, Lizzy, Betty..."

"I don't mind Beth."

"I don't, either. It suits you."

She looked at him warily. "So, you're going to call me Beth from now on?"

"Let's try it for a day, see how it fits."

She grimaced. "This is weird, but okay." After a while she said, "So, where are we going today, Peter?"

"Pennsylvania."

"Really?" She perked. "Where in Pennsylvania?"

"Wherever the road takes us."

"Penn Dutch country?" she asked, exaggeratedly batting her eyelashes.

He laughed and in a teasing Maine accent said, "Sorry. You cahn't get theah from heah."

"Why not?"

"I'm morally opposed to tourist traps."

"Well, I'm not."

"Too bad. Who's driving?"

"Whose RV is it?"

He growled.

"What a grump," she muttered happily as the motor home crossed the state line. Between them swung the lace potpourri ball, tied to the radio where Jerry Lee Lewis belted out "Let the Good Times Roll."

"You should call your brother and let him know I'll be coming to the wedding. They'll need to set another place at dinner."

"I know. I will."

They'd covered another mile when Pete asked, "Hey, Beth? Do you dance?"

"Sure. Pretty well, too. I had two years of ballroom lessons."

"Yeah, well, I'm not exactly a fox-trot kind of guy. Do you dance fast?"

"A little."

He pulled the RV off the road again, this time into the lot of a feed and grain store. "A little isn't good enough if you're going to be my woman." He gave her a teasing smirk.

"Huh?"

He unfastened his seat belt and got to his feet. "We should practice, Beth. People will be watching us at the wedding."

With a sigh of exasperation, she got up, but, in truth, she wasn't as annoyed as she pretended. The idea of picking up a few new moves from this man was rather exciting, in fact.

She followed him into the kitchen area, where she drew the blinds before they began.

For a long while, Pete ignored the music that was playing on the radio and simply walked her through his moves. They worked on steps they bungled, repeating them until they eventually flowed with instinctive ease.

They'd been practicing for fifteen minutes when the song "Splish Splash" came on. Pete grinned and said, "You're ready."

But apparently she was not. With the addition of music, her movements became too bouncy and loose. "Tighten up," he admonished, gripping her hand more securely, afraid that in her exuberance she might fly off and bash into the cabinets.

"What do you mean?" Undeterred, she beamed her incandescent smile at him.

"Don't be so perky, Beth. A little movement goes a long way."

"All right. I'll try." And she did. Still . . .

"Your arms," he said, waggling them up and down in easy ripples. "They're looser than spaghetti. Control them, Beth. Pull in."

"Okay," she chirped, bobbing like a bright balloon on the end of a string.

The problem, he realized, resided in her attitude. Didn't it always? It simply wasn't in her nature to be cool. Not that he was exactly an expert on what "cool" entailed, but he thought it had a lot to do with containment. Contained, her moves would become sinuous and seductive.

Pete's mood darkened when he realized he was thinking about Sue Ellen Carlisle, a woman who certainly understood her feminine powers and how to use them. No doubt about it, Sue Ellen had always been one helluva dance partner.

"This is so neat!" Mary Elizabeth ducked under his arm, twirled, and came up bobbing on the other side.

To his complete surprise, Pete found himself laughing, a rich satisfying laugh that came from a part of him he thought he'd lost. Maybe Mary Elizabeth wasn't cool, but there was a lot to be said for enthusiasm.

And for a willingness to learn.

And courage in the face of adversity.

And eyes the color of warm coffee.

The song ended. He caught her to his side, laughing and spinning. Under the span of his hand, her ribs rose and fell. He felt the heat of her exertion, caught her scent intensified, and before he could think, he'd dipped his head and pressed a kiss to her cheek. He wasn't sure why, except the urge just suddenly overwhelmed him.

She stood very still, eyes wide and fixed on the floor, a pulse racing at the base of her throat. *Oh, hell, what did I just do?* he thought. But before he could think of a way out of his dilemma, she broke away, beaming a smile that said she chose to ignore that dilemma.

"Thanks for the dance lesson, Peter. It was great fun." She was already heading back to her seat.

Pete breathed a lot easier.

They had covered a couple of miles when Mary Elizabeth, still thinking about the wedding, remarked, "What about our history? You know, how we met and all that?"

"Got any ideas?"

"A few."

"Good. So do I. But first, could you get me a cup of coffee?"

As the RV rolled along, they shared ideas and built a magical relationship out of thin air. They decided they'd met the previous winter while she was on a month-long vacation in Clearwater. *With a girlfriend,* Mary Elizabeth insisted. Vacationing alone smacked too much of man-hunting.

Before long they were bantering with enough friendly sarcasm to chase away any awkwardness still lingering between them because of that kiss.

"Now, let's suppose we met at a supermarket," she went on. "We were both shopping and you asked me..."

"Stop. Where'd you get the idea *anybody* meets in a supermarket—some silly woman's magazine?"

"Well, where do *you* want us to meet? A *bar?*"

"A bar's more believable. Besides, where *did* we meet, Mary Elizabeth?"

She fought back a grin. "All right, we met in a bar. A *nice* bar."

"A very nice bar." Pete's blue eyes laughed at her. "You were there to listen to the music, a jazz combo."

"My girlfriend, too. I don't hang out in bars alone."

Pete rolled his eyes. "God, you're such a Mary Elizabeth."

An M&M binged off the window to his left. He caught it in mid-ricochet and popped it into his mouth.

"Were you there for the music, too?" she asked.

"No. I stopped by to meet a client and lingered after he left." He spoke with conviction, as if the incident had actually occurred. "You'd noticed me earlier, and now that I was alone you asked the bartender to send over a drink."

Seconds stretched out, long and silent, and then she blurted, "In your dreams, Mitchell."

"You don't like that idea?"

"'Don't like' is too mild a term. I'd never buy a man a drink."

"That's too bad. It's a great way to break the ice."

"Not in my book." She drummed her long fingers on her thigh. Gradually her finger drumming slowed and she glanced at him in quick, speculative forays. "Has any woman ever bought *you* a drink?"

Sipping his coffee, he waggled his eyebrows at her over the rim of the mug.

"Figures," she muttered.

They rode on, continuing to add to their story long after it was necessary. Mary Elizabeth knew they were supplying details they would never use. The yellow roses he'd sent her on Valentine's day, for example, because she liked yellow roses best. A bed-and-breakfast at Bar Harbor, where they'd stayed in April when he flew up to see her. But it was hard not to get carried away. This project of creating a past was so much fun. Anything was possible and *everything* was possible—although she tried not to think as far as "everything."

They were well into Pennsylvania when a billboard advertising a flea market appeared on the side of the road. Five miles ahead, it said.

"Pay dirt," Pete exclaimed. "I had a feeling this route would lead to something interesting."

"A flea market?"

"A giant flea market," he corrected her.

Just beyond that billboard there stood another, advertising a comprehensive tour of Amish country. Mary Elizabeth eyed the turnoff with sad longing as it zipped by.

The flea market surpassed even Pete's expectations. It filled an entire barn, two floors. It being Sunday, the place was crowded with eager rummagers.

Pete loved flea markets. Didn't know why, except he always found the most extraordinary things when he visited one. This visit fell true to form.

"Serendipity-do-da!" he exclaimed, slapping his hands together when he spotted the tin roller coaster.

Mary Elizabeth, walking close by his side, laughed at his expression, which was precisely his point in using it. He loved hearing her laugh. The musicality of it fascinated him.

He approached the toy with feigned nonchalance, not wanting to appear too eager. "Does it work?"

The vendor seated behind the junk-heaped table nodded. Pete searched and found the built-in key, then wound the mechanism.

"Careful," the vendor warned. Pete nodded, and stepped back. The little car took off, zipping up and down and around the track.

"Oh, that's delightful, Peter," Mary Elizabeth whispered, leaning in.

He thought so, too, although at the moment his attention was more taken with the warm curves pressing against his arm. He'd been doing well today, he thought—except for that kiss and the little episode when she'd lifted her jacket. He'd realized then that knowing she was pregnant and *seeing* she was pregnant were two different things.

His mind had suddenly galloped out of control. Forward to how she'd look at six months, eight months, nine. Backward to a faceless man named Roger, whom Pete had suddenly disliked immensely. Forward again to the feel of a little person swimming around in there, pressing a foot or an elbow against his palm—*his* palm. He didn't admit it to himself often, but he missed having children of his own.

Other than those two episodes, he'd done well today ignoring Mary Elizabeth's feminine side. She'd just been a person who happened to be traveling with him, a sidekick he enjoyed the hell out of teasing. But walking through this flea market, he began to notice things, like how close she stayed by his side, how his senses stirred when she brushed against him. He was unaccountably fascinated by her height, too. Five-eight, maybe? He didn't see her in feet and inches, though, but rather in how well she'd fit him if they were standing together . . . kissing.

He also noticed the glances she drew from other men, even some who were there with their wives or girlfriends. Despite Pete's teasing about her hair and clothes, she was one class act. She just didn't seem to know it. She had a real wide gap where her ego should have been.

That didn't bode well. Ultimately, lack of self-esteem had been Cindy's problem, too. He remembered only too well the black hole it had created in their lives, a hole that nothing he did or said could fill. *You're beautiful, Cindy,* he'd tell her, and she'd want to know how beautiful. Would he pick her if he had a choice between her and Farrah Fawcett? He'd say of course he'd pick her, and she'd want him to say it again and again. Tell me, Pete. Hold me, Pete. Don't go in to work today, Pete. Love me, instead. Love me more. Prove you love me. Love me or else—

"Peter?" Mary Elizabeth's voice jolted him out of his dark thoughts. "Can I buy it for you?" she asked quietly.

"The roller coaster? I don't think so."

"But it's only seventy-five cents."

Pete dragged a hand over his twitching mouth. "That's dollars, Mary Elizabeth, not cents."

She swallowed. "Oh."

Her chagrin was just what he needed to banish Cindy from his thoughts. "It's probably forty years old, maybe fifty, and in excellent condition." Turning to the vendor, he said, "I'll give you fifty bucks."

The man shook his bald head, jowls waggling. Pete shrugged and began to walk away.

"I can't take anything less than seventy."

Pete slowed, turned and offered sixty. Again the vendor shook his head.

They finally settled on sixty-five, and Pete walked away a happy man.

He and Mary Elizabeth stayed at the flea market almost three hours. The time flew for him. Mary Elizabeth claimed to be having a good time, too, although he wasn't sure. Not until they reached a booth with an unusually large collection of fine china. She lingered so long, picking up this dish and that bowl, that she finally told Pete to go on; she'd catch up later. It was then he knew she'd caught the junking bug.

When she did find him, she was lugging a cardboard carton in two straining arms. "I'm sorry, I spent some of the money you loaned me, but I have a thing for china," she explained with a shy smile. "I don't know why I continually add to my collection—I certainly don't need the stuff—but I can't seem to stop. Whenever I do settle, my house will have to have an entire pantry just to hold dishes."

Pete took the heavy carton from her in exchange for his roller coaster. "Stop apologizing. I understand. I'm addicted to this collecting stuff myself."

She stared at him, quietly, her soft brown eyes fixed on his. The next moment those eyes filled with a luminosity he didn't recognize as tears until she swung away from him, blinking.

They walked on through the crowded barn, walking just to move. Finally Pete said, "What was that all about?"

She sniffed, then laughed, which seemed to be a familiar emotional pattern with her. "I like your company, Peter. I've never enjoyed a man's company so much."

Even as he felt an absurd flush of pleasure, he knew he ought to refute her. "But half the time we're fighting."

"I know. Isn't it wonderful?" She walked off, zeroing in on a Royal Doulton soup tureen, leaving Pete more baffled by her than ever.

"Would you care to explain that remark?" he asked later, as they tried to fit their purchases into a motor home that didn't need any more clutter. Besides the roller coaster, Pete had bought a yellow plastic radio from the 1950s that didn't work and a lava lamp that did. Besides the box of china, Mary Elizabeth had found three wine goblets that matched a set she already owned.

"I came from a polite family," she replied, closing the storage cupboard in the hall. "We didn't argue, no matter how angry we got."

Pete plugged his lava lamp into the toaster outlet. It would take a while to activate. "Were you and your family angry often?" He turned and found her standing stiff and red-faced.

"I didn't really mean *angry* angry, just, you know...."

"Angry," he supplied. He hooked his hands on his hips and gazed at her. She looked ashamed just for having admitted she sometimes felt anger. "Nothing wrong with ripping loose once in a while. What's stupid is *not* venting your anger, letting it eat away at you." He watched her nod and fidget and compress her lips. She was twitchier than a spider on a hot plate.

"Who were you angry at?"

She shook off his question. "I didn't mean to complain. I had a wonderful home, a wonderful family."

"But?" Pete wondered why he was probing. For days he'd been telling himself he didn't want to know her any better than he already did. So, why was he inviting her to mess up his peace of mind?

Surprisingly, it was Mary Elizabeth who backed off. "Let's just drop it, okay? I honestly don't know where I was going with that thought, anyway."

Somehow he doubted that, but he didn't argue. "Fine," he agreed, moving to the driver's seat.

When they were both buckled in, he opened the wrinkled map and laid it across her knees.

"Okay, Beth, find us the quickest route to Pennsylvania Dutch country."

Her head jerked upward, her eyes alight. "Are you serious?"

"Would I joke about something like that?" he said, turning the ignition. "You did say you wanted to go there, didn't you?"

She didn't answer, just hunched forward and began an avid study of the map. But as the RV left the flea market grounds, Pete thought he heard her mutter something—something that sounded suspiciously like "Serendipity-do-da!"

THAT NIGHT, AFTER THEY'D settled into a campground, Pete took his bike off the trailer and went for another ride, this one purely for enjoyment.

He was on a quiet country road when he spotted a pay phone beaming its lonely white light into the dark Lancaster County night. Suddenly he remembered he ought to call home and tell somebody he was bringing a guest to the wedding.

He called his sister Pam. She could contact the bride and make the seating adjustment as well as anybody.

Calling Pam was a mistake. Sue Ellen was there.

"Since when are you two friends?" he asked, sulking into the receiver.

As usual, Pam ignored him. "Want to talk to her?"

"No!" He straightened out of his slouch.

"Too bad. Here she is."

He was still cursing when Sue Ellen came on the line.

"Peter? Hello. What a surprise." Her voice brought to mind long mink-colored hair, soft pink lips, and betrayal.

"Uh . . . yeah."

"I heard you got the bike you wanted."

"You did, huh?" Pete wondered if monosyllabism was his usual mode of speaking, or if it only came on when he was talking to women he had loved and planned to marry.

"Any chance of me getting a ride when you get back? I don't think I've been on a motorcycle since, God, I don't know . . ."

Yes, you do.

"We'll see." His answer was noncommittal, his tone reserved.

Yet she replied, "Great. Thanks. So, where are you?"

"Sue Ellen, I haven't got a whole lot of change to feed this phone. Could you put my sister back on?"

"Sure enough. I'll see you at the wedding."

He remained silent and eventually she handed over the phone.

"Don't do this to me, Pam."

"I don't know what you're talking about."

"Sure you don't. The reason I'm calling is, I'm bringing a date to Brad's wedding, someone really special." Pete went on, telling her briefly about Mary Elizabeth, sketching in some of the background they'd made up earlier in the day. He thought he did a convincing job, too, until Pam laughed.

"You expect me to believe that? She's probably just somebody you picked up on the road."

Pete felt the blood drain from his face.

"Just give Jill a call for me, okay? Tell her to reserve another place at the family table. I gotta go." He slammed down the phone.

All around him the cool night pulsed with cricket sounds. A quarter moon hung like a silver charm at the end of the empty road, washing it with the palest of pale light. Objectively he knew it was a beautiful night, but he no longer cared whether he was a part of it or not. He got on his bike and rode back to Mary Elizabeth.

She was lying in bed reading, Monet curled up by her side. "Hi." She smiled when he strolled in. The smell of minty toothpaste hovered in the air. Tonight, he noticed, she wasn't wearing her robe, only pajamas—seersucker creations he associated with dry old spinsters.

And he still wanted her, God help him, seersucker pajamas and all.

He used the bathroom, and by the time he came out she'd turned off her light, which made undressing easier on both of them.

"Do you want to read?" she asked softly after he'd slipped between the sheets. "It won't bother me if you turn on your light."

"Nah. It's been a long day." He relaxed into the cool bed, feeling the ghosts of vibrations still haunting his muscles.

"It's been a good day, too." There was a smile in her voice. "We did so much!"

Pete imagined the smile reaching her eyes. "Yes, we did."

"Actually, this has been one of the best days of my life." She sighed. "Isn't life strange! Yesterday was one of the worst—the hospital part of it, anyway."

Pete wasn't sure he wanted to be someone with whom she experienced superlatives. But the truth was, today had been pretty high on his list of good days, too.

Actually, it was right at the top.

CHAPTER TEN

THEY REACHED BALTIMORE by 9:00 a.m.

Mary Elizabeth had tried to argue she didn't need a new dress for the wedding, but Pete insisted she did. He knew she probably *could* make do with what she had, but she'd seemed so down on herself, so depressed over her appearance, he thought buying something new might give her a brighter outlook. He suggested she visit a beauty salon, too, although he hoped she didn't do anything drastic with her hair. He sort of liked it the way it was.

He told her he'd spend the morning grocery shopping since they were running low on some basics. After that he'd visit the baseball museum or simply walk around and enjoy the architecture of the new harbor complex.

They left the motor home in a parking garage, picked up bus schedules and diagrams of the subway system, agreed to meet for lunch in front of the aquarium, and went their separate ways.

Peter had given her money, but Mary Elizabeth hoped she wouldn't have to use it. Coming into the city, she'd spotted a shop that bought gold and gemstones, and decided to make that her first stop.

She left the shop more pleased than she'd expected to be, having sold a pair of diamond earrings she'd never liked, as well as three gold chains, a class ring and several earrings whose mates she'd lost.

After the tranquillity of rural Pennsylvania, Mary Elizabeth found the bustle of Baltimore a pleasant contrast. Just walking through the downtown area energized her.

With little trouble, she located a quality salon that welcomed walk-in customers, went in and explained what she wanted. She had several pictures marked off in a fashion magazine but the stylist seemed more interested in studying the shape of Mary Elizabeth's face and fingering the texture of her hair.

The outcome of the woman's scrutiny was a trim that kept Mary Elizabeth's hair at shoulder length but added the wispiest of bangs and a few long layers curving toward her cheeks and jaw. Mary Elizabeth loved the look. It was straighter, fuller, more contemporary and, she thought, quite sensual. She immediately wondered what Peter would think.

On a whim she asked the stylist if she knew of any stores that specialized in skin analysis and customized makeup. She did, and after paying for her haircut, Mary Elizabeth walked up the block, had her skin and coloring analyzed, and subjected herself to yet another stranger's diagnosis.

The result was amazing. Gazing at herself in the mirror, Mary Elizabeth wondered why she hadn't done something like this sooner. She didn't look made up, which had been her fear coming into this shop. She just looked better, more vibrant, her mouth and eyes defined, her cheekbones polished.

From the cosmetics shop she went to The Gallery to shop for a dress for the wedding. She found just what she needed in one of the larger department stores that was running a half-price sale on its summer stock, a pale champagne two-piece ensemble whose full chiffon skirt was gathered in a comfortable elasticized waist and topped by a hip-length tapestry jacket. Very chic. Also very concealing.

Standing before the dressing-room mirror, gazing at her radiant reflection, she thought, *Yes, here finally is a woman Peter Mitchell would consider taking out.*

With time to spare before meeting him, she wandered the store, drifting inexorably into the maternity department. She dreaded it, imagining the racks full of huge flowered dresses with Peter Pan collars and big perky bows.

Mary Elizabeth was pleasantly surprised. She bought a pair of slim black leggings whose stomach panel would expand as she did. However, she passed over the matching jersey. She could make do with roomy shirts and long sweaters for quite a while yet.

She was almost out of the mall when she saw a sign for a sweater sale. Actually, she didn't have that many long sweaters. Two that were wearable, maybe? She went in.

Twelve minutes later she came out, not only having purchased a sweater—a cream-colored angora with a soft shawl collar—but wearing that sweater, too, along with her new leggings. *Won't Peter be surprised,* she thought, hurrying down the sidewalk. The next moment it hit her; she'd been thinking about Peter all morning. Every one of her choices had been made with an eye on his reaction.

Her steps slowed. She was doing it again—dressing to please him, believing it would make a difference. A difference in what?

She walked on, trying not to acknowledge the fact that she had been thinking of them as having a relationship. After all, they would be living less than two hours apart in Florida. It was certainly feasible that they could see each other beyond this week. But of course, Peter would have to want to see her, wouldn't he? And that was the crux of the matter, the point in her thinking where she always came out feeling like the fool.

She was pregnant. Why would Peter want to see her beyond this road trip? For that matter, how could *she* even consider it? Hadn't Charles made a valid point when he'd said a pregnant woman who dated ran the risk of appearing indiscriminate?

Her spirits were sinking fast, threatening to ruin what had been a wonderful day only moments ago. She took a purposeful look at her reflection in a store window, examined her swingy hair, her stylish new clothes—even her vibrant coloring was visible in the glass—and her cheerfulness returned. Even if her makeover generated no change between her and Peter, and it wouldn't, she'd done something nice for herself. That was enough.

Pete spotted Mary Elizabeth coming almost two blocks away. Funny thing was, he didn't recognize her at first. He only knew that one foxy lady was sashaying up the street in his direction.

When she waved, his gaze jerked upward to her face, away from those rounded hips swaying under that soft white knit stuff. In that moment of recognition he knew he was in deep trouble. He'd been trying to deny his attraction to her these last few days, but his libido apparently had its own agenda. The attraction had grown in leaps and bounds, waking him in the dead of night, dropping her into his thoughts at unexpected times throughout the day. He knew something had to give, soon. Trouble was, he also knew it would be a sweet, very sweet, surrender. That was why he'd begun to think that maybe the consequences of giving in wouldn't be as bad as he'd thought.

"Well, what do you think?" She put down her shopping bags and turned a slow circle for his perusal. A couple of lawyer types, passing on their way to lunch, applauded.

Her already glowing cheeks warmed to a higher tint. To Pete's utter delight, she paid them no attention but kept her gaze fixed on him.

"Oh, mercy!" For the life of him, Pete couldn't think of anything else to say. He guessed she understood, though. Catching her glossy coral-pink lips in her teeth, she smiled, pleased that he liked what he saw.

As his gaze roamed over her, however, he realized her beauty wasn't due directly to any of the physical changes she'd wrought. Those changes were too minor. Rather, her beauty was emanating from a source within.

Well, I'll be damned! Pete thought. She'd needed to feel better about herself, and although the changes were only physical, they'd worked. Maybe his sisters were right; shopping really was good for the soul.

He lifted his hand and fingered her newly styled hair. He liked it. She looked half pixie, half seductress. He caught her warm floral scent, became captivated by the curve of her graceful neck, imagined his lips pressed there right under her jaw—and for a moment forgot they were standing on a busy city thoroughfare.

He was going to kiss her. Kissing her would open a Pandora's box of woes, but the urge tearing through him was too overwhelming to curb. He was going to do it, right here, right now, and caution be damned.

She looked up quite suddenly as if sensing his thoughts. The moment froze and became measureless, an infinite expanse of mutual awareness and shared anticipation, echoing all the other moments of attraction they'd experienced over the last few days and denied.

And then she blinked and looked away, effectively breaking the spell. Pete cursed her common sense. But of course, she was right.

"Oh, here's your money," she said, reaching into her purse. "I didn't use it. I had my own."

"What did you do, hold up a convenience store?"

She cast him an impatient look. "I sold some of my jewelry at a pawn shop."

"Aw, hell, Beth!" He hoped she hadn't sold any heirlooms. Hoped she hadn't been ripped off.

"It's okay. I wanted to. It felt good doing this—" she flipped her hair "—on my own. So," she went on quickly, "where would you like to eat?"

"I got a recommendation from a cashier at the supermarket. A place that specializes in seafood. Come on, it's just a couple of blocks away."

In a city that made specializing in seafood a matter of pride, the restaurant they chose was truly superb. They ordered crab cakes, spicy steamed blue crabs and roasted oysters, served with rice pilaf and warm crusty bread.

While they ate they memorized the vital statistics of their lives: birth dates, height, weight, the names of their parents and siblings, a few family anecdotes, peculiarities of their hometowns, and whatever else they could think of that a couple who were in love ought to know.

They walked back to the parking garage testing each other. Mary Elizabeth fumbled only once, on the name of his best friend in elementary school. Pete, she realized, had a remarkable memory, which by now didn't come as much of a surprise.

She climbed up the steps of the RV feeling mildly euphoric, a mood she attributed to the delicious, leisurely meal they'd just enjoyed. When she stepped into the kitchen, her euphoria soared.

The first thing she noticed was the plush bear sitting on the counter, surrounded by pastel baby outfits still on their hangers. From there her gaze flew to the table, then the passenger seat up front. Gifts were everywhere, and not all of them looked to be for the baby.

She felt weak-kneed. She reached blindly for Peter, and when she found his arm, she closed her fingers around it. "Peter!" That's all she got out before her voice deserted her.

Pete cleared his throat gruffly. "After picking up the groceries, I had some time to kill."

She walked unsteadily toward the table where she found a set of soft bath towels, a squeaky yellow duck, a basket of baby toiletries and four dozen cloth diapers. She stared, happy, sad, mostly confused. "But... I'm not keeping the baby."

"That's okay." Pete stepped closer. "I just thought you might like to pass some things on to the new mom, let her know this is no ordinary kid she's dealing with. This one comes fully equipped and ready to rumble, compliments of her first—and best—mom."

Mary Elizabeth was choking on tears and affection for this man. She had to move away from him before she did something embarrassing. "What's all this?" Draped over the passenger seat were a pair of denim jeans—maternity jeans—and a large white T-shirt with bold blue letters that read Baby under Construction.

"Considering my occupation, I couldn't resist," Pete murmured, smiling almost shyly.

Mary Elizabeth fingered a second outfit, yellow cotton tights with a blue T-shirt that read Baby on Board, the words printed within a yellow square. On the seat she found two pairs of maternity shorts, two more tops and a book titled *What to Expect When You're Expecting*. She could contain her tears no longer.

"My sisters swear by that book," Pete said with casual disregard.

Before turning, Mary Elizabeth swiped at her eyes. She moved to the counter and picked up one of the baby outfits, a mint-green sleeper. So tiny. So soft. She held it up and for an instant actually imagined a baby filling it out. The image was so vivid she could almost feel the warmth and weight of it. Her eyes threatened to spill over again. Quickly she put the outfit down.

"Thank you, Peter. This is—" she spread her hands "—just overwhelming."

"Aw, hell, this is nothing compared to what—" He broke off abruptly, hitched his right shoulder and glanced aside, looking embarrassed again.

Compared to what? she wondered. What a baby would ultimately need? What he would like to buy?

She said, "I bet you didn't get to the baseball museum."

"If you've seen one, you've seen them all. Here, let me pick up this stuff so we can get rolling." He stepped toward the front seat.

"No, that's okay," she said, reaching at the same time. "I can do it." Their hands landed on the T-shirt simultaneously, their arms crossed one over the other.

In a college psychology class, she'd once seen a documentary about the aura that surrounds the human body. It included actual footage of auras, captured on a particular sort of film capable of photographing those strange energy waves. Mary Elizabeth remembered being especially fascinated by two people in the experiment who happened to be attracted to each other. Standing about a foot apart, their auras literally flared and elongated as if reaching out toward each other, trying to meet.

At this moment, with her right hand and his left resting on the shirt, she imagined a virtual bonfire of flares rising from the skin where their forearms crossed and touched.

Instantly, awareness was there, resonating between them more forcefully than ever. One minute they'd been just friends, the next a man and a woman alone, drawn to each other, minds and bodies rife with all the possibilities that existed between them.

Mary Elizabeth lifted her gaze to his face. She loved everything about it. Every angle and crease and curve seemed perfect. Even the imperfections seemed perfect.

Desire blindsided her and before she could disguise it, it was burning in her eyes, pulsing from her skin.

The moment will pass, she told herself, just as it had earlier when they'd met for lunch. All she had to do was move, resume talking. But the strange thing was, she didn't want to. She was tired of fighting it.

And so was Peter, it seemed. She watched his mouth soften, become serious and sensual. Watched his eyes darken and felt a shiver of anticipation while his head lowered, slowly, giving her ample time to pull away. She didn't. If anything, she swayed forward to shorten the agonizing wait. And then his lips met hers in a kiss that brushed and moved apart and brushed again, acquainting her with little more than the heat of his breath. It left her disappointed, leaning in, wanting more.

Pete's eyes glittered down at her, apparently pleased with her reaction. The next moment he angled his head and joined his mouth to hers again. This time there was nothing hesitant about the move. His arms slid across her back and gathered her close, while his lips continued to move on hers, smooth, warm, supple, and so very, very arousing.

Mary Elizabeth returned his kiss with a fervor that would have embarrassed her if she'd had time to think about it. But at the moment all she was capable of thinking was *Yes! Finally, yes!*

She felt Peter's body tauten against hers and happily let the kiss deepen and intensify. As it did, her body came awake . . . and she awakened to her body.

Suddenly she was aware that her breasts were crushed against Peter's chest—her swollen, tender breasts. Her *pregnant* breasts. Her pregnant belly arced against his jeans.

Pete felt a change in her and lifted his head. "What's the matter?" He watched a frown slide into her eyes where an instant ago there had been desire. Trembling, she pulled away.

He was rather shaken himself. He should have expected an unusually strong reaction. He'd wanted her for days. But he hadn't been ready for *that*.

"Peter, this can't happen," she said shakily.

"I know," he agreed, disgusted with his lack of control. "Come Sunday, we'll never see each other again."

She folded her arms and gazed at the floor. "It isn't just that."

Pete tried not to ask. He lasted about two heartbeats. "What is it, then?"

"I'm pregnant." Her voice scratched with anguish.

"I know you're pregnant. Believe me, I know." He thought about little else these days. "But that doesn't mean you aren't still desirable." He slouched against the counter and crossed his legs, trying to diminish the visual proof of exactly how desirable she was.

She groaned and shook her head again. "I'm sorry. I should never have let that happen. I feel so embarrassed."

Should I ask? he wondered. Oh, hell, in for a dime . . .

"I'm not sure I understand where that's coming from, that embarrassment."

"Isn't it obvious?"

"Would I be asking if it were?"

She thought awhile, her mouth working. "It's just wrong, that's all."

"What is? Kissing?"

"Yes!"

"It felt pretty right to me."

She started to pace, arms clutched tight under her breasts. "But don't you find it cheap?"

Pete's mouth dropped open. Cheap was the last thing on his mind. Before he could tell her, though, she added, "Most men would, no matter how broad-minded they say they are."

"Whoa. I'm not following this. Come over here and sit."

They slid into the banquette, taking different sides of the ell. "All right, now let's try that again. Most men would find *what* cheap?"

She sat huddled, arms still crossed, her hands gripping her elbows. The proud glow she'd acquired as a result of her makeover was gone, confirming his suspicion that what needed mending resided at a far deeper level. "Well," she said, "to begin with, nice girls don't get pregnant outside marriage."

Pete emitted a choked laugh.

"Okay, they do," she amended, "but they usually marry the guy who got them pregnant, fast. A woman who chooses not to go that route is still the exception. She has to, well, really watch what she does."

"Why? Because she's chosen an unconventional path?"

She lifted one shoulder halfheartedly.

"So people won't talk?"

Two shoulders lifted. "Sure. And because guys might get the wrong idea and think she's..."

"Cheap?"

"Well, yes." She kneaded her upper arms, nervously twisting the soft white sweater. "That's definitely a risk she runs. Her pregnancy is obvious proof she's recently been with another man."

Pete frowned incredulously. "Do you think, because you let me kiss you, I now consider you easy or immoral? Do you think I see your pregnancy as the result of indiscriminate behavior? Is that it?"

She swallowed again. "I guess."

"You know something, kid." He leaned far over the table, his eyes fixed hard on hers. "You're nuts."

She backed away. He leaned even closer. "It's the intimacy of this arrangement, the close quarters," he explained. "It was bound to happen. We're only human."

"You think what we did was right?"

"No, I believe it was wrong, too, and I'll try not to let it happen again—but for different reasons. As I've said before, I don't have one-night stands."

Her face took on a hard, belligerent look that stymied him. "We'll only be a two-hour drive from each other." She let the logical conclusion tumble through the ensuing silence. She was daring him to admit he just didn't want to continue seeing her.

There was no use in trying to refute her. Although lately he'd been toying with the idea of seeing her through her pregnancy, he still believed he lacked the fortitude. "I like my freedom, Mary Elizabeth. I don't enjoy serious, long-term relationships. They take too much time and energy. In your condition, you deserve better than that."

He saw her ice up right before his eyes. "In other words, what I 'deserve' is a guy who's willing to take on used goods and a brat who's somebody else's. Well, let me be the first to inform you, that animal doesn't exist."

"Lady, you *are* crazy."

"Am I? Tell me, what do *you* think my worth is on the dating scene these days?"

Pete suddenly surged with anger. "You have as much worth as you give yourself, Mary Elizabeth."

He saw her eyes fill and felt his heart contract. "What happened to calling me Beth?" As if that was the issue here!

"You can change your hair and your clothes, but I'm afraid you're still a Mary Elizabeth inside." He tipped her face so she had to look at him. "What you need is a serious attitude adjustment, kid."

She jerked away from his hold. "Yeah, well..." she said vaguely, blinking away tears.

"Who was he?" Pete asked sharply.

"Who was who?"

"The person who did the tune on you."

"I don't know what you're talking about."

"Yeah? Well, somebody sure did a bang-up job on your self-esteem. I'm gonna take a wild guess and say... your father?"

The color drained from her face. Still, she managed to say, "Where did you ever get an idea like that?"

"From you, things you've said. The way he pushed Roger at you. The extremes you went to to make that relationship work. I can't help thinking the entire Roger fiasco was just an attempt to please your father. Then, when you told me he wasn't upset to see you leave home, well, what else could I think except the guy's a royal jackass. Oh, by the way, you also stammer whenever you mention him."

"I do not."

"You do."

She sagged into the seat, sighing. "All right. I admit my father had a few things to say to me before I left, but..."

"Did those things happen to include words like 'cheap' and 'used goods'?" Pete was still amazed that she'd used such phrases. "Is he the one who told you no man would want you because you're pregnant? That's all crap, Mary

Elizabeth, and if that's the sort of line he dished up while he was raising you, then you damn well *should* be angry with him. You should be fit to be tied."

A knock at the door brought a curse to his lips. "Who the hell can that be?"

Opening the door, Pete found a young security officer with his knuckles poised, ready to knock again. Pete looked past him, remembering quite suddenly that they were parked in a garage in Baltimore. "Yes?"

"Just checking to see if things are all right here."

"Things are fine."

The young man poked his head in warily. "That right, ma'am?"

Mary Elizabeth had risen from the bench. "Yes. We were just about to set off."

Pete closed the door, grumbling. Damn kid looked about fifteen years old. When he turned, Mary Elizabeth was already in the passenger seat, her cheeks flushed. Maybe, he decided, her attitude adjustment would begin today.

CHAPTER ELEVEN

THEY DROVE OUT of Baltimore in tense silence. The countryside was beautiful. Lots of thoroughbred horse farms, but Mary Elizabeth wasn't interested. All she wanted was...what? For this trip to be over? Was it still only Monday? She closed her eyes, knowing only half of her wanted that. The other half wouldn't mind if her journey with Pete went on forever. She sighed, longing for relief from this tug-of-war between her heart and her brain.

She awoke sometime later, not having realized she'd drifted off to sleep. The motor home had stopped and Pete was unbuckling his seat belt.

"Where are we?"

"A park. Somewhere in western Maryland. It seems a nice quiet place to walk." He uncoiled from his seat. "And talk."

She wasn't sure she liked the sound of that, but she was awfully stiff from riding, so got up, anyway.

They walked at a revitalizing pace, past flower beds and jungle gyms, down one path and another. It was just what she needed. Her blood was flowing again, her head clearing. Eventually, though, their pace slowed to a conversational amble.

"I don't know a hell of a lot, Mary Elizabeth," Pete drawled, squinting ahead, hands tucked in his back pockets, "but I have learned it's easier to live with certain situations if you talk about them to somebody."

She threw him a skeptical glance. "Like you?"

"I'm a great listener. Why I was born with big ears."

Her lips twitched.

He guided her off the path, across a springy lawn to the shade of an ancient beech tree, where he spread his flannel shirt and they sat.

"It's nice here," she admitted softly as Pete fit himself behind her and began massaging her shoulders.

"You're so tight," he said, and then, pressing forward, grumbled against her ear, "you don't need this. Neither does the baby. Why not get rid of it, all this old emotional baggage? You're supposed to be starting a new life, so do it. Throw it overboard."

She sighed. "I wish I could."

"Well?"

"How?" she challenged, shrugging off his hands and turning to face him.

"Tell me about it. Talk to me."

She sat for several minutes, still as the afternoon sun on the grass, legs crossed Indian-style, fingers loosely interlaced under her gently protruded belly. Pete watched her sink into herself, examining her thoughts, weighing her trust in him. *Come on, you can do it,* he assured her silently, willing her to take that first step. He saw her wet her lips, take in a breath, and thought jubilantly, *Yes!*

"The day I told my father I was pregnant, I learned something about myself I didn't know, something that changed my life irrevocably." She paused. He waited. "I learned I'm not his daughter." Her eyes darted to Pete's to measure his reaction. He kept his expression set, although inwardly he was reeling.

"Go on," he urged gently.

She returned her gaze to the safe middle space between them. "It seems my mother had an affair during their marriage and I was the result."

"Do you know your biological father?"

She shook her head. "He was someone working at the house, adding on a sun room." The corners of her mouth turned downward. "A guy just passing through, hired for the season by a local contractor."

"Was your mother in love with him?"

"Mrs. Pidgin, our housekeeper, claims she was, but I have my doubts. She stayed with my...with Charles, didn't she?" Bitterness slid into her voice. "She even went on to have another child with him."

"Well, dissolving an established marriage isn't always an easy matter."

The bitterness spread to her eyes.

Pete frowned. "Are you angry at your mother?"

He watched her emotions gather and rise until finally she couldn't contain them any longer. "Yes! She had no right to do that to me."

"Do what to you?"

She focused on him with startled eyes. "I...ah...have me, I guess." Her brow creased. "Get pregnant by someone just passing through and then let her husband know about it."

Pete watched her swallow convulsively, waiting till she seemed more composed to say, "You think it would've been better for her not to tell him?"

"For me it would have been." Her features appeared chipped from ice. Pete imagined a wealth of heartache behind her statement, behind all that ice. Charles had probably put her through hell, playing her for a scapegoat.

"The other day," he said carefully, "when you were telling me about Roger and your reasons for not wanting him to know about your pregnancy, you mentioned several times you feared he'd resent the baby, think of it as a burden and an embarrassment.''

She plucked a blade of grass and pulled it apart again and again.

''Does that fear have anything to do with the way your father raised you?''

She tossed the shredded grass. ''Charles had his reasons.''

''That's not what I asked. Did he resent you, make you feel unwanted?''

''My mother betrayed him. She had an affair. Every time he looked at me he must have been reminded of that infidelity.''

''And that's why you're mad at *her?*''

He knew he'd confused her. He'd meant to.

In her continued silence he said, ''You remind me of my sister Lindy. Her husband has a drinking problem, but for a long time she refused to admit it. She used to make excuses for him. It was his job, his friends. Most of the time she felt guilty as sin, too, thinking his problem was really her fault, that there was something wrong with her that drove him to drink.'' Pete knew he had Mary Elizabeth's attention.

''Then one day I convinced her to go to Al-Anon, and she learned drinking was *his* problem and had nothing to do with her. She stopped making excuses and, to make a long story short, eventually got her life together.''

Pete could see thoughts moving behind Mary Elizabeth's eyes, memories churning, the pain deepening.

''Okay, maybe Charles did make me feel unwanted,'' she admitted, blinking rapidly. ''How could he not? I *was* unwanted. When we were talking about my options, the day I told him I was pregnant, one of his suggestions was for me to go away, have the baby and give it up for adoption. When I refused, he said I was just like my mother. I guess they had discussed options, too." Her voice went faint. "Ways of getting rid of me."

"But she refused?"

Mary Elizabeth's eyes swam with tears. "Yes."

Pete let her mull over that thought for a moment before he said, "But you're doing just what he suggested. Going away, giving up the baby."

"I know, but now it's my decision. I didn't like the way he was dictating something so important."

"I see." Pete mentally chalked one up for Mary Elizabeth. "How did Charles make you feel resented? Do you remember any specific things he did or said?"

She breathed out a sharp laugh. "Millions of things."

"Like?"

She waved a hand at him. "What's the use in digging up trash like that now?"

"Although talk won't change the past, sometimes it can change the future."

She shook her head. "No, I wouldn't feel right talking about it now."

"Why not?"

"I don't know. It's just . . . unbecoming."

"Unbecoming?" Pete almost laughed. "Do you see it as whining or something? As slandering Charles's character? Or being a . . . a bad girl?" he mocked.

She twisted her lips and scrunched her nose. Pete wanted to take her in his arms right there and smother her with kisses. Instead, he plucked some grass and, like her a moment before, began shredding.

"The past has a hold on you," he said, regaining his seriousness. "*Charles* has a hold, one of the most destructive there is, too. He seems to be dictating what you think about yourself, and most of it is negative. What you've got to do is take that power away from him, kid. It doesn't belong to him."

"That's why I left home," she mumbled, chin tucked.

Her statement caught him from an unexpected angle. His fingers stilled. "Of course! I'm just beginning to realize ... That was a really big step for you, wasn't it, physically removing yourself from him. It was your way of saying you weren't going to take his guff anymore. You were sick of the guilt and the pain."

"Yeah, well, I don't see my leaving as anything to be particularly proud of. In fact, I see it as sort of selfish."

"Well, stop it, dammit," he mock-scolded. "Start thinking of it as right, as strong, as an affirmation of your self-worth." He paused. "Did I just say 'affirmation of self-worth'?" He gave an exaggerated shudder. "Next thing you know I'll be listening to New Age music and wearing crystals."

Her glance could only be called coy. "Or maybe taking your sister to some other group meeting where the phrase 'self-worth' might happen to come up?"

Pete whistled through his teeth. "You really are smarter than you look."

Smiling, Mary Elizabeth stretched her right leg and kneaded the calf.

"A cramp?"

She nodded. He got up and helped her to her feet. When they'd resumed walking, he said, "One thing I've found that helps me when I've been hurt is to stop thinking of myself as a victim. I do that by turning my pain into anger."

She looked at him askance. "That doesn't sound very enlightened."

"What can I say? It works."

"So, what do you do? Go around punching people?"

"Ah, the damage of first impressions. No, what I usually do is confront the person who's wronged me and let him know exactly how I feel. It gets a weight off my chest and usually leads to our clearing the air."

She was shaking her head. "Oh, I couldn't do that, Peter. Not with Charles."

"I understand. Some people you just can't confront. That's why I own a punching bag."

She laughed, a sound that poured through him like warm brandy.

"I've converted one of the bedrooms in my condo into a gym, and when somebody or something's bugging me and there's no other way I can get rid of my frustration, I pound a punching bag for about an hour. The madder I get, the better I feel afterward. So, as I'm punching, I'm saying things like, 'You sonuvabitch. You *promised* me, you *swore on your mother's grave* that you'd deliver those special shingles by Monday! And I only gave you the order as a *favor*. As a reward for my generosity, I had to face the owner. *I* had to tell him why we won't be finished with his house on time! And he wasn't happy.'" Pete paused. "I really focus on what happened, too, let my memories get as specific as possible so that I can feel the original emotions flowing through me again. And all the while I'm punching away."

"And that helps?"

"Yep. By the time my hour is up, I'm feeling much better."

"Yeah, well, I don't own a punching bag, Peter."

"Maybe you can find a substitute... not me," he added quickly, shielding himself with his raised hands.

When they reached the RV, she said, "You really think it'll help?"

"It's worth a shot."

She nodded. "I'll give it some thought."

Inside, they microwaved a bag of popcorn, got bottles of apple juice from the fridge, and soon were under way again.

"I have one other suggestion I think'll help." Pete tipped back his bottle and swallowed some juice. "Call Roger."

She stiffened. "Uh-uh. I don't even want him to know where I've gone, never mind that I'm pregnant."

Pete glanced at her, puzzled. "But he's bound to find out where you are, working with your father and all."

She sighed heavily. "I told Charles I was going to Chicago."

Pete slumped away from her, staring at the road. After a moment he began to laugh, a dark, wicked rumble. "There's no end to the mess you've created, is there. Do I dare ask why?"

She stuffed her mouth with popcorn, making him wait for the answer. "When I refused to tell Roger, Charles threatened to tell him himself and bring about a marriage. That's how badly he wanted this little unpleasantness taken care of." She patted her waist. "He seemed to be appeased when I said I'd leave the area, but that didn't last long. He's afraid I might return with the baby. I knew he'd started thinking about telling Roger again. I think he still might."

"All the more reason for you to call the guy and tell him yourself. Right now you're running scared. Charles is calling all the shots. Take that power away from him. A phone call'll do it."

She knew he was right. Keeping this news from Roger had been bothering her from the beginning of her pregnancy. Guilt was weighing her down, exhausting her. "I'll consider your advice."

"Good. And if you decide to take it, do yourself a favor. Decide how *you* want to handle the matter before you call. Don't wait for Roger to tell you what to do. Have a plan of your own."

"That's it? You're not going to tell me I should keep the baby or give Roger joint custody or—"

"Hell, no. Those are your decisions."

She moaned, sinking into her seat.

"Nobody ever said growing up was easy, Mary Elizabeth."

Pete turned on the radio, hung his wrist over the wheel and let The Shirelles and The Platters carry them over the Virginia line and on into the Shenandoah Valley.

It was dusk when they arrived. They hadn't quite made it to the national park, but Pete found an adequate campground, anyway. It was small and privately owned, and on this Monday evening in late September, only sparsely occupied. He parked at a distance from the other campers in a secluded spot by a rushing stream. The site lacked the convenience of hookups but offered a view of the Alleghenies that was beyond price.

Mary Elizabeth had started their supper while still on the road—a porterhouse steak, brown rice and broccoli, provisions Pete had bought that morning in Baltimore. By the time he had the RV settled into its site, the meal was done and laid out on the table. She had hoped they'd be able to eat outside, but night was simply coming on too fast.

Their dinner conversation was quiet and thoughtful, and revolved on the subject of her illegitimacy. Though they'd tried to ignore it, it had been on their minds all afternoon.

"Don't you ever wonder about your father?" Peter asked. "Who he was, what he was like, things like that?"

Reluctantly, she nodded and told him the few crumbs of information Mrs. Pidgin had given her, that his name was John Avery, that he was originally from Minnesota, that he liked to travel and worked as a carpenter mainly, it seemed, to support his love of wandering. "Aside from that..." She fell silent again, moving the food around on her plate, then suddenly tossed down her fork. "I know absolutely nothing about him."

Pete looked at her, surprised by her fit of pique. She was thinking about her mother again. He knew it without even asking. *How* he knew, he wasn't certain, but their wordless communications were increasing, their empathetic instincts deepening.

He asked quietly, "Do you blame your mother for that?"

"Yes." She pushed aside her plate. "She had no right to withhold that information. It was part of my very identity. I feel cheated. I feel betrayed." Pete watched pain crease her smooth face. He reached across the table and took her hand in his. He didn't care if it was the wrong thing to do. It was what felt right at the moment.

"Something tells me you're not so much mad at her as hurt."

Slowly, she gave in and nodded. "You know what really hurts? She kept *her* identity a secret from me, too. I used to think I knew her. All those years, the memories I carried, memories I *treasured*..." Mary Elizabeth's voice thinned as some of those memories crowded her.

Giving her head a small shake, she continued, "But suddenly I learn she wasn't that person at all. It's like..." Her hand had gone lifeless in Pete's. "It's like she's died for me all over again."

Her grief tore at him. She'd been through a lot, more than most people had to endure in twenty-seven years. What made it worse was that she was extremely sensitive.

"Have you ever considered that she believed not telling you was the best thing for you? Whether it was or wasn't is irrelevant. It's what she believed was best."

Mary Elizabeth nodded reluctantly. "It couldn't have been an easy decision."

"You would know."

Her eyes met his and filled. "Mrs. Pidgin says Charles threatened to fight for custody of Susan if my mother left him. She believed he'd win, too. That's why she stayed with him and told my real father it was over between them. After that Charles made her promise she'd never tell anyone about her affair. He's an extremely proud person, very conscious of the family's reputation. Mrs. Pidgin thinks that's why they went on to have a third child, so he could show the world nothing was amiss with the Drummonds." A tear spilled down her cheek. "My mother died seven years later—pneumonia that got so bad her heart failed her. Mrs. Pidgin claims it was her heart all along, a problem that started when my father, my real father, left town."

The silence lengthened, made soothing by the plash of the stream outside their open window.

"Sounds like one pitiful mess," Pete finally commented.

"Yes, it does." Embarrassed, she looked aside. "I'm sorry."

"For what?"

"Being such a drag."

"You apologize too much."

"Yeah, but..."

"Yeah, but," he mocked. "Honestly, I don't mind. Who knows, maybe I'll need your shoulder to cry on some day."

Mary Elizabeth broke into a smile that ignited a small fire in his chest. "That, I would pay to see." She got to her feet and began clearing the table. Unexpectedly she said, "Peter, would you mind leaving me alone for about an hour tonight?"

He studied her through narrowed eyes. He was about to ask why and then it happened again; without exchanging a word, he understood. She had an appointment tonight, with Charles Drummond.

"Not at all. My bike needs a workout, anyway."

They took their dishes to the sink and left them to soak. Pete went to the bedroom for his jacket, gloves and helmet. When he returned, Mary Elizabeth was still standing at the sink, eyes fixed on the darkness outside. She looked inconsolably alone.

He swayed on his feet, physically wavering with the indecision that rocked inside him. Finally he just came up to her from behind and wrapped her in his arms.

She stiffened, as he knew she would. "It's okay. I just want to hold you."

He felt her relax. Her shoulders released, her arms softened, she exhaled a held breath. Fitting himself closer, he laid his cheek against her hair. He was surprised to realize he was nervous for her.

Holding her the way he was, he was something more than nervous, but that didn't surprise him. He was getting used to being in a near-constant state of arousal.

Before Mary Elizabeth found that out, though, he gave her a squeeze of encouragement and said, "Give 'em hell." Then he released her and slipped out the door.

Mary Elizabeth waited until the roar of his bike faded before going in search of her tennis racket. She felt distinctly foolish, but it was the best substitute for a punching bag she was able to come up with.

She found the racket deep within the bunk bed over the cab. To get to it, she had to take down her rocking chair, which Pete had fit in there somehow, and two boxes of books.

In the bedroom she tried lifting the racket over her head. It thumped the ceiling. Slowly she swung it downward toward her mattress. On the way it hit the over-the-bed cupboards and grazed a light fixture. No, this wasn't going to work.

A few minutes later she had solved her problem. Outside, working by the pale light that streamed from the RV's windows, she placed a bed pillow, minus its embroidered case, atop a hip-high rock by the stream. Her sense of foolishness had grown acute, even though no one could see her. The nearest campers were too far away, and the RV shielded her from view, anyway.

She lifted the racket in two hands and brought it down experimentally. It landed on the feather pillow with a satisfying wump.

Exhaling, she adjusted her stance, wiggling her bottom and planting her feet like a ball player at bat. Then she lifted the racket again and thought, *Okay, Charles Drummond, this one's for you.* Wump!

In the ensuing stillness, she looked around self-consciously. Nothing stirred. No eyes peeked out of the woods. No twitters arose.

She raised the racket again and thought, *I lived in your house for twenty-seven years without complaining about the way you treated me, but I guess the time has come. You made me miserable, Charles.* She whacked the pillow. *No matter how I tried to please you, you found fault. And I did try. Pleasing you practically became my life's work. But you always made me feel I'd failed or there was something inherently wrong with me.*

She hit the pillow again and paused to take measure of her feelings. Guilt had joined her self-consciousness. What right did she have to complain, she who'd been given the best of everything? Most of the world had it so much worse.

"Excuses," she said out loud, cutting off that train of thought.

Gripping the racket handle, she focused on her grievances again. *Mrs. Pidgin was right. She said if you hadn't given me those things, people would've wondered why not, why you'd singled me out. And we all know the worst fate in life is to have people talk.* She beat the pillow very hard, then paused once again. She was beginning to feel genuinely irate. *But you did single me out, didn't you? At home where no one could witness it.*

An episode sprang to mind so unexpectedly, bringing with it an upsurge of forgotten pain, that she'd pummeled the pillow several times before she'd even examined the memory.

How old had she been? Eight, maybe? Nine? She was riding her bicycle out on the road in front of their house when Charles approached from the other direction returning from work. She remembered pedaling hard to meet him at the mailbox, so hard her leg muscles burned, then bringing the bike to a skidding stop using the hand brake and ultimately her feet. She was beaming, happy because she'd made it; she'd gotten to him in time to say hi and give him a welcome-home hug.

But, reaching for the mail through the open window of his Lincoln, he met her with a thin-lipped scowl that was followed by a lecture on how she mustn't drag her feet when she was riding her bicycle. Didn't she know she was wearing out her shoes? And shoes were expensive, he said. What did she think, money grew on trees? He'd gone on and on, until even now at twenty-seven, Mary Elizabeth felt shriveled with embarrassment and guilt. She felt ... unlovable.

Damn you, Charles! She clubbed the pillow. *I didn't deserve all those lectures on the cost of things—books, clothes, even food. You made me feel like a burden just for breathing. Susan and Charlie were downright careless with their things, but you never lectured them.*

Her insides were shaking and that frightened her. But before she could decide whether to stop or continue this exercise, another memory assailed her—the Father's Day she'd spent hours in her room making a greeting card for Charles, a card she'd found later that night still lying on the chair where he had opened it earlier in the day. It was creased and flattened as if it had been sat on, while on the mantel Susan's and Charlie's store-bought cards were on proud display.

Tears stung her eyes as she remembered that hand-painted gift into which she'd poured so much love.

Damn you, Charles. Maybe you were hurt, too. I was the product of an affair, proof of a betrayal. But I was only a child. I just wanted your love. You shouldn't have taken your feelings out on me.

She hit the pillow so hard she felt the twang of impact up her arms and right into her chest. But she was beyond stopping now. Memories kept rising, pain seizing her, anger pouring out.

And this is for all the A's I got that you never mentioned and all the C's that you did. Mary Elizabeth began to perspire. Her clothing stuck to her back.

And this is for all the times I heard "Why can't you be more like Susan?"

Feathers were beginning to shoot through the ticking.

And this is for the time I had a crush on Kevin Manchester in eighth grade and you said I looked trashy. This memory elicited a double wump, and then one more, a backhand, for good measure. For she truly felt thirteen again, infatuated with the opposite sex for the first time, and totally insecure about the whole business. She remembered the hours she spent studying fashion magazines, felt again the misery of looking at herself in the mirror, the frustration of rearranging her hair, her clothes, her facial expressions. And then, just when she'd thought she might have done something right, Charles had said, "What's wrong with you these days, Mary Elizabeth? You're looking so trashy.''

Well, Charles Drummond, let me finally tell you. You're the one who had the problem, not me. I only wish I'd known it then. What you did to me was sick, sick, sick. With each "sick" she pounded the pillow. Her muscles were quivering, her eyes blazed, and feathers were now flying like snow through the torn ticking. Yet she didn't stop.

As the stars grew big in the sky above, she continued to travel the dark roads of her life, reliving old hurts and some that weren't so old, as well.

And about my job, maybe you did pull a few strings, but I was qualified, too, and I did good work. But you never stopped reminding me you'd pulled those strings. You couldn't let me forget that even as an adult I was beholden to you, a burden you had to provide for.

She seemed a woman possessed. Every memory she brought to light was tied to a dozen more, reaching deep into murky places in the heart she hadn't known existed.

And Roger—oooh, now there's an issue that's long overdue....

There were so many grievances she'd buried, so many unkind words that had accrued until she'd actually believed them herself.

But as was inevitable, she eventually gave the racket a swing that would be her last. *It's over, Charles,* she thought. *You're history.* Then she just stood there, breathing hard, arms weak, staring at the battered pillow and the bent racket, and feeling absolutely empty.

After a while, when no other thoughts came to fill the void, she gathered up what she could of the pillow, stuffed it in a trash bin and went inside. She drank a full glass of water, noticing that the hand that held the glass was shaking, like her stomach and her legs.

Turning from the sink, she bumped her knee on the rocker she'd taken down earlier from the bunk. It seemed to be waiting there on purpose.

The chair had come from her bedroom back home and was the only piece of furniture she'd felt comfortable removing from Charles's house. Her mother had bought it when Mary Elizabeth was born and had used it to rock her while she was nursing. Mary Elizabeth didn't remember those days, but she did remember being rocked to sleep as a toddler, especially after nightmares. She also recalled sitting in her mother's lap and being read to in that chair, and later being taught to cross-stitch.

Too weary even to sigh, she sank into the padded seat and huddled like a person pulled to safety from a raging sea. She set to rocking and closed her eyes, seeking balm in the rhythmic movement. Instinctively, she crossed her arms over her stomach, as if comforting and protecting the child within.

And that was exactly how Pete found her when he returned—asleep, arms wrapped around herself, a childlike peace reposing on her face.

CHAPTER TWELVE

PETE DIDN'T HAVE TO ASK how she felt the next morning. He found her wading in the cold stream, singing "Oh, Shenandoah" off-key at the top of her lungs. Standing on the bank, he scratched his bare chest and grinned.

She'd been so wiped out the previous night she hadn't even awakened when he'd carried her to bed. Which was no surprise. Their day had started early and had been active right to the end.

Pete thought back on all they'd done, all the ground they'd covered—both physical and otherwise—and felt something close to astonishment. Time had never seemed so elastic, so unbounded or saturable to experiences, not even when he was a boy. Either he was having one helluva vacation or Mary Elizabeth had taken him clear into another dimension.

She noticed him standing on the bank and broke into one of her thousand-watt smiles. His stomach hollowed out with the sensation he imagined he'd get if he were falling off a sixty-story building.

"Good morning," she said, her long honey-and-ash hair gleaming with morning sun. Her eyes met his, and when he should have looked away he didn't. Neither did she. They just stood there, openly taking pleasure in each other, and in that moment Pete felt a sense of inevitability about the course of this day.

"Oh, your eye is looking so much better today. There's just the slightest tinge of yellow."

He nodded, glad she'd noticed, glad she liked what she saw. She was wearing the maternity jeans he'd bought her, rolled to the knees, and the shirt that read Baby under Construction, with a bulky red cardigan slung over it all.

She plucked at the shirt. "I know I don't really need it yet but..." She just shrugged.

But you're feeling pretty damn good this morning about being pregnant, he finished silently.

"Looks nice on you."

She waded to shore and dried her feet on a bath towel. Admiring the curve of her ankle, he noticed the ground nearby was strewn with feathers. Had a duck or bird been mauled here by some woodland animal?

"Where are we going today?" Her warm brandy voice scattered his thoughts of ducks and maulings. Morning sun lit flecks of gold in her brown eyes.

"I thought we'd get on the Skyline Drive and head south. It's the touristy thing to do, but in this case I'll make an exception."

"Oh?" She tilted her head, drawing attention to the sweeping length of her neck, a neck that seemed made for kissing. "Nice driving?"

He clicked his tongue. "Most scenic route there is through these old mountains. It becomes the Blue Ridge Parkway farther south."

"Oh! Are we heading toward the Blue Ridge Mountains?"

"Uh-huh."

Her expression took on a dreamy softness as she said, "There's just so much..." She didn't finish her thought, just lifted her arms to the horizon as if she were embracing all that it encompassed.

Yes, so much, he thought, realizing with some surprise he was enjoying showing her the world. Enjoying? He was having the time of his life.

"Is there anything in particular you'd like to see today? Any place you'd like to go?"

Mary Elizabeth's smooth brow furrowed in thought. Suddenly she brightened. "I remember reading about some wonderful caves in this region. You know, the kind with stalagmites and stalactites?"

"Caves?" Pete nodded. "Sure. Why not?"

Coming around the RV, Mary Elizabeth noticed his Triumph parked by the door where he'd left it the previous night. "Can we also spend part of today riding?" she asked, swinging her leg over the leather seat.

Pete grinned. "You look mighty pretty sitting there, Mary Elizabeth." After trying out other names, he'd decided he liked "Mary Elizabeth" best, after all.

"Well?" she prodded. "If I'm supposed to be a serious girlfriend of yours, won't your family expect me to ride with you?"

"Sorry. In your condition you don't need all that shake-rattle-and-rolling." *Besides, motorcycles are dangerous.* The thought popped into his head from out of nowhere.

No, not nowhere. He couldn't count the number of times he'd skidded on roadside sand or hit a pothole and almost gone over the bars—and he was a careful driver. And what about his friend Mark who'd tangled with a Buick? A minor collision if he'd been in a car, but instead he'd died.

Pete scrubbed his face with two hands. Where were these thoughts coming from? He'd never worried about being hurt before.

"Can I at least sit here awhile?" She clutched the handlegrips and hunched forward, trying to look menacing.

And Pete thought, *If I died now, I'd never see that funny face again, never know if she had a boy or a girl. And what if she needed my help . . . ?*

Suddenly he began to think that maybe it wouldn't be such a big chore to drive from Tampa to Sarasota every once in a while. Maybe he did have the staying power to see her through her pregnancy. He might even go to Lamaze classes with her, be her birthing partner if she wanted. He'd gone to a few classes with Lindy, so it wasn't as if he didn't know what he was getting into. And after the baby was adopted, she'd need someone to help her adjust, get back in the swing . . .

Pete emerged from his thoughts with a start. Oh, hell! He couldn't mean what he was thinking. He couldn't really want to complicate his life by getting involved with a woman who had so many needs. Could he?

He noticed Mary Elizabeth looking at him curiously, still waiting for an answer. "Sure you can sit there. Have a ball," he said with more gruffness than her simple question should have elicited. "But it goes back on the trailer right after breakfast."

They were rolling again by nine. Mary Elizabeth felt wonderful. Much of her exhilaration came from having unburdened herself of the grievances she'd harbored while living as Charles Drummond's daughter. Well, some of the grievances. She wasn't naive enough to think that beating up one bed pillow had rid her of a lifetime of anguish. But it certainly had helped.

Just being on the road gladdened her, too. As Pete had predicted, the scenery along the Drive and the Parkway was magnificent—the endlessly rolling peaks, the mysterious, mist-shrouded valleys, the silver-blue sparkle of lakes and streams.

That day they stopped at three scenic lookouts and snapped innumerable pictures of each other with her Pentax. They visited a cavern and were appropriately awed by its soaring walls and immense columns of colorful, glittering stone. They saw a natural bridge purported to be a wonder of the world, and at a roadside stand bought gaudy key chains in the shape of the state of Virginia.

But mostly what Mary Elizabeth saw that day was Peter Mitchell. He filled her eyes, consumed her thoughts, and made everything else a minor distraction.

When he spoke she hung on every soft, dark note. When he walked, she reveled in his manly stride. She loved the way his clothes fit, how the blue of his shirt picked up the blue of his eyes. She loved the habit his hair had of curling over his ears. She even loved the size and shape of his feet. What Mary Elizabeth had trouble admitting, though, was that, quite simply, she loved *him*.

The thought stymied her. How could that be after less than a week? In six days people could discover they were attracted to each other, maybe even blindly infatuated. But love, real love, took time.

So maybe what she was feeling was just attraction?

Well, if that was so, it was the damnedest attraction she'd ever experienced! When in her life had she ever been fascinated by how long a man brushed his teeth? When had she daydreamed about his feet?

It was the intimacy of this arrangement, she told herself, leaping on Peter's excuse from the previous day. She'd never lived in such tight quarters with a man before, and the man in question wasn't just any ordinary man. Peter was very nearly overwhelming.

Improbable as it still seemed to her, she knew sparks were jumping both ways. She felt it in the heat of his eyes as they followed her, in the countless times he touched her for no apparent reason, his hand lingering, fingers stroking. And of course there was that kiss yesterday, that sweet, drugging kiss that had left her addicted and craving more.

The trouble was, as the day wore on, she became less and less sure what she would do if he kissed her again. The issue wasn't that she still felt "cheap." She'd laid that warped idea to rest last night. The issue was making love, which was where any degree of physical contact between them now would lead. She wanted to. Oh, how she wanted to. But where would that leave her emotionally when they parted on Sunday?

Despite her misgivings, the idea of making love with Peter occupied her mind with increasing frequency. What would it be like? she wondered a dozen times that day. He was so different from Roger. Physically, he was so much larger. His hands were calloused, the tendons of his arms hard as oak.

She imagined that what he knew about lovemaking lifted him head and shoulders above Roger, as well. Which led to some fairly warm images cropping up in her mind . . . which lengthened to steamy scenarios . . . which had her sweating in her seat more often than she cared to admit.

Would it happen, then? The question hung between them every time they spoke or even just looked at each other.

Lord, what was she thinking? Of course it wouldn't happen. Peter had made it perfectly clear he didn't get involved with anyone he wasn't going to see again. It was a matter of principle with him. He'd also said he wasn't interested in serious relationships, and in her condition she deserved more from a man.

But Peter had said lots of things these past six days and then changed his mind, and in his eyes she thought she saw a change of mind. So, ultimately, would their making love be up to her? Would it depend on whether she was willing to accept an on-the-road affair? Strong enough to let it go in four days? It was a question that rode with her all day, unanswered.

They made it all the way to the North Carolina border that day, compensating for the slow-going scenic route by switching to the interstate for the last two hours of their drive. They found a state park about ten miles from the highway and settled in with a couple of hours of daylight to spare.

They were cooking up their supper—linguini and clam sauce from a can—when Mary Elizabeth suddenly announced, "I've decided I'm going to call Roger."

For some reason Pete's lungs seized up on him. "When?"

"Right after we eat."

The spoon he was stirring the sauce with scraped faster against the pan. "Hey, there's no need to rush."

"Yes, there is." She stirred the pasta and their elbows bumped. "I'm eager to get it over with, to be free of this whole mess."

Pete walked away from the stove to set the table and try not to think of the alternative, that she might not end up free but mired even deeper than she was now.

GOLD FROM THE SETTING SUN gilded the tops of the towering pines that edged the clearing outside the recreation hall. Mary Elizabeth stood inside, phone cord stretched to its maximum, gazing out the window, waiting for Roger to pick up at the other end. Outside, Peter was shooting baskets with two teenage girls and a boy. The girls were flirting.

"Hello?"

The smile dropped from her lips. She swung from the window and stammered, "R-Roger?"

"Who's... Mary Elizabeth?" His voice slid up an octave.

"Yes. Hi." Sweat trickled down her sides. "How are you, Rog?"

He ignored her polite inquiry. "Where are you, for God's sake? People here are pretty worried. Are you all right?"

She wet her dry lips. "Yes, I'm fine. I'm in North Carolina, just over the Virginia border." She laughed nervously. "Why are people worried?"

"North Carolina? My God, Mary Elizabeth! Your father told me..."

"I know. Chicago. Never mind that right now. Why are people worried?"

"Oh. Oh, well, your wallet showed up a couple of days ago. Some woman in upstate New York found it on her front lawn. Your housekeeper almost had a stroke, and your father's ready to notify the FBI. You'd better call home."

Mary Elizabeth clutched her head. "I will. I promise." Poor Mrs. Pidgin. She'd forgotten, the woman had been expecting her to phone when she reached Chloe's, two days ago.

"Listen, Roger, the reason I'm calling... I have something to tell you."

"Oh?" He sounded wary.

"It concerns you and me and the last week we were dating."

"Oh?" he repeated, his wariness intensifying.

"I don't know any painless way to say this, so I'll just come right out and say it. Roger, I'm pregnant."

Silence roared between them for several incredulous seconds.

"Are you sure?"

"Yes. I'm almost three months along."

"Three..." Another span of silence enfolded them. "Is that the reason you've moved?"

"Yes. One of the reasons."

"To North Carolina?" He seemed to want to find something in her location to be astounded at.

"No, I'm on my way to Florida, to my friend Chloe's. I'm just taking my time, going the tourist route, you know?" She heard him swallow, and swallow again. "I'm calling because I thought you might want to know." She massaged her forehead. "About the baby, I mean."

"Oh, uh, yes, of course. Do you need money?" Roger's voice had lowered, although she was pretty sure he was alone in his apartment.

"No," she said. "I'm planning to have the baby and give it up for adoption."

"In Florida?"

"Yes." What was this obsession he had with states? "Do you have a problem with that? Adoption, I mean."

"Uh...no." He exhaled so hard the sound of rushing air hurt her ear. "Actually, that seems like a very wise plan." His voice had loosened noticeably. It struck her as almost comical that for weeks she had feared he'd want to marry her. Apparently, that was the furthest thing from his mind.

He sounded practically magnanimous when he asked, "Would you like me to fly down there for the birth or anything?"

"No. That isn't necessary. I'll have Chloe. But thanks for offering. It's really decent of you." And it was. Why had she been so frightened to call?

"Your father doesn't know about this, does he?"

"Yes, he does."

"But not that I'm..."

"Yes, that too."

"Oh, God. I had lunch with him just this afternoon. He didn't say a word."

"That's Charles Drummond for you. He doesn't exactly like information of this sort getting around. If you don't say anything, I guarantee he won't, either."

"Well, that's something, I suppose." Roger was quiet awhile. "If I tell you something in confidence, will you promise to keep it under your hat?"

"Roger, I'm a thousand miles away. Who am I going to tell?"

"Okay. All right. It's just that nobody knows yet except my parents. I'm thinking of running for town council next fall. I don't need to tell you how damaging this news could be if it leaked during an election campaign."

Mary Elizabeth felt disillusionment creeping over her, like spidery frost over a window. "You needn't worry, Rog. No one will hear it from me."

"Thanks. I knew you'd understand. Now, are you sure you don't need anything?"

"I'm sure."

"Well, if you do, let me know. How've you been feeling?"

"Very well, thanks. I—"

He interrupted with a nervous laugh. "God, this is just so weird, you pregnant. It still hasn't fully registered. It's been hitting me in bits and pieces."

She held her breath, wondering if paternal feelings were coming in bits and pieces, too. "Rog, I've got to ask you something—purely hypothetical, of course. What if I were to keep the baby?" She heard a small gasp. "It's just a what-if."

"Okay," he responded shakily. "What if?"

"Would you acknowledge it or want to help me raise it?"

"Gee, I don't know."

"I don't mean to put you on the spot. I know it's a difficult question, especially when you factor in running for political office."

He sighed. "I suppose I would. It would be my child. Yes, I guess I'd make room for it."

"But would it be an imposition?"

"Well, sure. You can understand that, can't you? A child would be an imposition on you, too. More so. You'd be its primary parent. Think of the effect it would have on your career. And what about your social life?"

Mary Elizabeth watched a parade of ants scurrying single-file along the baseboard.

"Aw, hell, Mary Elizabeth. It isn't just my running for office. It's..." He hesitated.

"It's what, Rog?"

"Well," he hemmed, "I've met somebody."

"Ah. Say no more."

"I'm sorry for feeling the way I do. It's just..."

"No need to apologize. I understand."

"I hope so. Well, maybe it's a good thing your question was only hypothetical." Tension with an undercurrent of challenge buzzed over the wire.

"Mmm. Good thing." She poised the toe of her shoe over the line of ants, feeling momentarily evil, then drew it back. From the other end of the line came the familiar ring of Roger's door buzzer.

"Sounds like you've got company."

"Yes."

"You'd better go." Irrationally, she felt a pang of regret, for him, for her, for the love they'd never quite achieved.

"Stay in touch, Mary Elizabeth," he said softly. "I mean that."

"Sure. You, too." Mary Elizabeth hung up the receiver and dropped back against the wall. Her emotions were so tangled she didn't know whether to laugh or cry.

Roger's disinclination to acknowledge the baby left her hollow with disappointment. Peter had almost convinced her that her dismal opinion of Roger was incorrect, that it had been unfairly tainted by her relationship with Charles. But Roger had just confirmed her conviction. He *would* consider the baby a burden, and though he hadn't said it, he *would* resent it in time. She knew it as surely as she knew anything.

Oddly, however, Roger's disinterest also put her at ease. Without his interference, she was now free, really free, to go about her life and make her own decisions regarding the baby.

But most of all, Mary Elizabeth felt relieved. She'd done it, made the call, faced the dragon, and in so doing had rid herself of the guilt she'd lived with while Roger had remained in the dark. She'd also beat Charles to the punch and jettisoned her fear of not knowing Roger's reaction. Peter was right; she'd taken the reins of her life into her own hands and become empowered.

How did one man get to be so smart? she wondered, pushing away from the wall and gazing out the window. He was still shooting baskets with the teenagers. A little girl, four or five years old, had joined them, and Peter had lifted her onto his shoulders. Her giggles, as she dunked the ball, brought a smile to Mary Elizabeth's eyes and an unsettling image to her heart—of Peter as a father.

She gave her head a hard shake. What foolishness was that, casting a confirmed bachelor into the role of parent? She swung back to the phone with a stern reminder she had one more call to make.

Pete was waiting for her on the steps outside. "Well?" he asked as they walked the path back to their campsite.

"Roger took the news well. He offered me money and his company during labor. But bottom line is, he isn't really interested in becoming a father."

They continued to walk, the silence between them so dense it practically throbbed.

Without warning, Pete stopped, hooked an arm around her neck and pulled her to him, holding her close, holding her tight. His muscles trembled. He didn't say anything, and neither did Mary Elizabeth. She was rather too astounded to speak. She hadn't realized he was so concerned about the outcome.

As they stood on the path, the resinous scent of pine spiced the dusk. The trill of a bird she'd never heard before rode the warm southern air. And Mary Elizabeth thought, *This is a moment I'll remember forever. This piny scent. That bird. And Peter's wordless rejoicing.*

Back at the campsite they built a fire. The sun had just dipped behind the farthest ridge, but an afterglow of peach still warmed the western sky, throwing the distant peaks into hazy relief.

Pete and Mary Elizabeth sat on a blanket, watching the fire, talking quietly about her call to Roger and nibbling on a late dessert of cheese and green grapes.

Pete was grateful she hadn't asked him to explain that incident on the path. He still found the depth of his relief unsettling. It confirmed his suspicion he was beginning to have feelings for Mary Elizabeth. Not just appreciation of her fine looks. Not just physical desire. *Feelings.* He hadn't let that happen since his divorce.

Mary Elizabeth sank her teeth into a grape, and while she was chewing mumbled, "Oh, I called home, too." Pete's head swung around. "Well, to Mrs. Pidgin's. I wasn't ready to talk to Charles." She then explained how her wallet had been sent to the house in Maine. "I needed to let Mrs. P. know I was all right. She has too fertile an imagination for her own good." She smiled, betraying her deep affection for the housekeeper.

"My license and other important ID were still in it, so I asked her to ship it to your sister Pam's first thing tomorrow."

"Oh, is that why you interrupted the best game of one on one I ever played to ask for her address?"

"Uh-huh. That way I'll be able to drive legally from there to Chloe's after the wedding."

"Smart thinking." Pete noticed her arching and pressing the small of her back. "Come here. Scoot around front and rest against me. You look uncomfortable." Bending one knee, he made a cradle for her between his legs and held out a hand.

She smiled. "Thanks." With a sigh of relief, she settled back, into the rise and fall of his chest, into the warmth of his arms lying crossed over hers.

"Did you also tell your Mrs. Pidgin how you've been traveling?" Pete rubbed his chin over the silk of her hair.

"No. I hate lying to her, but she'd just worry herself sick, wondering who you were and if I was all right."

Pete adjusted their fit, tucking her closer, his arms coming to rest right under her breasts. Under her voluminous new T-shirt she was all womanly curves, soft and enticing. It took a moment before he found his voice. "You did well today, Mary Elizabeth. Got a lot done."

"I guess. At least I handled the mess I left behind me. Now all I need to tackle is the future." She moaned and buried herself deeper in his safe, encircling embrace.

He laughed. "You'll be all right."

"Easy for you to say. You've got a job. You've got a condo."

"There you go again, underestimating yourself."

"I'm not underestimating myself. I'm simply being a realist."

He chuckled. "Yeah, but your vision of reality is skewed."

She tilted back her head and gazed up into his fire-lit face. "Spoken by a man who buys lava lamps and thinks they're neat."

"Cool, Mary Elizabeth. Cool. *You* think things are neat."

He bent forward, smiling against her cheek, and she thought, *This is reckless. But frankly, I don't care anymore.*

She laid her hand on his knee, and he thought, *This is going to get us into trouble. But when have I ever run from trouble?*

They sat in silence, listening to the crackle and hiss of the fire, feeling their heartbeats accelerating, both gripped by that strange sensation of inevitability that had begun the day.

"Mary Elizabeth?" Peter's voice rumbled, deep and soft, but something about it sounded different, a note that hinted at . . . vulnerability?

She sat up and turned to face him, laying her hands on his chest. She needed to see what that uncharacteristic note was about. "Yes?"

His brows were low slashes over his eyes. All the lines of his face had gone serious. "The other day when I said I was against marrying . . ."

Her pulse quickened.

"I want you to know that isn't a decision I made casually simply because I like my freedom."

She could see that whatever he was thinking about was distressing him. She combed her fingers through the hair over his ears and watched his eyes. For a moment she thought he'd changed his mind. He looked past her, his mouth tight.

But then he said, "The reason I intend to stay single is—" he swallowed "—I've been married already."

Mary Elizabeth felt the earth spin. Everything blurred with the speed of it, and then abruptly settled. "Married. Ah." Her composure amazed her.

"I was young and it lasted only a couple of years. But it was a painful-enough experience to turn me off marriage for a lifetime."

Under her hands his chest heaved like a bellows. "What happened?" she inquired. Her face warmed immediately. "I'm sorry. I shouldn't pry."

"It's okay." His face looked craggy in the flickering firelight. He drew a long breath and then proceeded to tell her about Cindy, about her endless insecurities, about everything.

"Toward the end of our marriage, things were really bad." By this point in his narrative, his eyes appeared lost, his face bleak. "She knew I wanted to leave her, so she upped the ante in her games. She said if I left, she'd kill herself."

Mary Elizabeth hadn't expected that. She flinched. "Dear Lord, she...didn't, did she?"

He shook his head. "But that wasn't for lack of trying. They were feeble attempts, though. She wasn't really suicidal. She only meant to scare me." He looked into Mary Elizabeth's eyes and his mouth lifted in a sad, lopsided smile. On that look rode a wealth of things unsaid, a wealth of pain undivulged.

"Her behavior also convinced me to leave the marriage as soon as possible, not just for my own good, but for hers, too. I wasn't familiar with the term 'enabler' back then, but I must've understood the basic concept and realized that's what I was for her."

He paused, eyes fixed on the past. "Thank God we didn't have a baby. I can't imagine how that would've complicated things."

After a protracted silence, Mary Elizabeth asked, "What happened to her?"

"Oh, I made sure she moved back with her folks and got psychiatric help."

A muscle pulled in his cheek, the slightest of reactions that nonetheless caused Mary Elizabeth to wonder what he meant by making sure she got psychiatric help. Had he paid? And for how long?

"The last I heard, she'd moved to Denver and married and divorced twice more."

Pete stroked Mary Elizabeth's arm, his fingers coming to rest over hers against his chest. "So, that's the way it is with me." He gazed straight into her eyes. "I just thought you ought to know."

Under her hand his heart beat hard, an echo of her own. She suddenly knew exactly why he'd shared this part of himself with her. He wanted her to understand, really understand, he was serious about not wanting to ever marry again, so that if she got involved with him she did so with eyes wide open.

So it *was* up to her, just as she'd feared all day. But as she sat there watching this magnificent man, she realized she had already arrived at a decision. She leaned forward, slowly, and pressed a kiss to his firm, dry lips.

Backing away, she momentarily feared she'd misread the situation—he sat so still—until he said, "You're sure?" The dark undercurrents of passion in his voice sent heat spilling through her. With her eyes wide open and fixed on his, she nodded.

CHAPTER THIRTEEN

WATCHING THE SOFT CORONA of firelight shining off Mary Elizabeth's pale hair, Pete thought she was just about the most beautiful sight there was. Angelic almost. He might live to regret this some day, a day when he was facing the long drive to Sarasota, or sitting through another boring Lamaze class. And what if he discovered she really didn't interest him, after all?

Unfortunately, he didn't care about any of those what-ifs at present. He only listened to the need coursing through him, thrilling in the knowledge that it coursed through her, as well.

He dipped his head forward and finally took what he'd been dreaming about night and day, sighing his pleasure into her mouth. What a sweet mouth it was, too, warm and soft and eager. He immediately wanted to immerse himself in its mysteries and ravage its secrets.

But he didn't. He was too concerned about rushing her. Although she wasn't a novice to lovemaking, he sensed limitations to her experience that caused him trepidation. The last thing he wanted was to overwhelm her. He needed to move carefully. He wanted this first time to be special.

He was somewhat confused, therefore, when she tipped back onto the blanket, taking him down with her. And he was more than confused as she plowed her fingers through his hair, her nails scraping his scalp, and joined her open mouth to his once more. Pete momentarily lost control. The night swirled, the stars and the earth and everything between, with Mary Elizabeth at its center.

Fighting for breath, he broke the seal of their kiss and buried his face in her hair. He needed to catch his bearings.

"We don't have to do this if you don't want." She sounded a little embarrassed.

"Don't want?" Pete laughed, rolling onto his side and pulling her against him. "You enjoy seeing men explode, do you?" He felt her smile against his neck.

He got to his feet, towing her with him. "I think we ought to go somewhere less public, though."

While she folded the blanket, he doused the campfire. He felt like a raw kid again, excited and scared, and the feeling amazed him. In thirty-six years he'd had lots of first times with women, but this felt like *the* first time.

As soon as the door of the RV closed behind them, he turned her into his arms and kissed her. Mary Elizabeth dropped the blanket and kissed him back, fitting herself to him, winding her arms around his shoulders, holding him tight. Her lips glided over his, supple and seductive, then opened, inviting him to deepen their union.

Pete started to burn, a fire that kindled at his center and quickly spread to the rest of him. Tipping his head to the side, he fit his mouth to hers more aggressively, tasting her, circling the inner softness of her lips, delving the deeper secrets within. She responded with a low wanting sound, and then her tongue ventured forward to meet his. He let her explore, and explore she did, her forays becoming more emboldened with each passing second. Dear Lord, what was she doing to him? Maybe he was wrong about needing to move carefully. He was beginning to fear he was the one who was being swept along too fast.

He tried to slow down, tucking her head under his chin while he caught his breath. But even the innocent slide of his hands across her back became for him an erotic act. He spread his hands wide, palms rasping against her cotton shirt, fingers exploring each ridge and hollow from her nape to her firm little bottom.

He soon realized that trying to slow down was impossible. He couldn't remember the last time he'd wanted a woman so badly. He kissed her again, caressing her breasts with one hand while he held her to him with the other. The hunger roaring inside both of them radiated like heat from a furnace.

He left her mouth to trail kisses along her neck. She moved against him, arching, inviting him to continue his journey south. He obliged, kissing her through her clothing, feeling her respond even through layers of fabric.

Looking up, he saw her eyes were passion-glazed, her lips full and flushed with desire. He returned to them, kissing her deeply, deeper, backing her up to the refrigerator and resting against her—although resting was hardly the term for what they were doing.

What *were* they doing, he wondered with the last part of his brain that was still functioning—two grown adults, behaving like oversexed teenagers? She was so responsive though, he couldn't help himself. God, so responsive.

He thrust against her, consumed by a building, driving lust. With a soft desperate cry, she lifted her left foot off the floor and wrapped it around the back of his right knee.

Pete curled his hands under her and lifted her to meet him. She made it easy, practically shimmying up his body, using the refrigerator for leverage. She looked wild and wanton, and Pete wanted nothing more than to be wild and wanton with her.

Against her mouth he growled, "Let's go someplace more comfortable."

But she shook her head, blond hair flying. "No time," she gasped.

He didn't realize how close she was to completion until she emitted a breathless little cry and her body tautened in his arms. He watched, somewhat dazed, as her head fell back and she cried out, her moist heat burning through her clothing and his.

He held her tight, and when she finally finished shuddering, he gently eased her to her feet. Holding her close, Pete stroked her hair and smiled in satisfaction, even though his own body still thrummed with need.

Her head lay heavily on his breastbone while she fought to catch her breath. Her hands rested on his arms, slack-fingered. He could feel her racing heartbeat slowly decelerating.

She remained in that position so long that Pete finally tipped up her chin, thinking she might've gone to sleep. He wanted to see her face at this moment, wanted to look into her eyes.

What he saw was not what he expected. Instead of a soft-mouthed, dreamy-eyed woman floating in the afterglow of orgasm, Mary Elizabeth looked distraught, her eyes luminous with unshed tears. His first thought was that he'd hurt her.

"Are you all right?" He pulled her away from the refrigerator, checking to see if maybe he'd driven her against the door handle. He smoothed his hands down her back, up her arms, touched her cheek, her hair, wanting to find the source of her pain.

She shook her head, never meeting his eyes. "I'm all right."

His second fear was that she was still a victim of Charles's warped influence, that she was feeling she'd done something tawdry.

"I'm all right," she repeated. "Just feeling a little ridiculous."

"Oh, sweetheart." He pulled her to him in relief, folding her close, wanting to laugh but knowing better. "You should never feel ridiculous about what just happened."

Her breath warmed his chest in a long, displeased sigh. "Oh, really. How would you feel if it had happened to you?"

"If you had held out for half a minute more, you might've found out." He smiled gently. "But you're right. I'd feel ridiculous." He released her but continued to hold her by the shoulders. "But with you... It's different with a woman. I feel flattered, Mary Elizabeth. Honest-to-God flattered." He scrunched down a few inches to meet her sullen eyes and let her see he was sincere.

"Yeah, well..." Her gaze slid off to one side. But he could see she was thinking about it. One corner of her mouth tightened, forming a dimple in her cheek. "Some society we live in. A man prematurely climaxes and he's considered a flop. A woman does it and the man's ego gets pumped up."

"It *is* kinda crazy, isn't it." Pete smiled as the comedy in the situation struck him. He watched her emerging from her embarrassment, her face melting into a matching smile.

"Then you're not disappointed?" she asked. "You don't think I'm a failure at this sort of thing?"

"Are you kidding? How can I be disappointed when you've just proved you're absolutely crazy about me?"

Her eyes widened. "Oh! The arrogance of the man!" she gasped, swatting his arm and suppressing a laugh, which bubbled out, anyway.

Pete caught up her wrists. "You are. Admit it."

"In your dreams," she scoffed. They were both laughing now for no apparent reason Pete could discern, and he thought, *This is amazing, this relationship we have, this resilient, always-surprising relationship.*

The thought made what happened next flow as naturally as breathing. He released her wrists, gathered her close, rested his cheek on the crown of her head and rocked her in an embrace of pure affection. Their jovial mood slipped away, and when they gazed at each other a moment later it was as a man and a woman aware of their mutual respect and shared need.

Pete lightly fingered a strand of her hair, then traced the contour of her cheek while she stood before him, immobile, shivering under his sweet exploration. With his thumb he outlined her lips, coming to rest on the lower one full center. His eyes darkened and his soft, sinful voice whispered, "How about we try doing it right this time, Mary Elizabeth?"

She swayed on her feet like a woman under a hypnotist's trance. "I thought you'd never ask."

To AWAKEN IN THE ARMS of Peter Mitchell defied description. Mary Elizabeth's gaze roamed his face, from the suncreases around his still-closed eyes to his irregular hairline to the small mole on his right cheek. She thought she could look at that face forever and never get enough.

They lay on their sides on her narrow bed, his arm heavy across her waist, hers tucked against his chest, their legs entwined.

They'd tried to be sensible last night, tried separating after they'd made love, but she hadn't gotten any sleep with him gone from her bed. She'd just lain there in the dark, eyes wide open, restive, thinking about what had happened.

She'd never known making love could be that wonderful. Peter had taken such slow, thorough care with her, lifting her to a height of arousal she'd thought she might die from—and then keeping her there until she was mindless and virtually begging for release. And when it came, oh . . .

She hadn't realized he was still awake and restive, too, until he whispered her name. She'd answered by throwing aside the covers and making room for him. Then, what had been on their minds became reality for a second time, and a third.

Buttery morning sunshine poured across the room, spilling over Peter's smooth shoulder and into his tousled black hair. Outside, mockingbirds experimented with song. Other campers were stirring. Pots and utensils clinked. Voices carried on the early stillness. And Mary Elizabeth thought, To be able to wake like this every day of one's life would be better than having all the riches on earth.

She was so deeply happy that she began to think she'd made a grave mistake in making love with Peter. Already she didn't know how she was going to say goodbye to him come Sunday. But say goodbye she would. She had no choice. She wanted to think that he shared what she felt, that there was something that drew them and bound them that went beyond mere sensuality. But no words of love had been spoken last night, no mention of a shared future. But then, she hadn't expected any, so she had no reason to complain now. And she wouldn't. Knowing what he'd gone through with Cindy, she wouldn't ever push the issue. She couldn't ask of him what he couldn't give.

She eased onto her back and stared out the window at the brightening sky through the trees. No, making love with Peter hadn't been a mistake. It had been beautiful and special, a memory she would treasure all her life.

As she lay there, with the glow of his loving still lighting her eyes, she realized also that *she* felt beautiful this morning, *she* felt special.

Her hand drifted to her stomach, and she smiled. Her entire being seemed to be singing with emotion—happiness, optimism, and yes, maternal love for the little person developing inside her. She couldn't deny it any longer. Her love for this baby—her baby—had been growing steadily, day by day. So had her hopes for it and her dreams.

As she lay there watching the golden sunlight slide into the high branches of the trees, the truth quietly slid into her heart: she wanted to keep this baby. She wanted to love it and nurture it and share in its life. Until now she had felt inadequate, unable to provide for a baby. But she wasn't inadequate. She had a great deal to offer as a mother. In fact, she might even become a great mother. Why hadn't she seen it sooner?

She turned her head and let her gaze caress the man beside her. She wanted to wake him and tell him how she felt. She wanted him to know she'd just arrived at a miraculous new decision, to keep her baby. She wanted to run outside and shout the news to the world.

But she didn't wake Peter. He might think her idea was imprudent or consider her fickle. Neither did she run outside. Her decision to keep her baby was no one's business but her own. Besides, the idea was so new she needed to hold it to herself a little longer. So she just closed her eyes, tucked herself into Peter's warmth, and when he woke and asked her why she was smiling, she only kissed his cheek and said it was because of him.

In a sense, that was right.

THEY MADE IT ALL THE WAY to Georgia that day. Pete considered taking a swing into the Smokies. He loved those misty old mountains and wanted to share them with Mary Elizabeth. But visiting the Smokies would take them too far off course, so he continued on a southerly route through the Carolinas.

It wasn't very interesting driving—he could've made it so if he'd had a mind to—but the scenery didn't seem to matter that much anymore. Everything that was important in the world had condensed to the interior of this RV. To Mary Elizabeth.

He had hoped making love with her wouldn't be as good as he'd suspected. But it was. And then some.

You're in deep trouble now, boy, he admitted as they crossed the South Carolina line. But funny thing was, he was laughing when he admitted it.

They made love twice that day. That, ultimately, was what Pete remembered about Wednesday. They'd pretended interest in food or a certain tourist site, but all they'd really wanted was an excuse to stop and surrender to their rekindled needs.

Somewhere along the way—was it during the tour of that restored antebellum mansion they visited?—Pete decided he definitely wanted to continue seeing Mary Elizabeth after they got to Florida. They had something truly special going on between them, something he couldn't possibly say goodbye to on Sunday. As for seeing her through her pregnancy, of course he had the staying power. And of course he'd help her through the birth. He couldn't imagine not helping her. And after the adoption, they would have all the time in the world just to enjoy each other.

That night as he was showering, he decided he should broach the subject soon. Sooner than soon. Immediately. He had noticed her sinking into a pensive mood a few times that day and suspected she was feeling secretly upset about their relationship. How could she not when he'd led her to believe he didn't want to see her after this road trip?

With a towel tucked at his waist, he sat on the edge of her bed where she lay reading. She put down her book and stroked his damp arm.

"Hi." She rolled toward him and pressed a kiss to his knee. "Something on your mind?"

"Mmm." He clasped her hands to stop their roaming. "I've been doing some thinking about us, and I've come to the conclusion that not seeing each other after Sunday doesn't make sense."

She looked up at him with a startled sort of expression on her face. "You want to continue seeing me?" she repeated. "Dating, you mean?"

"Yes."

"Oh."

It wasn't quite the reaction he'd expected. His disappointment must have shown because she sat up and pressed her cheek to his. "Of course. That would be lovely."

Pete wondered why getting closer to this woman felt so much like drifting apart. "Are you sure that's what you want?"

Her eyes filled quite suddenly. "Oh, yes." Her voice broke over the affirmation. But again Pete sensed a contradictory tug within her that he couldn't explain.

"That leaves us with a slight problem, though," he said, lying down alongside her. "It renders the story we made up about ourselves pretty useless."

She turned on her side, looking confused. "How so?"

"Well, if we go ahead with it and tell my family we met last winter while you were on vacation, et cetera, et cetera, what will they think when we continue to see each other and your pregnancy begins to show? I'll tell you what they'll think. Either the baby is mine, or it's someone else's and you were fooling around while you were supposed to be pining away for me up in Maine. Either way I'm mincemeat."

She didn't smile. "Oh, I see. What do you want to do, then?"

"As I've said before, the truth keeps things simple." He lifted himself over her and kissed her long and deep. She didn't respond. She seemed a shell of herself.

He backed away, frowning. "Do you have a better idea?"

Mary Elizabeth stared at his chest, trying to calm her speeding heart. *I've got to tell him,* she thought. *My wanting to keep the baby will make a difference.* She bit her lip, her mind racing ahead to the consequences. *But not yet. Oh, please, not yet. Let me enjoy him one more day.*

"No," she said softly. "Your idea is fine." The last few syllables were lost as her lips met his.

THEY WOKE TO A GRAY drizzle on Thursday that seemed to reflect the mood that had descended on the RV. For much of that day Mary Elizabeth sat at the kitchen table alternately reading or embroidering while Peter drove. Occasionally, Peter tossed a remark over his shoulder, and sometimes those remarks lengthened to entire conversations.

But mostly she just rode along in silence, staring out the window at field upon field of red Georgia mud, wondering why she hadn't told him yet. The baby would make a difference. Why did she have this persistent fear of consequences?

Because consequences hurt, she answered herself, and this one would be a humdinger. He was going to renege on his offer to keep seeing her.

For a while she let herself entertain the possibility he'd be happy with her decision, that he'd say it made no difference to him. At one point she even ventured so far as to imagining him confessing he'd love to be the baby's father. It was a beautiful daydream, the three of them living as a family. But reality brought her down with a thump. If Roger, the baby's very own father, didn't want it, did she think a stranger would?

She lowered her head as Charles's words crept into her fantasy: "What man wants to take on another man's child?" She didn't want to be influenced by Charles anymore. His bitterness had warped his outlook. But she knew there was a grain of truth to what he'd said. Babies were a heavy responsibility. They were expensive and taxed one's time and patience and stamina. Did she really think Peter would enjoy taking on all that responsibility? He seemed to already have enough on his plate with his family and his construction company. And what about that remark he made when he was telling her about Cindy? *Thank God we didn't have a baby.*

Her thoughts jumped. Would he resent her baby? If he continued to see her, would he be annoyed by its crying? Begrudge how it cut into their time together?

Her thoughts took another leap. TV news was rife with stories of men being abusive to their girlfriends' children—beatings, molestation, murder. Nearly every night, she tuned in to another terrible incident.

Of course, those stories represented the extreme, and she couldn't imagine Peter being physically abusive. But Charles hadn't been physically abusive, either. Distrust began to build inside her, alongside a deepening protectiveness.

Was it a choice then between the baby and Peter?

And what about any other man who might come into her life in the future? She couldn't imagine other men, didn't want other men, but she forced herself to consider the possibility, anyway. What sort of relationship would they have with her child? Would it always be a choice? The thought of raising a child alone was intimidating, but it didn't disturb her nearly as much as the thought of raising that child in partnership with someone else, someone who'd be emotionally abusive.

They crossed the Florida line late in the afternoon, and as if obeying a cue from a benevolent god, the sun came out, slanting under the canopy of quickly dissipating clouds and momentarily chasing Mary Elizabeth's brooding thoughts. She moved up to the passenger seat and leaned forward on the dash, gazing in wonder at palm trees and Spanish moss and pastel stucco houses. Florida! She'd finally made it!

They stopped at a restaurant to celebrate their arrival, and over a dinner of sweet coconut shrimp talked about the upcoming day. The thought of meeting Peter's family put Mary Elizabeth on such a sharp edge she almost suggested they call off their bargain. But Peter had gotten her here; she'd be a welsher to cut out before repaying him.

That night they made camp in Osceola National Park. The air was hot and still and heavy with humidity. As if on cue, but from a different and decidedly malevolent god, the air-conditioning system broke down. Pete and Mary Elizabeth opened every window as far as it would go, and would've left the doors opened, too, except for the army of mosquitoes outside.

Flopping into bed wearing only his shorts, Pete grunted. "Welcome to Florida, sweetheart."

He looked across the way. She was wearing a burgundy nightgown—short, satiny, spaghetti-strapped. He hadn't thought she owned such a thing. Oh, hell! It was too hot to make love.

It was too hot not to.

He swung out of bed and went to her. But as soon as their kisses reached the melting stage, she sat up, shaking her head.

"I can't do this anymore, Peter."

He'd known something was brewing all day. "Why? What's the matter? Have I done something wrong?"

"No. It's me. I just...I feel uncomfortable being with you."

His eyes narrowed and burned into her, stripping her defenses.

"What I mean is, I've decided maybe...no, *definitely*, I'm thinking about keeping the baby." She didn't breathe. Just watched Peter's face, watched his eyes.

What she saw tore at her. He looked as if he'd been sucker-punched. Well, what had she expected? she chided herself. Him to be happy?

But then it hit her. Yes, she *had* been expecting that, or perhaps *hoping* was a better word. She'd hoped he'd be different from Charles and Roger and the other men she imagined were out there waiting to reject her. Peter had so many wonderful facets that had surprised her, she'd hoped he would surprise her again by embracing her decision.

She watched the astonishment leave his eyes as fast as it had appeared, to be replaced with a smile as thin as water on glass. "That's wonderful, Mary Elizabeth."

"Yes, well, I just thought you ought to know."

Peter retreated to his own bed and sat hunched forward with his elbows on his knees. "Okay. Now I know. So what's the problem?"

She sat facing him, frowning in thought. "Don't you see it as a complication to our relationship?"

"I'd be blind not to. But I'm still not sure I understand what you're getting at."

Oh, don't you? As hot and sticky as the night was, Peter seemed to be losing color.

"The problem, I suppose, is I want more." Later she would realize how poorly phrased her answer was, but at the moment she was too taken with her insight to censor her words.

"More? What more?" A bead of sweat trickled down Pete's left temple.

"Oh, sometimes I fantasize about having the baby, a home..." She swallowed, and swallowed again. "And a man who'll love us both forever."

Peter laughed, a chuckle as thin as his smile had been. "Hell, Mary Elizabeth, I'm not in the habit of marrying a woman unless I've known her at least a full week."

She burned with humiliation. "I said it was a fantasy. I didn't mean I expected you to marry me, for heaven's sake. Just the opposite. All I was trying to say was, now that I'm planning to keep the baby, I feel uncomfortable being intimate with a man knowing the relationship is a dead end." Her eyes quickly shifted, but not before they'd dropped the question into the space between them: *And this is a dead end, isn't it?*

When she looked back, Peter's face was an unreadable blank. He reached for his jeans, tugged on one leg, then the other, and rose to fit them over his narrow hips. She noticed he was breathing hard. He pulled on his boots, found a musty shirt, polished his helmet with a sleeve and drifted toward door.

"Where are you going?"

He paused but didn't turn when he said, "For a ride. It's mighty close in here tonight. I just... need some air."

CHAPTER FOURTEEN

THE RV PULLED UP to Pam's pink suburban ranch house just after noon on Friday. Since Peter and Brad lived in Tampa and Lindy's household was too chaotic, Pam's house had become, by default, the center of operation for the Mitchell side of the wedding party.

Mary Elizabeth ran her palms down her thighs as she scanned the battalion of cars already parked around it. "Do I look all right?" she asked nervously.

"Sure, you look great," Peter replied without even glancing at her. He wasn't in the best of moods. Not bad, just quiet. Distant. He'd been that way since the previous night when she'd told him about her decision to keep her baby.

She wanted to ask him what they were doing, where they stood, if he still intended to see her after this weekend. But whenever she was about to ask the question, it stuck in her throat. She'd grown uncomfortable with him, put off by the shell he'd closed around himself.

Uncoiling from his seat, he finally gave her a glance. "Stop worrying." He placed his hand on her head and gave it a friendly back-and-forth tug. "They're my family, all jerks, just like me."

She smiled at that, some of the tension melting from her face, but not all. Hardly all. On an instinctive level, she felt he'd abandoned her somewhere down the road, and from here on she was on her own.

"Come on," he urged. "Folks are waiting to meet you."

And they were: Pam and Lindy, Brad, who'd taken the day off work, and three of the five children, the oldest two being in school. There were also two cousins and an aunt in the kitchen helping with preparations for the rehearsal dinner, which Pam would be hosting that evening.

Peter and Mary Elizabeth weren't even in the house yet when conversation erupted. "Hey, look who finally came home," Brad called out the door, while Pam, gaping at the RV, said, "Oh, my God! You *are* traveling in a motor home." Meanwhile, two nephews and a niece were climbing up Peter's legs and hanging on his neck, to the tune of Lindy's ineffective "Behave yourselves. Uncle Petie's not a jungle gym."

Mary Elizabeth found them a most outgoing, likable bunch. They welcomed her into their midst, insisted she have some lunch and accepted her help afterward as if she were an old family friend. Still, she felt a tension buzzing under the surface of their smiles, a curiosity they held in polite reserve. She saw it in the way they looked from her to Peter, and in their shrugged eyebrows when they looked at each other. She got the feeling she wasn't what they'd expected.

By midafternoon they had apparently banked their curiosity long enough. Peter was fitting the extra leaves in the dining-room table when Lindy said, "Pam says you told her you've been seeing Mary Elizabeth since last February. Is that right?"

Mary Elizabeth was carrying in an extra chair from the garage at the time. She tensed, suddenly remembering the flaw in the fiction they'd created. If they continued to see each other, how would they explain her increasingly evident pregnancy? Would Peter go with the truth? Embarrassing as it was, the truth would ultimately make their relationship easier to understand and accept.

Across the room their eyes met. She waited, sensing his reply to Lindy's question would answer the one that had been haunting her since last night: what were they doing, where did they stand?

Peter blinked, cutting off their connection, and said, "Yes, we met while she was on vacation in Clearwater."

She grabbed a polishing rag off the floor and began to clean the chair she'd just carried in, while Peter went on, reeling out the story they'd invented to give their romance dimension—a story that would end with them parting in two days and only pretending to see each other afterward.

Their eyes never really met again that afternoon.

If anyone noticed, they didn't comment. The children came home from school, Pam's and Lindy's husbands returned from work, and the happy tumult expanded. Which was fortunate, Mary Elizabeth decided. It drew attention away from her and Peter and the fact that they hardly ever spoke. It also made it easier for Mary Elizabeth to conceal the heartache that was building inside her.

At five o'clock, with those who would be going to rehearsal arguing whose car they'd take, and the coffee urn refusing to perk, and the children chasing Monet around the kitchen table with doll's clothes, a voice called from the living room, "Hello-o. Anybody home?"

Mary Elizabeth felt a reaction jump through the people around her like an electric current. There was a hush, a sense of the room holding its breath....

And then, from Pam, "In here, Sue Ellen."

Mary Elizabeth swiveled just as a woman balancing a half dozen white florist boxes appeared in the kitchen doorway.

"Hi. Just came by to drop off..." Her words slowed noticeably when her eyes met Peter's. She smiled. "Hello, Peter. What a surprise."

Peter? Mary Elizabeth glanced from one to the other. Sue Ellen called him Peter?

Sue Ellen tossed back her full head of dark waves. "Here are your flowers for tomorrow. Boutonnieres for the men, corsages for the women. They were delivered to the bride's house by mistake along with the rest of the flowers. Jill was so busy though, I thought I'd run them over here for her."

"Thanks, Sue Ellen." Pam took the boxes to the refrigerator, while everyone else resumed breathing and going about their business.

Sue Ellen was tall, shapely and absolutely gorgeous, Mary Elizabeth decided, but in an approachable sort of way, with big green eyes that looked right at a person and a forthright femininity that existed in perfect harmony with an air of strong independence. She'd been eyeing Mary Elizabeth unashamedly from the moment she'd walked in.

"Since no one else seems inclined to introduce us—" she stepped up to Mary Elizabeth, smiling confidently "—I'm Sue Ellen Carlisle, an old friend of the family. And you're...?"

Through a sudden avalanche of feelings—jealousy foremost among them—Mary Elizabeth somehow found her voice. "Mary Elizabeth Drummond." She shook Sue Ellen's hand, which clasped hers firmly.

"Nice meeting you." Then stepping away, Sue Ellen teased, "I said hello, Peter." She placed two graceful hands on his biceps as if to kiss him. "So far I haven't heard a hello back."

He flicked a glance at Mary Elizabeth—why, she'd never know, because when his eyes returned to Sue Ellen they positively smoldered. "Sue Ellen," he greeted with a lazy half smile.

"So, are you ready to see that baby brother of yours tie the knot?" Her hands still hadn't left his biceps.

"I guess."

Mary Elizabeth left the room then to rescue her cat, who'd taken refuge in the living room. Or maybe she left so she wouldn't have to listen to Sue Ellen asking Peter to save her a dance tomorrow, and Peter replying he'd save her two. *And that's the last time I think of him as Peter!* she decided, carrying Monet out to the RV where she fed him and cuddled him until they both felt better.

When she returned to the house, Pete was ready to leave for rehearsal. "Would you like to come along?" he asked her.

When she replied no, she'd stay behind to help with the buffet, he didn't push the issue. Push? He barely gave it a shrug as·he walked by her. Sue Ellen left at the same time, chatting up a storm.

"Sorry 'bout Sue Ellen dropping by like that," Pam apologized later when she and Mary Elizabeth had a rare moment alone. She'd asked what Mary Elizabeth planned to wear to the wedding, and Mary Elizabeth had brought her out to the RV to show her.

"Nothing to be sorry about," she replied, draping her new outfit over the kitchen table. "She was just doing the bride a favor by delivering the flowers."

Pam snickered. "If I know Sue Ellen... Oh, never mind. No sense in bad-mouthing somebody I myself wanted to set up with Pete—until I met you." Her eyes, as blue as her brother's, roamed the RV, picking up evidence of him everywhere. "There's something really strong between you two, isn't there?"

Mary Elizabeth's throat ached. "I thought there was, but now..." She shook her head.

"Have patience with him. That's the only advice I can give you. He's had a couple of really bad experiences with marriage and..."

"A couple?" Mary Elizabeth's heart contracted. "He's told me about Cindy. Who else is there?"

"Sue Ellen, of course." Hearing Mary Elizabeth gasp, Pam hastened to add, "Oh, but they never actually made it down the aisle. They were supposed to get married, though. He asked her the night of their senior prom, and naturally she said yes. They were crazy about each other, had been for years. But then he went into the army and she went to college." A frown slid into Pam's expression. "She sent him a Dear John letter while he was stationed in Central America, poor guy. It was a cruel way to break up, him being so far away and all. And then to say she was getting married to somebody else." Pam shook her head. "It close to broke that poor boy's heart."

If Pam's intention was to cheer Mary Elizabeth, she was failing. "I may be way off base, but do you think that's why he married Cindy?"

"Afraid so. He admits it himself, although at the time he didn't realize he was acting on the rebound. He thought he really loved her. That's why he feels so shaky about his judgment in women now, why he's so terrified he'll make another mistake. He already has two strikes against him."

Just then a car pulled up to the curb, its horn beeping playfully. "Company," Pam murmured. They started for the door, but at the steps she paused again. "Until today I thought what my brother needed was to have Sue Ellen back in his life. But I was wrong. You're what he needs. Only thing is, he might not admit it for a while. Hang in. He's a great guy. He'll be worth the trouble."

Mary Elizabeth tried to keep Pam's encouraging words in mind, but matters only got worse that evening. Sue Ellen had apparently followed the wedding party to the church and finagled an invitation to the gathering afterward. She reentered the house draped on Pete's arm and remained there through most of the evening. Although he didn't forget Mary Elizabeth altogether and occasionally wandered over to ask if she was all right, he seemed happier to be sitting with Sue Ellen, talking and laughing over old times.

And why shouldn't he? Mary Elizabeth admitted, watching them from across the living room. Sue Ellen was a beautiful woman—confident, feminine and highly entertaining. Pete had planned to marry her once. Why wouldn't he be sitting with Sue Ellen, looking as crazy about her as he'd been at eighteen? What did Mary Elizabeth have to offer in comparison? She'd overheard them talking about taking a spin on his new bike. Because she was pregnant, Mary Elizabeth couldn't even ride it out of the driveway. *Why did he bring me here?* she asked herself time and again. *What was this past week all about?*

As hurt as she was, Mary Elizabeth still managed to hang on to her pride. She drew on her vast store of social skills, and mingled and chatted as if nothing was wrong.

By dessert, however, she'd had enough. Not only was she hurt, she was quietly seething. Pete had one hell of a nerve to treat her so poorly.

She hated slipping out without saying goodbye to anyone, but she thought it was best. She didn't want to upset the celebratory mood of the occasion. She'd be sure to write to Pam and extend her thanks and apologies as soon as possible.

She was struggling with the hitch at the back of her RV, trying to detach the trailer that still carried Pete's precious

Triumph, when a familiar voice cut through the evening shadows. "What are you doing, princess?"

"What does it look like I'm doing?" she snapped. She hadn't thought he'd noticed her leave. She'd hoped to get away without a confrontation.

"Step aside," he said, nudging her away. With a few effortless moves, Pete had the contrivance free. "Now, let me ask you again, what are you doing?"

Red-faced with pent-up anger, Mary Elizabeth stomped past him without answering, flung open the door of the RV and stomped inside. She returned momentarily and pitched his duffel bag onto his toes. "You needed protection, huh? Wanted me to keep her away, huh?"

In she went again, to appear at the door a moment later with a bundle of laundry. Pete ducked, but her aim was good. The bundle came apart on his head and spilled over him like a cracked egg.

Tossing aside a pair of black B.V.D.s, he bounded up the steps, slamming the door so hard the RV rocked. Mary Elizabeth wasn't intimidated. She met him chin first.

"What kind of game were you playing?" she demanded. "Lying to me about her, not telling me you really wanted to get back with her and only brought me along to...to what? Make her jealous?"

Pete frowned in deepening puzzlement. "I didn't lie to you. I don't want to get back with her."

Mary Elizabeth folded her arms tight. "You think I don't know you two had planned to get married once? Your sister Pam is a very talkative person, Pete. So you want to try telling me again what you needed protection from?"

"Goddammit, Mary Elizabeth!" He planted two fists on his hips. He was breathing heavily but looked more frustrated than angry. "Wise up."

She gasped when his meaning came clear. "Me? You needed protection from me? Well, thank you very much." With that she marched to the bedroom and returned bearing his tin roller coaster. "You could've just told me to get lost, y'know. You didn't have to embarrass me in front of everybody in order to get rid of me."

Pete lunged forward and snatched the roller coaster from her before she tossed that, too. He went outside and carefully set it on the lawn.

He came back in recharged. "How long have we known each other, Mary Elizabeth? Seven days?" He followed her into the bedroom. "And yet you went ahead without the slightest compunction and put me on the spot last night. Well, I'd say you've got some damn nerve."

She thrust his helmet into his midsection. "On the spot? What spot?" The lava lamp came next, dropping into the bowl of the helmet with a clatter.

Pete's face darkened. "You know what I'm talking about."

She paced the room, searching for the rest of his belongings, shaking her head continuously. "You don't listen, do you. I said I didn't expect you to marry me. That's why I suggested we end our relationship."

"Sure. Right after saying you wanted more—the baby, a home, a husband, the whole enchilada."

"I said that was a fantasy."

"Yeah, right." His eyes blazed. "You realize what you were doing, don't you?"

"Oh, please, enlighten me."

"You were upping the ante in our relationship. Just like..."

"Cindy? Oh!" She gasped in outrage. "Is that what you think?"

"It's what I know. Just when I was getting used to the idea of seeing you through your pregnancy, bingo, you drop a whole new scene on me. It's been that way from the beginning. There was always just one more little favor I could do. Well, I'm sorry, princess. You've pushed me one time too many."

Mary Elizabeth felt she'd been struck physically. "You big, dumb jerk!" She threw his can of foot powder at him. "I'm leaving. Going. Right now." She spun away, clutching her arms. "Pam gave me my wallet. I have my license...."

"What about the wedding?"

She lowered her head and shook it, suddenly fighting a lump in her throat. "Congratulate your brother for me. Under different circumstances I'd love to attend his wedding. I like him. I like all your family, but, no—" she gazed at her bed where they'd made love so often and so well "—I won't subject myself to any more humiliation."

"Leaving isn't necessary."

She spun around. "You just don't get it, do you. You think I'm playing a game, trying to trick you into marrying me. Well, I've got news for you. I wouldn't marry you if you begged me. Sorry to disillusion you, but this baby is far more important to me than you are."

Pete stared hard at her, frowning. "What the hell is *that* supposed to mean?"

She pushed past him and entered the bathroom to pack up his shaving kit. "It means," she said crisply, "I don't want any man, even you, interfering with my child."

When his toiletries were stuffed in the bag she turned. Pete was shaking his head. "Still letting Charles color your world, aren't you."

"No, I'm just calling it the way it is. If the baby's natural father has no interest in it, how do you think a stranger will feel?"

"You still don't think there are any decent men out there?"

She looked straight at him, feeling mean. "I haven't found one yet."

He flinched ever so slightly, but then rallied with, "You're living in the past, kid. Letting Charles call the shots."

"You have a nerve, accusing me of being stuck in the past, you, a man who can't get over a marriage he walked out of fifteen years ago."

"Thirteen."

"Oh, that makes a big difference! Here." She stuffed his shaving kit in the bowl of his helmet. "I think that's everything. Now, get out of my house."

His eyes glittered coldly. "Gladly." But he continued to stand there, filling the passageway. He pulled a cigarillo from his shirt pocket and one-handedly lit the tip. "You know how to get to the highway from here?"

She crossed her arms. "I can read a map."

He took a long, disrespectful pull before answering, "Fine."

"I'll send a check for everything I owe you within two weeks."

Pete puffed a cloud of foulness into the air. "I'll count on it."

She turned her head. "Well, have a good life, Pete."

"You, too." He walked into the kitchen, his helmet caught under one casually draped arm. "Wherever the road takes you."

When she turned her head again, the door was just clicking shut.

Mary Elizabeth slumped against the wall in abject mortification. *Have a good life?* What did she think she was doing, auditioning for a soap opera?

Outside, Pete gathered his laundry with a grimace. *Wherever the road takes you?* Judas Priest! Why not just quote her the last scene from *Casablanca*?

Mary Elizabeth tiptoed to the front seat, where she watched Pete from the corner of her eye. When he'd stuffed his clothes in his bag, he tossed it toward his bike and headed for the house. *Good riddance,* she thought.

Hearing the engine of the RV turn over, Pete hitched his shoulders and thought, *At last.* He felt like a man who'd escaped a physical danger, a convict on death row receiving a reprieve at the eleventh hour. No more potpourri balls swinging from the radio knob. No more cat hair making him sneeze.

But as the RV chugged down the street he turned to gaze after it. "And no more Mary Elizabeth looking all soft and warm in the morning when I open my eyes," he whispered into the empty night.

MARY ELIZABETH'S FIRST month in Florida was a time of rapid adjustment and change. She arrived at her old roommate's door not only distraught over her debacle with Pete but also uncertain of her welcome. They'd roomed together for only two years, and that had been long ago. After an hour with Chloe, though, Mary Elizabeth wondered where her uncertainty had come from.

They talked long into the night, rediscovering a cherished friendship, and Mary Elizabeth finally understood why her first instinct, when she'd decided to leave home, had been to call here.

She was met with one disappointing bit of news, however. The job at the dentist's office had already been filled.

But on the up side, her new credit cards had arrived and she was able to draw a cash advance to tide her over. She made sure to draw enough to also write out a check for Pete.

She remained with Chloe for a week. They shopped and went to the beach, drove around to acquaint her with the area, and talked until their jaws were sore. It was wonderful, but by the end of the week Mary Elizabeth insisted she move to a campground. It was time she started getting her life together.

The first step she took was to file a résumé with a temp agency. Living on credit made her nervous. Her next move was to buy a cellular phone so the temp agency could contact her. While she was waiting to hear from them, she scoured the help-wanted ads in various local newspapers.

Though she'd started with a bang, by the end of her second week in Florida Mary Elizabeth was feeling pretty low. The temp agency hadn't called, not even once, and she hadn't found anything in the want ads she felt qualified to do. She had never been a waitress, couldn't type sixty words a minute, knew nothing about selling cars, and she was beginning to think Charles was right—she'd never survive on her own.

One of the few joys in Mary Elizabeth's life those days was the weather. Having lived in cold, rugged Maine all her life, she thought she'd never get enough of the heat and sun.

Another joy was phoning Mrs. Pidgin, which she did often. She was astounded to hear that after thirty-two years of service, the woman had quit her job with Charles. Her husband was already retired, she said, and she wanted to enjoy his free time with him.

"I only stayed on because of you, anyway," she explained to a speechless Mary Elizabeth. "Your mother asked me to before she died, to watch over you. She knew Susan and your brother would be all right with Charles, but you she worried about."

"Oh, Mrs. P., I had no idea." Mary Elizabeth's heart overflowed with love and gratitude. If it hadn't been for this woman, her life would've been bleak, indeed. "How can I ever repay you?"

"Just be happy, love, and don't look back."

Mary Elizabeth tried to follow that advice. She submitted her résumé to a job placement service. She found an obstetrician and went for a physical exam. She visited with Chloe and went to the beach. But abiding happiness eluded her—even when, at the end of her third week, a promising job opportunity came through.

The placement agency had found an opening on the staff of a small museum in St. Petersburg, a position that seemed custom-made for Mary Elizabeth. The salary wasn't anything to write home about, her placement officer explained, but on the other hand, the personnel director was agreeable to paid maternity leave.

Mary Elizabeth went for an interview and spent the next three days on tenterhooks. When her acceptance came through, she danced around the RV with Monet, crying and laughing in relief.

But throughout her days, beneath her determination and busyness and momentary upswings, there remained a dark undercurrent of sadness, a barely heard but always present murmur that things were not right in her world.

"It's because of Pete," she finally admitted one night a week after she'd been working. She was lying in bed reading when she glanced toward the empty bed alongside hers and admitted, "I miss him. More than I can bear."

Cleaning the RV, she'd found a stray sock of his, a red bandanna, the can of foot powder that had ricocheted off his chest when she threw it at him, and a pair of dark glasses. Vaguely planning to mail the forgotten items to him, she'd placed them on his bed and there they'd stayed. Artifacts, she thought. Her own private Pete Mitchell museum. A memorial to the deepest happiness she'd ever known.

Reaching, she plucked the bandanna off the bed and buried her nose in its soft folds. It still smelled faintly of Pete. She closed her eyes, used the bandanna to wipe the tears that squeezed through her lashes, and then held it clutched in a fist at her mouth.

Four weeks away from him had given her ample time to rethink their parting argument, and each time she did she felt worse. Pete had had a valid case.

She hadn't meant to cast him in the role of husband and father, but subconsciously that was exactly what she'd done. She'd been so fixated on the baby and on the sort of relationship it would have with any man she became involved with, that she'd leapt miles ahead of where she and Pete were and started speculating whether he would resent her baby or not. She'd had no right to do that. It *had* been only a week since they'd met. No wonder he'd reacted negatively. Any man would've run.

She should have been satisfied with his suggestion they continue to see each other. Satisfied? She should have been jumping for joy. That was quite a step for him after just a week, offering to stand by her through her pregnancy, even go to Lamaze classes with her. A step that might have led to more, eventually.

But did she give their just-seeded relationship time to take root? Time to grow at its own natural pace? No, she'd poisoned it right at the outset by leaping ahead, rushing him, scaring him half to death.

And what *about* that obsession she had regarding her baby, her fear that any man she became involved with would resent it? That might be true in some cases, but Pete? Pete was an incredibly giving person. His family depended on him in innumerable ways, but he didn't resent them. He *loved* them. And he loved children. She'd seen with her own eyes how he interacted with his nieces and nephews. So what was her problem? Why wasn't she able to trust that he'd be just as wonderful and unresentful with her and her baby? *Was* she still living in the past? Was Charles still somewhere inside her telling her she was an unlovable burden?

"Damn!" She shot straight out of bed. She wasn't unlovable. She wasn't ugly or stupid or helpless. She had lots of fine qualities and more strength than she'd ever dreamed possible. In the five weeks since leaving home, she'd had to face and overcome so many obstacles, she felt downright proud of herself.

As she stood there between the two beds counting her virtues, it suddenly struck her. She was free of Charles. She'd freed herself.

Unfortunately, her relationship with Pete had perished in the struggle to reach this point.

Or had it? Was there any possibility it could be salvaged? Hope began a light, rapid cadence in her heart. Of course, she had to keep in mind Pete's aversion to marriage. She shouldn't start thinking he might get over that aversion someday. His radar would pick up her expectations and he'd bolt again.

That was presuming he'd even talk to her.

A sudden fear snaked around her newly risen hopes. What if he was back with Sue Ellen? The woman was lovely and spirited and...

Mary Elizabeth stopped abruptly, realizing what she was doing. She was comparing herself, selling herself short. She refused to do that anymore. Pete might very well be back with Sue Ellen, but that didn't diminish her own unique qualities.

She walked into the kitchen and made herself a cup of chamomile tea. While she was sipping it, she decided to call Pete from work the next day to see if they could meet somewhere to talk. He might say no, or their meeting might lead nowhere, or if he agreed to resume a friendship, that friendship might end next month. There were no guarantees when it came to matters of the heart. But she'd never know unless she gave it a shot. If nothing else, she would apologize for causing their friendship to end so badly. He'd done a lot for her on the road. He deserved at least that much in return.

She finished her tea, went back to bed and was asleep almost before her head touched the pillow.

PETE WALKED OUT of the beachside restaurant in Clearwater with the middle-aged couple whose three-quarter-million-dollar house he was building. They had fiddled with the blueprints again and figured a meal and a couple of drinks would smooth his ruffled feathers. He took them up on their offer. These days, eating with people, even pains in the butt, was far better than eating alone.

After the couple drove off, he mounted his Triumph and set off down the busy coastal road. The sun was just a small orange crescent on the horizon, but its radiance still managed to flood the Gulf and the sky above with blushing color.

Inadvertently he wondered if Mary Elizabeth was watching the sun go down. Wondered what she thought of it, if she liked her new home, if she was all right.

He gave his head a quick snap. Damn! He didn't know why he continued to worry about her. He was sure she'd landed on her feet. She had more lives than a cat. Besides, he had his own life to look after, his own obligations. The fact that he and Mary Elizabeth had met at all was simply a quirk of fate. An accident. A meaningless detour in the course of their lives. Now it was time to move on.

And he did, for about half a mile. Then he let himself admit he was throwing up a smoke screen to avoid what was really bothering him, those feelings he had for Mary Elizabeth. They hadn't gone away. If anything, they'd grown, and he didn't know what he was going to do about them anymore. They were interfering with everything—his sleep, his appetite, his work.

He'd thought of calling her at her friend's, dozens of times. Thought he might at least apologize for his jackass behavior at his sister's. He'd even gotten as far as dialing the number a few times, but he'd always lost heart before anyone answered. And the longer he didn't speak to her, the worse it got. By now she was probably mad enough to spit through the phone.

Maybe he should go see her in person. Or maybe take an extended trip somewhere, like Australia...

Or maybe he would simply drop into that little bar he'd just passed. Jimmy's Shack, it was called. It looked like his kind of joint. He made a U-turn and pulled into the lot.

The place was dimly lit and sparsely filled. The whizzing and binging of an intergalactic war, played out on a pinball machine, intertwined with a twangy song thumping from the jukebox. Pete's mouth twitched when he recognized Ricky Skaggs' "Highway 40 Blues."

Out of habit he chose a bar stool close to the back exit. Two men looked at him with subdued curiosity. He nodded a benign hello and they turned back to the game show they were watching on the TV behind the bar.

Pete ordered a beer, put a quarter in the jukebox and sat back to enjoy the ambience of Jimmy's as "Since I Met You, Baby" began to play. This was exactly how he liked spending his life. Alone, freewheeling, discovering charming pockets of America like this here Jimmy's Shack.

Only problem was, he wasn't having such a good time anymore. He hadn't for a while. After Brad's wedding he'd taken a few days off by himself down in the Keys. He'd needed to put some distance between himself and Sue Ellen. After the stupid stunt he'd pulled at Pam's, she'd expected all sorts of things from him. She'd even invited him to stay at her place that night, and he'd had to tell her point blank he wasn't interested—which didn't exactly make Brad's wedding an easy day to get through.

So he'd gone off to the Keys. But he hadn't had fun even there and had returned early. He'd never done that before. He felt restless, discontented. Uncharmed. Pete scowled and wondered why. What had changed?

He lifted his beer glass and took a long swallow. Simultaneously, he met his reflection in the mirror behind the bar. He tilted his head to better catch the light. It picked up the crow's feet at his eyes, a few strands of silver in his hair.

Maybe he was having a midlife crisis. With Brad getting married and all, it was understandable. Brad was the youngest of the bunch, and his marriage just underscored the fact that Pete, the oldest, was still at loose ends. Still coming home to an empty house. Still buying Christmas gifts for other people's kids. Hell, he'd always wanted kids. He'd always seen himself with a wife and a home.

No, that wasn't what was eating him tonight. Those things were certainly true, but they didn't cover the whole picture. He knew damn well what had changed. He'd met Mary Elizabeth, a woman he had feelings for.

Go on, admit it, Mitchell, you fell crazy in love with her. And the reason he'd treated her so badly at Pam's was that, like her, he'd already begun to fantasize, too—about the baby, a home, the three of them together—and it had scared him out of his skin.

He tipped back the glass, drained it dry and set it down. He'd run like a coward, proving he was no better than the imaginary jerks she feared she'd meet up with who would reject her because of the added burden of her baby. Instead of helping her see that not all men were like Charles, he'd confirmed the crippling legacy Charles had imparted. He'd deepened her distrust.

And why? Because he was afraid of being burned again? Mary Elizabeth was nothing like Cindy. Sure, she had needs, but she didn't have that desperate, hungry edge that Cindy had hounded him with. She'd left Charles, she hadn't married Roger, and she'd walked away from *him*, proving she was prouder and more independent than most people he knew.

Pete was staring at the foamy dregs in his glass when another revelation struck him. There was nothing wrong with needs. Everybody had them, one kind or another. They didn't necessarily mean a person was needy.

Neither was there anything wrong with two people depending on each other, in a healthy way. That's what friends and family were for—and what marriage was all about. Trouble was, Cindy's dependence on him hadn't been healthy. He shouldn't have let his experience with her pollute his entire attitude toward marriage.

He swore under his breath. Had he messed up the best opportunity of his life?

He was still staring into his empty glass when the bartender came over and set down a fresh, brimming mug. Pete frowned. He hadn't ordered another beer.

"Compliments of the lady down the end of the bar." The man gave Pete a sly half smile before walking off.

Pete felt none of the pleasure he should have felt. He didn't want to talk to a strange woman in a strange bar, wasn't in the mood to play seduction games. He wasn't even sure he wanted this beer. But the least he could do was acknowledge the woman's generosity.

He leaned forward, resting his forearms on the thickly varnished bar, and scanned the line of faces to his far right. The place was filling fast, he thought idly...right before he found her and his heart exploded through his chest.

CHAPTER FIFTEEN

MARY ELIZABETH WAS a bundle of nerves. She sipped her club soda, kept her eyes on the TV screen and hoped she didn't jitter right off this bar stool.

Finding Pete had not been easy. His home phone was unlisted, so she'd called his office. But he'd been out, working at a remote job site all day. When his secretary asked if Mary Elizabeth wanted her to page him, she'd said no, she'd call back later. And she had, at five, which was the time the secretary had said Pete was most likely to be there. But he wasn't. Luckily, Brad was. In fact, he answered the phone. He seemed quite pleased to hear from her, too.

It was Brad who'd informed her Pete was scheduled to have dinner with a client over in Clearwater. He'd also suggested she try to meet up with him at the restaurant. When she'd asked rather doubtfully if that was a good idea, he'd laughed and declared it a great idea.

On that encouraging, if somewhat mysterious, note she'd changed her outfit, repaired her makeup and hurried up the highway, cursing the fact that the only vehicle at her disposal was still her cumbersome RV.

When she'd arrived at the restaurant nearly two hours later, however, Pete had been nowhere in sight. Dejected, she'd started back, calling herself every kind of fool she could think of.

But a few miles down the road, she'd thought she'd spotted a bike like his parked outside a bar. She'd turned around and investigated...and finally stopped calling herself a fool.

She'd wanted to run straight in, but then reminded herself to show a little restraint. Pete might take one look at her and bolt out the back door, or worse, he might be here with a woman, maybe even Sue Ellen.

Mary Elizabeth had decided to slip in as unobtrusively as possible. When she'd found him, not only was he quite alone, but he appeared so melancholy she had ached for him. He looked tired, too, and he'd lost some weight. Was it possible he'd been as miserable as she? Her heart raced with hope mixed with fear and anxiety.

What that overburdened heart lacked, however, was the courage to look down the bar to observe his reaction to her being here—to her buying him a drink. What if he was angry? What if he was laughing in ridicule? No, she couldn't look. If he wanted to slip out the back door, she would leave the way open for him.

From over her left shoulder, someone asked, "Would you care to dance?"

She swiveled quickly in the direction of the voice, her pulse accelerating, only to find a stranger standing there, a young man with a very bright sunburn. She flicked an uncertain glance down the line of bar stools and her heart plummeted. Pete's was empty. Her instincts had been right.

But suddenly, a voice behind her answered, "Sorry, son. The lady's taken." The voice was soft as a prayer, dark as sin.

The young man backed off immediately.

Pete watched Mary Elizabeth set her glass down with a slow, very shaky hand. He had to use every ounce of willpower he owned to keep from reaching out to her and gath-

ering her into his arms. She took in a long breath, exhaled
in ragged shudders, then turned to face him.

"Hello, Pete," she said calmly.

The corner of his mouth lifted. "Mary Elizabeth," he
replied with painful restraint.

God, she looked great. Really pulled together. Sexy as
hell, too, but in a classy sort of Mary Elizabeth way. She was
wearing something he'd never seen before, a jade green,
watered-silk pants-and-shirt outfit that was drapey and
flowing. It didn't quite conceal her pregnancy, though. One
month had made a big difference. The sight of her and her
rounded belly filled him with indescribable joy.

He watched her tip back her head so that her hair grazed
her shoulder blades. He remembered the silken feel of that
hair, not with his mind, but with his body. With the tips of
his fingers, the flat of his cheek, his lips. Every part of him
that had touched her hair suddenly remembered...as it also
remembered her hands, her breasts, her feet, her lips.
Without realizing it, Mary Elizabeth had burned herself into
his sense memory.

And into his life, because the joy he was feeling wasn't
just sensual. Here before him was everything he'd ever
wanted—friend, lover, partner.

He set the beer she'd bought him on the bar. "What are
you doing here?"

"Oh, I saw your bike, thought I'd stop in, say hello."

Mary Elizabeth watched Pete's eyes narrow to two glittering points of doubt as he said, "With all the roads you
and I could've traveled, do you know what the odds are of
our meeting up like this?"

"Small," she agreed, fighting off a smile. "Astronomi-
cally small. It makes a person wonder, doesn't it?"

"About what?" His eyes had become seductive and
heavy-lidded, teasing her, burning into her.

Still, she answered with cool insouciance. "You know, about things like chance and fate and maybe we were meant to travel together?"

Pete had been thinking along pretty similar lines, but he only grinned and said, "Or maybe you tracked me down because you're nuttier than a box of Cracker Jack about me."

He held his breath, waiting for a snappy comeback. Joking would be good. But apparently she wasn't in a joking mood. She merely lifted her long blond lashes and said quite seriously, "Maybe."

They stared at each other until the air fairly sizzled between them. Abruptly Pete declared, "I am *so* sorry, sweetheart," just as she was saying, "I hope you'll forgive me." They paused a heartbeat, smiled uncertainly and then fell together into a laughing embrace that made explanations unnecessary.

"Oh, lady, you feel so good," Pete whispered against her hair.

"Mmm," she agreed, holding him tight, unable to speak for the lump in her throat.

In deference to the other patrons in the bar, they moved apart, but they didn't quite relinquish each other.

"Would you like to dance?" Pete asked softly.

She glanced toward the small open area where five other couples were swaying to a slow jukebox number. "I'd love to."

Reaching the dance floor, Pete took her in his arms and she nestled against him.

"How have you been?" he murmured. He felt her smile against his neck.

"Miserable," she replied, "but at least I have a job." She then proceeded to fill him in on the latest developments in her life.

Pete was pleased for her but not surprised. "I knew you could do it."

"And how have you been?" She drew back to look into his eyes.

"Pretty damn miserable, too, if you want to know the truth." He adjusted their fit and encircled her with both arms. "Mary Elizabeth, I need to apologize for what happened at Pam's."

"You already did that."

"Explain, then."

"I think I already understand. You were right, I *did* put you on the spot. After knowing you only a week, too. That was grossly unfair of me. And for that I can only say I'm sorry."

Pete's weathered face took on an uncharacteristic softness. "It's true, I was worried that it had only been a week. But I learned something this month away from you."

"Oh? What's that?"

"I learned that sometimes a week is enough time to know."

She tilted her head. "Know what?"

He held her a little tighter. "When you've found the person you want to spend the rest of your life with."

Mary Elizabeth stood absolutely still, afraid she hadn't heard right. The music receded, the other dancers ebbed from their awareness, leaving them in a private, spellbound dimension where only they existed.

"The baby, too?" she asked hesitantly.

Pete smiled softly. "Of course, the baby, too. Mary Elizabeth, you've got to understand, part of me might have turned coward when you said you wanted to keep the baby. That was the part of me that had been burned twice. But another part wanted to shout alleluia to the rafters." Pete laughed. "My God, a baby!" he said, awestruck. "A brand-new little person."

Mary Elizabeth ran the knuckles of her index fingers under her eyes and gave a snuffling laugh. "With any luck, it won't be anything like me."

Pete folded her close and began to dance again, swaying, barely scuffing the floor. "No. That's what I'm looking forward to especially, having another person around as wonderful as you."

Her smile abruptly dropped. "What'll we do about Roger? He thinks I'm giving up the baby."

Pete gave her a pointed what-do-you-think look.

"I know, I know. Honesty keeps things simple. But telling him might open a whole new can of worms."

"Don't worry about Roger, we'll handle him together."

The number ended and they walked off the dance floor.

"There is one area where I'll bend my policy on the truth," Pete offered, turning to face her when they reached the bar. "If you'd rather not let on who the father is around my family and friends, I understand. I don't mind pretending the baby's mine."

Mary Elizabeth bit her lip. "Would *you* feel better if they thought it was yours?"

He shrugged. "Makes no difference. I intend to be enough of a father to it to make even us forget I'm not."

"In that case, it makes no difference to me, either. We can tell people to whom it might matter, and let others assume what they like."

"Does that include the baby?"

"Uh-huh. When the child is old enough to understand and handle the news, I intend to tell him, or her. That's the one thing I'm still not at peace with, my mother's not telling me about my real father. Even if I'd never gotten to meet him, it would've been nice to hear about him from her. It would've explained a lot about Charles, too, and maybe I wouldn't have let him affect me as deeply as he did.''

Pete opened the door and stepped aside for her to pass through. The late October night was warm and humid. Sultry. But a fresh breeze was sliding in off the Gulf. The traffic on the strip wasn't as heavy as it would be in winter, but it still ran steady. Lights from high-rise hotels and condominiums blotted out the stars.

Pete strolled with Mary Elizabeth at a snail's pace to the RV. It was parked alongside his bike.

He paused, studying the two vehicles. ''Hmm. Seems we have a problem, sweetheart.''

''Oh?'' Her heart tripped.

He rubbed his chin. ''Well, I guess you'll just have to follow me.''

''Follow you? Where?''

''To my place, of course. You can leave the RV parked there—there's great security—and take my car to work. It'll be a lot easier than trying to maneuver this elephant through the city every day.''

She planted her hands on her hips. ''Whoa. Wait a sec. What are you proposing? That I move in with you? Tonight?''

Even in the tinted light cast by the neon sign flashing Jimmy's Shack—Jimmy's Shack—Jimmy's Shack, she was able to see Pete's color deepen.

''Talk about jumping the gun! Sorry, sweetheart.'' He hitched a shoulder. ''So, what are you going to do? Return to your campground?''

''Yep,'' she answered, imitating him. ''I don't ever want you saying I rushed you into anything.''

''But I don't feel . . .''

She shook her head. ''Besides, a woman deserves at least a few weeks of courtship, don't you think?''

"Courtship?" He looked as if he'd swallowed a bug. "You mean, flowers and candy and going to the movies?"

"Yep." Her smile grew wide and wicked. "I want every bribe and seduction ever devised by the mind of man."

"But we're already...I mean, back there, weren't we discussing...?"

"I don't remember being proposed to, and I definitely don't remember giving you an answer." She shook back her hair, her chin lifted.

Pete thrust his hands in his jeans pockets and scuffed the gravel. "Aw, hell, Mary Elizabeth, are you gonna give me a hard time for the rest of my life?"

She opened the door of the RV and took one step up before looking over her shoulder. "If you're lucky."

She was about to close the door when he bounded in and took her in his arms. "Guess what, princess," he said, laughing a low, dangerous laugh. "I feel lucky." His eyes glittered. "So, what do you say? Will you marry me?"

She shrugged unenthusiastically, trying to pretend her heart wasn't turning cartwheels.

He tried again. "Will you *please* marry me?"

She rocked her head in a considering manner.

Pete held her tighter. "Please. I love you, Mary Elizabeth, and can't live without you. You'd make me the happiest man alive if you'd do me the honor of agreeing to be my wife."

"Well!" Mary Elizabeth didn't need to pretend astonishment. "I...I'll give your offer serious consideration."

Apparently, Pete wasn't satisfied with that answer because the next moment he was kissing her, subjecting her to the most powerful argument of all, his sexual proficiency.

By the time he lifted his head, she was as limp as seaweed.

"Y—" Unable to speak, she merely nodded.

"Is that a yes?"

She nodded again and managed to croak, "I love you, too, Pete."

"Glad to hear it." Pete gathered her close. "Very, very glad," he said as he fit his mouth to hers.

EPILOGUE

MARY ELIZABETH LOOKED down from the second-story window. Mrs. Pidgin was lumbering along the walk that led from the condominium to the parking area, a plastic grocery bag gripped in each hand. The bright June sun beamed down on her newly permed hair and radiated off the roof of the waiting RV.

"What's all that?" Pete inquired, slamming shut the hood where he'd been checking the oil.

"Oh, just a little something extra. You never know."

Upstairs, Mary Elizabeth chuckled. She and Pete were about to set off on a drive that would include a visit to the Grand Canyon and Yosemite National Park. They planned to be gone only three weeks, but Mrs. Pidgin had already packed enough food to last them three months.

She heard Pete say, "Thanks, doll." He always called Mrs. Pidgin doll, and she always blushed.

She and her husband, Alfred, had ventured to Florida on a rare vacation the previous November to spend Thanksgiving with her sister in Gainesville. Mary Elizabeth suspected her real motive was to inspect "this new fella, Pete" Mary Elizabeth had been seeing. Whatever the reason, after a week of sunshine and shuffleboard, she and Alfred had stunned everyone by announcing this was the life for them. They made the move in time for the wedding in December, which they would've attended, anyway, since Mary Elizabeth asked them to serve in place of her parents.

They'd done so beautifully, too, walking her down the chapel aisle, right behind Chloe, her matron of honor, and giving her away in a touching ceremony that was witnessed by nearly one hundred and fifty guests. Among those guests was a contingent from Maine—friends Mary Elizabeth had left behind, a few relatives, and most moving of all, her sister and brother, who were outraged that their father had refused to attend.

Mary Elizabeth had called Charles to tell him she was getting married and to ask if he would walk her down the aisle. But he'd declined. Drummonds, he said, did not walk down church aisles dressed in white when six months pregnant.

Mary Elizabeth hadn't argued. She hadn't been angry, hadn't even been hurt. All she'd felt was pity. "That's too bad," she'd replied in a calm, dispassionate voice. "You're going to miss a great time. We'll send you pictures."

And they had, and apparently Charles had taken a good look at what he'd missed, because a couple of days into February, he'd called to see how she was feeling. He'd called after the baby was born in March, as well, and sent a sizable savings bond as the beginning of a college fund.

"I don't know what to make of this," Mary Elizabeth had said, looking at the bond in a daze.

Pete had replied, "You can make of it whatever you'd like, Mary Elizabeth."

The better she got to know her husband, the more she learned to listen. Often, a casually tossed remark resonated with profundity that only hit her later and stunned her when it did. *You can make of it whatever you'd like.* Wasn't that a prescription for life?

She decided that what she would make of the call and the savings bond was a cordial line of communication. After all,

Charles had been an integral part of the first twenty-seven years of her life. She couldn't just pretend he didn't exist.

But she found writing letters easier than phoning, and did so about once a month, sending a photo of the baby each time. It was hardly a warm relationship, but that didn't bother her. It was enough. Besides, she was too busy and too happy these days to let anything bother her.

Below the window, she heard Pete mutter something about coming up to see what was keeping them.

"What's keeping them is little Miss Eliza." Mrs. Pidgin laughed. "You can't rush that child. She already has the appetite of her daddy." The remark poured out with such total spontaneity, Mary Elizabeth wondered if Mrs. Pidgin had actually begun to think of Pete as Eliza's father. He'd like that.

She heard him enter the house, jog up the stairs . . . then silence. She looked up to find him standing in the bedroom doorway, watching her with that goofy, awed, lovestruck expression she was beginning to think wasn't ever going to go away.

Pete cleared his throat and approached. Mary Elizabeth was sitting in her Salem rocker by the window, the very chair her mother used to rock her in. The baby had just finished nursing. Her plump left cheek was flushed from pressing against Mary Elizabeth's warm skin.

"Hey, Eliza," Pete said softly. He went down on one knee and cupped the baby's downy head in his right hand. "Are you ready to go on your very first vacation?" The baby beamed a gummy smile at him that turned him to mush right before Mary Elizabeth's eyes.

"Oh, are you in trouble. She's got you wrapped right around this." Mary Elizabeth raised and wiggled her little finger.

"You've got that right. Tell Daddy what you want him to buy. A pony? Is that what you want? A Porsche?"

Mary Elizabeth gazed at Pete, murmuring to the baby, and fell in love all over again. He had taken to fatherhood faster and with more enthusiasm than she'd ever dreamed possible...although she should have expected it from the zeal he'd poured into preparing for Eliza's birth.

And that moment when Eliza had slipped into the world—oh, what a look on his face, what a look in those eyes! She could only call it transcendent.

It had been a normal pregnancy, and an equally normal labor, but Mary Elizabeth had been exhausted by the time the baby was born, drifting in and out of consciousness as the doctor placed Eliza on Mary Elizabeth's stomach and Pete cut the cord. She vaguely recollected the baby being there, on her stomach, and fearing she didn't have the strength to hold her and keep her from sliding off. She'd wanted to tell Pete so, warn him, ask him to take charge, but he was less help than she was.

It was a sight to see—a six-foot, three-inch man, broad as a barn, with muscles like oak and a face as hard as granite, this man, slumped in a chair, holding his head in his hands and bawling his heart out. Mary Elizabeth would cherish the image forever.

"She had a great feeding. Should leave us in peace for at least a couple of hours." Mary Elizabeth handed the baby to Pete and fastened her clothing. Eliza was sizable for her three months, yet she looked tiny against Pete's shoulder, and so fair.

Mrs. Pidgin had offered to baby-sit, but Mary Elizabeth couldn't imagine parting with Eliza for three weeks. Traveling with her at this age would probably be as easy as it was ever going to get, too. They would, however, leave Monet behind in Mrs. P.'s care—with Pete's deepest gratitude.

Mary Elizabeth looped the diaper bag over her shoulder, scanned the room and declared them ready to leave.

Pete had made a few alterations to the interior of the motor home—a queen-size bed in place of the two narrow singles, and a two-person bench where the passenger seat had been. It wasn't quite as comfortable as its bulky, contoured predecessor, but now Eliza could ride with them up front, securely fastened in her car seat.

Pete turned the ignition. Mrs. Pidgin stepped farther back on the sidewalk, pulled a rumpled tissue from the pocket of her housedress and mopped her eyes. Mary Elizabeth smiled and blew her a kiss.

"Okay, I'm ready." Mary Elizabeth slapped her thighs. "More than ready." She loved being a wife and mother, but after months of near-confinement, she was eager to get rolling.

"Wait. There's one thing I've got to do first." Pete leaned across Eliza, who was gurgling happily, and took Mary Elizabeth's face in two hands. The next moment he was kissing her, a kiss that was bold and sensual yet sweetly familiar.

Backing away, he opened his eyes slowly and sighed, "Okay, now I'm ready." He put the vehicle in gear and moved carefully away from the curb, waving goodbye to Mrs. Pidgin.

They'd covered only a few miles when Mary Elizabeth said rather pensively, "You know, if you ever want to do this alone, take one of your bike trips, I mean, I'll understand."

Pete hung his wrist over the steering wheel and thought about it awhile. "No, those days are over."

"Are you sure?"

He nodded. "There's no need. There's nothing to run away from anymore, nothing to go searching for. When I met you last September," he murmured, his eyes soft with love, "I reached my destination."

His image rippled through her tears.

Returning his eyes to the road, Pete said, "This is the only kind of traveling I want to do from now on. The three of us together."

She cleared the sentimentality clogging her throat and smiled. "How about four of us?"

"That sounds good, too." He sobered immediately. "You aren't—?"

"Good heavens, no. I was just speaking hypothetically."

"Oh." He blew out a sigh of relief. "Since we're in a hypothetical mood, how about five for the road?"

She took a long considering moment before replying, "Yeah, I could handle that."

"How about six?"

"Don't push your luck, Mitchell."

He threw back his head and laughed.

Mary Elizabeth settled into her seat with a contented smile and let her gaze fix on the horizon. What a strange journey her life had taken since leaving Maine. How rootless and alone she'd felt then. How blessed she felt now.

She no longer thought of Maine as home. Nor did she really think of Florida in that way, either. Home, she'd learned, was not so much about place as it was about people. Home, as the old adage said, was where the heart was.

She gazed at Eliza, who'd drifted off to sleep, looked over at Pete fiddling with the radio, trying to find an oldies station, and her heart overflowed. It didn't matter where the road took them. They were home.